THE BARREN GROUND

OF

NORTHERN CANADA

Ready for Tracking

THE
BARREN GROUND
OF
NORTHERN CANADA

BY

WARBURTON PIKE

NEW YORK
E. P. DUTTON & COMPANY
681 FIFTH AVENUE

PUBLISHED, 1917,
BY E. P. DUTTON & CO.

AUTHOR'S PREFACE TO THE ORIGINAL EDITION

In many of the outlying districts of Canada an idea is prevalent, fostered by former travellers, that somewhere in London there exists a benevolent society whose object is to send men incapable of making any useful scientific observations to the uttermost parts of the earth, in order to indulge their taste for sport or travel. Several times before I had fairly started for the North, and again on my return, I was asked if I had been sent out under the auspices of this society, and, I am afraid, rather fell in the estimation of the interviewers when I was obliged to confess that my journey was only an ordinary shooting expedition, such as one might make to the Rocky Mountains or the interior of Africa, and that no great political reformation depended upon my report as to what I had seen.

In talking with officers of the Hudson's Bay Company, many of whom had been stationed for long periods in the Athabasca and Mackenzie River districts, I had often heard of a strange animal, a relic of an earlier age, that was still to be found roaming the Barren Ground, the vast desert that lies between Hudson's Bay, the eastern ends of the three great lakes of the North, and the Arctic Sea. This animal was the Muskox, but my informants could tell me nothing from

personal experience, and all that was known on
the subject had been gathered from Indian report.   Once or twice some enthusiastic sportsman had made the attempt to reach the land of
the Musk-ox, but had never succeeded in carrying out his object; specimens had been secured by
the officers of the various Arctic expeditions, but
no one had ever seen much of these animals or of
the methods of hunting them employed by the
Northern Indians.

   This, then, was the sole object of my journey;
to try and penetrate this unknown land, to see
the Musk-ox, and find out as much as I could
about their habits, and the habits of the Indians
who go in pursuit of them every year.   But
the only white men who had succeeded in getting
far out into the Barren Ground were the early
explorers,—Hearne, Sir John Franklin, Sir
George Back, and Dr. Richardson, while long
afterwards Dr. Rae and Stewart and Anderson
went in search of the missing Franklin expedition.   With the exception of Hearne, who threw
in his lot with the Indians, these leaders were all
accompanied by the most capable men that could
be procured, and no expense was spared in order
to make success as certain as possible; yet in spite
of every precaution the story of Sir John Franklin's first overland journey and the death of Hood
are among the saddest episodes in the history of
the Arctic exploration.

   My best chance seemed to be to follow

Hearne's example, and trust to the local knowledge of Indians to help me; and I think, as the sequel showed, that I was right in not taking a crew from Winnipeg. The Indians and half-breeds of the Great Slave Lake, although very hard to manage, are certainly well up in Barren Ground travel; they are possessed of a thorough knowledge of the movements of the various animals at different seasons, and thus run less danger of starvation than strangers, however proficient the latter may be in driving dogs and handling canoes.

In following out this plan I naturally passed through a great deal of new country, and discovered, as we white men say when we are pointed out some geographical feature by an Indian who has been familiar with it since childhood, many lakes and small streams never before visited except by the red man. I have attempted in a rough map to mark the chains of lakes by which we reached the Barren Ground, but their position is only approximate, and perhaps not even that, as I had no instruments with which to make correct observations, and in any case should have had little time to use them. Let no eminent geographer waste his time in pointing out the inaccuracies in this map; I admit all the errors before he discovers them. All that I wish to show is that these chains of lakes do exist and can be used as convenient routes, doing away with the often-tried method of forcing canoes up the swift and dangerous streams that fall into the Great Slave Lake from the northern tableland.

The success of my expedition is to be attributed entirely to the assistance which was given me by the Hudson's Bay Company, and I take this opportunity of thanking them for all the hospitality that was shown to me throughout my journey; I was never refused a single request that I made, and, although a total stranger, was treated with the greatest kindness by everybody, from the Commissioner at Winnipeg to the engaged servant in the Far North. My thanks are especially due to Lord Anson, one of the directors in London, to Messrs. Wrigley and William Clark at Winnipeg, Mr. Roderick MacFarlane, lately of Stuart's Lake, British Columbia, a well-known northern explorer who put me in the way of making a fair start, Dr. Mackay of Athabasca, Mr. Camsell of Mackenzie River, Mr. Ewen Macdonald of Peace River, and most of all to Mr. Mackinlay of Fort Resolution on the Great Slave Lake, who was my companion during a long summer journey in the Barren Ground.

My only excuse for publishing this account of my travels is that the subject is a reasonably new one, and deals with a branch of sport that has never been described. I have spared the reader statistics, and I have kept my story as short as possible. I hope that in return anyone who may be interested in these pages will spare his comments on faulty style, and the various errors into which a man who has spent much time among the big game is sure to fall when he is rash enough to lay down his rifle and take up the pen.

I have also cut out the chapter with which these books usually begin,—a description of the monotonous voyage by Atlantic steamer and Canadian Pacific Railway, and start at once from Calgary, a thriving cattle-town close under the eastern foothills of the Rocky Mountains.

LONDON, 1891.

LIST OF ILLUSTRATIONS

MAP

THE BARREN GROUND

OF

NORTHERN CANADA

THE
BARREN GROUND
OF
NORTHERN CANADA

CHAPTER I

In the middle of June, 1889, I left Calgary for a drive of two hundred miles to Edmonton, the real starting-point for the great northern country controlled by the Hudson's Bay Company, and, with the exception of their scattered trading-posts, and an occasional Protestant or Roman Catholic Mission, entirely given up to what it was evidently intended for, a hunting-ground for the Indian.

My conveyance was a light buckboard, containing my whole outfit, which was as small as possible, consisting almost entirely of ammunition for a 12-bore Paradox and a 50-95 Winchester Express, besides a pair of large blankets and a little necessary clothing.

Forest fires were raging in the Rocky Mountains close at hand, and the thick smoke obscuring the sun, the heat was not nearly so fierce as usual at this time of the year; the road was good for a prairie road, and comfortable stopping-places each night made the journey quite easy. About sixty miles out the country loses the appearance of what is known among cattlemen as the bald-headed prairie, and is dotted with clumps of poplar, and occasionally pines; half way to Edmonton the road crosses the broad stream of the Red Deer, and passes through the most attractive country that I have seen in the north-west territories. It is being rapidly settled, and, with the convenience of a railway now building between Calgary and Edmonton, cannot fail to be an important farming and stock-raising district within a few years.

On the morning of the fifth day I reached Edmonton, a pleasant little town scattered along the far bank of the North Saskatchewan, and historical in the annals of the Hudson's Bay Company, by whom it was established as a fur trading-post many years ago; it is fated shortly to lose its individuality in the stream of advancing civilization, and will probably develop into an ordinary prairie-town of some importance.

Finding that I had no time to spare if I wished to catch the steamer down the Athabasca river, I left again the same evening, after buying a small supply of flour and bacon. I changed the buck-board for a wagon, having for driver a French

half-breed who had spent his early life on the
prairie in buffalo-hunting, but, on the extinction
of the game, had been earning a living by freight-
ing for the Hudson's Bay Company, and farming on a small scale. He was a much pleasanter
companion than the smartly dressed young man,
"come of good folks in the East," who had been
my driver from Calgary, and many an interesting
tale he told me on our three-days' journey to the
banks of the Athabasca; tales of the good old
times when the buffalo were thick, and the Crees
waged perpetual war against the Blackfeet, and
whisky formed the staple article of trade for the
Indian's fur. At the present day the Prohibition
Act orders that even the white men of the north-
west territories must be temperate, thereby causing whisky to be dear and bad, but plentiful
withal, and it is surprising how such a law exists
in a country where nine men out of ten not only
want to drink, but do drink in open defiance of
the commands of a motherly Government.

A fair road some hundred miles in length has
been made by the Hudson's Bay Company
through a rolling sandy country, crossing several
large streams and passing through a good deal
of thick pine timber where some heavy chopping
must have been necessary. The flies bothered us
greatly; the large bulldogs, looking like a cross
between a bee and a blue-bottle, drove the horses
almost to madness, and after our midday halt it
was no easy matter to put the harness on; fortu-

Old Hudson Bay Post at Edmonton

nately we had netting, or the poor beasts would
have fared much worse: as it was the blood was
streaming from their flanks during the heat of
the day. The mosquitos appeared towards evening, but as the nights were usually chilly they
only annoyed us for a few hours. There were no
houses along the road, but plenty of firewood
and feed for the horses; we had a good camp
every night, sleeping in the open air, starting very
early and resting long in the middle of the day.

Two days took us over the divide between the
Saskatchewan and Athabasca rivers, and now the
water in the little streams that we crossed eventually reached the sea far away in the frozen Arctic Ocean at the mouth of the great Mackenzie.
Early on the fourth day we came in sight of the
Athabasca running between high pine-clad banks,
and, dropping down a steep hill, found the Company's steamer loading up with freight for the
far north. This spot is known as the Athabasca
landing, and consists of a large depot for goods,
trading-store, and several workmen's houses,
while the house of the officer in charge stands on
the hillside a little way back from the river.
From the landing there is water communication
down stream, broken of course by portages, to
the Arctic sea, while the Lesser Slave Lake lies
within a few days' travel up stream, from the
north end of which a road seventy-five miles in
length has been cut to the bank of Peace River. I
spent a pleasant enough day loafing about, Mr.

Wood, who was in charge, showing me great kindness and giving me much useful information about my route, and at twelve o'clock the following day we started down stream. The only other passengers were a Mr. Flett and his wife and daughter, who were on their way to take charge of Fort Smith during the coming winter. Mr. Flett was just returning from a visit to his native country, the Orkney Islands, after an absence of forty-four years in the service of the Company, all of which time was spent in the wildest part of the North. He was full of the wonderful changes that had taken place since he was a boy, but finding himself completely lost in civilization, had hurried back to the land of snow. Unfortunately Mrs. Flett had been unable to stand the climate of the old country, and was quite broken down in her health. I was sorry to hear during the winter that she died a few days after we left her at Fort Chipeweyan.

Owing to the very light snowfall in the mountains in the winter of 1888-89, the water in the river was unusually low, and, as we expected, on the third day the steamer, a large light-draught stern-wheeler, after striking several times on shallow bars, had to abandon the attempt to reach the Grand Rapids. We accordingly tied up to the bank, and, sending a skiff down to take the news, awaited the arrival of boats from below to take our cargo. For ten days we lay at the junction of Pelican River, a small stream coming in on the north side of the Athabasca. There was absolutely nothing to do; the low gravelly banks on each side were fringed with thick willows backed by a narrow belt of poplars, and behind these the gloomy pine woods, with here and there a solitary birch, stretched away in an unbroken mass as far as the eye could see. The forest was alive with mosquitos, although owing to the low water in the river they were said to be much less numerous than usual; they were sufficiently thick however to make any exploration in the woods a misery. Fishing we tried without much result, and everybody was pleased when at last Mr. Scott Simpson, who was in charge of the river transport that summer, arrived with two boats. The steamer's cargo was unloaded, partly into the boats and partly on to the bank, and early in the morning she started back for the landing while we proceeded on our journey down stream.

These inland boats, as they are termed, are extraordinary specimens of marine architecture, long open craft, classified according to shape as York boats, sturgeon-heads, and scows, capable of carrying a load of ten tons, manned by a crew of eight oars and a steersman, rowed down stream and tracked up, running rapids and bumping on rocks. Planks, nails, and pitch are always kept ready to effect repairs, and are in frequent demand. The crews are generally halfbreeds from the Lesser Slave Lake and Lake La Biche, both of which pour their waters into the

Athabasca; but there are also volunteers from all parts of the North, as the wages are good and the work is suited to the half-breed's character, besides the certainty of receiving rations every day, which is a great attraction in a land of scarcity. Sometimes crews of Locheaux Indians are sent up from the Mackenzie, and have the reputation of being the best workers; they certainly seemed to me to be less given to rebellion and more easily managed than the half-breeds. The boats are steered with a huge sweep passed through a ring in the stern post, and great responsibility rests on the steersman, who at times requires all his skill and strength to throw the heavily-laden boat clear of a rock in a boiling rapid.

In three days, without accident, we reached the island at the head of the Grand Rapids, just in time to rescue a Company's clerk named Mackay from a very unenviable position. He had come up with the boat-brigade from Fort Mac-Murray, and, provisions running short, had travelled over-land accompanied by a half-breed to meet the steamer from which they expected to get supplies to take down to the crews. On reaching the island they were unable to attract the attention of the man left in charge of the freight lying there, so they walked a couple of miles up the north bank and built a raft on which to cross the river. They thought they would be able to pole the raft, but the water proved too deep, and being

The Hudson Bay Fort at Edmonton

unable to get steerage way on her, they soon broke
their unmanageable vessel to pieces against a rock.
It was now a case of swimming in a strong current that was forcing them over the big rapid
where certain death awaited them; the half-breed
succeeded in fetching the island, but Mackay, seeing he was being swept over the fall, swam to a
rock and managed to climb on to it.   The half-
breed found the sole inhabitant of the island in his
cabin, but there was no boat in which to go to
the rescue, and if there had been it was no easy
matter for two men to lower it down, without
all going over the rapid.   They were engaged in
building a raft to make the attempt when they
saw our brigade coming down the river.   By the
aid of a long line and plenty of hands the smallest
boat was lowered down to the rocks, and what
might have been a very serious accident was luckily averted.   Mackay was much chilled by sitting
on the rocks for several hours in wet clothes after
two days without eating; but, when he had had a
good meal he was none the worse for his rough
experience, and, as is always the case when the
danger is past, had plenty of chaff to put up with.

The channel on the south side of the island can
be used for dropping a light boat down with a
line, but all cargo has to be portaged; the north
channel is quite impracticable for navigation, having a heavy overfall with an immense body of
broken water.   The whole river-bed above the
island is covered with round boulders of soft

sandstone, many above water, which make the approach to the landing difficult. The north bank is a sand-bluff with many similar boulders protruding from the steep cliff, the south bank lower and timbered close to the water's edge. Many perfect specimens of petrifaction are to be seen on the island and along the river-banks.

The portage is the whole length of the island, about one thousand yards, and a rough tramway has been built to save the labour of carrying cargoes such a distance on men's backs; this tramway is a splendid plaything for the crews, and they spend hours in running the trolley down the hill and poling it up on the principle of a canoe ascending a rapid. Here we passed two weeks in waiting for the boats from below to take the whole of the steamer's load, which during this time was brought down by the same boats that we had used. The time slipped away quickly, though we did nothing but smoke and yarn, and towards the end of July the brigade turned up, bringing the first consignment of furs and the news from the North. We were soon off on our hundred-and-fifty-miles' run to Fort MacMurray, and the travelling was now exciting enough, a succession of rapids making hard work for the men, as several had to be run with half loads and the boats tracked up for the other half, and at a small cascade everything had to be portaged while the boats were dropped over with a line.

The worst rapid goes by the name of the Boiler

Rapid, from the fact of the boiler for the steamer
Wrigley which plies on Mackenzie River having
been lost here through the breaking of a boat.
Here the channel has a bad turn in the strong
water, and neat steering is required to clear two
reefs of rocks which lie in an awkward position
in the middle of the stream. Sometimes there
were long stretches of quiet water between the
rapids, and the boats drifted with the current
while the men smoked or slept; occasionally some
one would strike up a snatch from one of the old
French-Canadian *chansons,* which seem to be
dropping out of fashion entirely since the steamers have to such a large extent done away with
the old style of boating. Four, five, and on long
days sometimes six times we put ashore to eat;
a wonderful amount of flour, bacon, and tea being
consumed by the fifty men composing the brigade. Considering the distance from which the
provisions are brought, the inability of this part
of the country to supply any of the necessaries of
life, and the importance of forwarding trading-
goods to the northern districts before the short
summer closes, it is not surprising that there
should be at times a scarcity. On the present occasion, however, there was no stint, and fine
weather made the trip delightful. At night the
boats were run ashore, and each crew lighting
their own fire, the encampment presented a most
picturesque appearance, the gaudy belts and head-
gear of the swarthy crews as they moved in the

firelight showing in strong contrast to the dark
background of tall pine trees. We generally chose
as exposed a place as possible for the camp, to get
the benefit of any wind there might be to blow
away the mosquitos, which were bad in this part
of the river. I had the post of honour in the
leading boat steered by the guide of the brigade,
a Swampy Indian from the Red-River country
who had spent many years in voyaging for the
Hudson's Bay Company. In former days the
guide was absolute dictator and had full control
over all the boats, but nowadays discipline is slack
and he seems to have little authority.

It was a pretty sight to see the long string of
boats leaping the rapids behind us, the bowsman
standing up and pointing the course to the steersman, while the rowers plied their utmost and
broke out into the wild shouts that can never be
suppressed in moments of excitement. The Cree
language forms the medium of conversation, although many of the half-breeds talk fluently in
Red-River French; English is little spoken in any
part of the North that I visited.

On the afternoon of the fourth day we arrived
at Fort MacMurray, a small post of little importance, standing at the junction of the Athabasca
and the Clearwater River, a large stream coming
in from the southward, and until the completion
of the Canadian Pacific Railway to Calgary the
main route to the North. The outfits sent from
Winnipeg used to reach the waters falling into

the Arctic Sea far up the Clearwater at the northern end of what was known as the Long Portage,
but the present route is much simpler, as there
is no up-stream work with loaded boats. After
leaving Fort MacMurray the old course is maintained, following down stream the main artery of
the northern watershed.

The stern-wheel steamer *Grahame* was waiting
for us in the mouth of the Clearwater, with Dr.
Mackay, the Hudson's Bay Company's officer in
charge of the Athabasca district of which Mac-
Murray is the most southerly post. It extends to
the north as far as Fort Resolution on the Great
Slave Lake, and also takes in Fort Chipeweyan,
the head-post of the district, situated at the west
end of the Athabasca Lake, Fond du Lac at the
east end of the same sheet of water, Vermillion
and Little Red River on the Lower Peace River,
and Fort Smith at the foot of the rapids on the
Slave River. It is no sinecure for the man that
has to keep this vast extent of country supplied
with everything necessary for the existence of
the Indians, making the best bargain he can for
the products of their hunts, and endeavouring to
please the Chipeweyans in the woods and the
shareholders of the Company in England at the
same time.

The cargo was put on board the steamer in the
evening, and in the early morning we started
once more for the North. The water was still
exceedingly low, but not so much so as to be an

impediment to navigation, as the stream increases in size after the junction of the Clearwater, and beyond scraping once or twice on sandbars, our progress was uninterrupted. About twenty miles below MacMurray we stopped to take on wood and pitch from the natural tar deposits which are just beginning to attract a little attention in Eastern Canada, and the geologists, about to be sent from Ottawa to examine into the resources of this part of the country, will doubtless make a thorough investigation of the amount and quality of the deposit.

The whole of that day we steamed through a wilderness of pine timber presenting exactly the same appearance as in the upper reaches of the river, but on the following morning the banks became low and swampy, the stream sluggish and divided into various branches, and a few miles of intricate navigation brought us out on to the Athabasca Lake. Across on the north shore we could make out the white houses and church of Fort Chipeweyan, and after a couple of hours' steaming, with smooth water, we were alongside the rather rough apology for a landing-place.

Fort Chipeweyan was established in the early days of fur-trading, and a hundred years ago was the starting-point of Sir Alexander Mackenzie's voyage of discovery that resulted in the exploration and naming of the immense stream discharging from the Great Slave Lake. It was the scene of many stirring events during the rivalry of the

North-West and the Hudson's Bay Companies, and since their amalgamation has always been an important trading-post. At the present day it consists of a long row of white painted log-houses occupied chiefly by the Company's servants; at the southern end are the officers' quarters in close proximity to the large trading and provision stores; at the north end stand the Protestant church and Mission buildings, and farther along the lake is the Roman Catholic establishment. The numerous houses form quite an imposing sight in contrast to the surrounding desolation. The settlement is almost at the west end of the Athabasca Lake which stretches away some two hundred and fifty miles to the eastward, with Fond du Lac, a small outpost, at the far end.

Since the steamers have been running Chipeweyan has been partly supplied with the provisions of civilization, but is still chiefly dependent on its fisheries for food, and great pains are taken in the autumn to store as many whitefish as possible. At the commencement of cold weather every available net is working and the fish are hung on stages to freeze; a large number are spoilt for eating if the weather turns warm during hanging-time, but they are always available for the dogs. Trout-lines are worked all the winter, and if the supply seems to be running short, nets are also set under the ice, but usually without such good results as at the Fall fishery. Caribou from the Barren Ground sometimes wander near

Fond du Lac, and whenever this occurs the fort is kept well supplied by the Indians, but an occasional moose affords as a rule the only chance of fresh meat. Many geese and ducks are killed and salted during the spring and autumn migration of wild-fowl, which come to the Athabasca Lake at these periods in vast numbers. Chipeweyan has a large population for the part of the world in which it is situated, and as there is a proportionate consumption of food no chance of laying in a stock is missed. The lake still affords an excellent field for exploration, as beyond the main route to the east end and some of the nearer fisheries very little is known to the Whites, and the country in every direction from Fond du Lac is mapped chiefly on information derived from Indians. It is unlikely that there are any startling discoveries to be made, as the general character of the country seems to be the same as that of the district lying to the north and east of the Great Slave Lake, developing gradually into the Barren Ground; but there must be many geographical features in the form of streams and lakes to be noticed, which might amply repay the trouble of a summer's exploration. All supplies can easily be taken by water-carriage as far as the east end of the lake, though of course the well-known difficulty of transporting provisions into the Barren Ground would commence as soon as the main lake was left.

CHAPTER II

AFTER a stay of a few hours at the Fort, we started again in the *Grahame* on our voyage to the head of the rapids at Fort Smith, a distance of perhaps a hundred miles, and almost immediately passed into the main stream leaving the lake, and until the junction of the Peace bearing the name of the Rocky River. During the high water in summer part of the water of the Peace finds its way into the Athabasca Lake by a passage known as the Quatres Fourches, but as the floods subside a slight current sets in the opposite direction; the lake thus has another outlet into the Peace, which eventually joins the Rocky River about thirty miles below; the combined stream is then called the Slave River till it debouches into the Great Slave Lake, on leaving which it becomes the Mackenzie.

A distinct alteration in the appearance of the country is visible on leaving Fort Chipeweyan. The red granite rock shows up and the pine timber is smaller and more scattered, burnt in many places, and mixed with a thick growth of willows and berry-producing bushes; the scenery from the river is monotonous and without landmarks, although a wider view can be obtained than in run-

16

ning down the Athabasca, where the big pine-
trees prevent all chance of seeing far in any direction. The current is of no great velocity with the
exception of two small rapids formed by the contraction of the channel; both are navigable, although at certain stages of water it is necessary
to put out a rope to assist the steamer in mounting
the more formidable of the two. We had a very
merry passage down, Dr. Mackay and several of
the officers of his district accompanying us, and
in good time on the second day we tied up to the
bank on the west side of the river, just at the
head of the rapids.

I must take this opportunity of congratulating
the Hudson's Bay Company on the efficient manner in which their steamers are managed. Considering the utter incapacity of the Indian and
half-breed crews when they first come on board,
great praise is due to the captains and engineers
for their success in overcoming obstacles in navigation and carrying on the Company's business
in a country so remote from civilization. Everything is done in a quiet and orderly way, and a
very noticeable feature is the total absence of the
swearing and profanity so essential to the well-
being of a river-steamer in other parts of the
American continent.

The next day the work of portaging began, as
the whole cargo had to be transported sixteen
miles to the lower end of the rapids. In former
days the goods were taken down by water, neces-

The Grahame Towing Freight-scows on Lake Athabasca

sitating many portages and great delay; but within the last few years a road has been cut through the woods on the west side of the river, and the portage is made with Red-River carts drawn by oxen. Twenty carts are in use, starting loaded and returning light, on alternate days. The road is fair in a dry summer, but full of mud-holes in bad weather, and celebrated as the worst place for mosquitos in all the North.

While this was going on we amused ourselves with duck-shooting on some lakes and muskegs a few miles back from the landing, and our bag was always a welcome addition to the table, as no other kind of fresh meat was to be had. Big game is very scarce along the main route, and though there are still a few moose and bear it is rarely that an animal is seen close to the banks of the river. As soon as the cargo was all over we went across to Fort Smith, standing just below the rapids, to await the arrival of the Mackenzie River steamboat which was expected at any time. Dr. Mackay took me down the old boat-route in a canoe, and I had a good opportunity of seeing what labour and risk there must have been with heavily-laden boats; we made some fifteen portages in all, which occupied a long afternoon, with only a light canoe. A large colony of pelicans have taken possession of some islands among the rapids, and rear their young without fear of molestation.

Fort Smith, in spite of its fine situation on an

open flat high above the river, is the most disreputable establishment I came across in the North, and the contrast was more striking as most of the forts are kept rather smartly. Several half-breeds have settled close round, and a large band of Indians, known as the Caribou-Eaters, whose hunting-ground lies between the two big lakes, get their supplies from here. Within a short distance is Salt River, which produces all the salt consumed in the country, and saves the expense of importing this necessary article.

On August 13th, after several days' waiting, the steamer *Wrigley* arrived, bringing up the Mackenzie River furs and several of the officers from that district. Among her passengers was a French half-breed, King Beaulieu, who afterwards became my guide to the Barren Ground. He agreed to go in this capacity at a consultation held in Dr. Mackay's presence, swearing eternal fidelity and promising to do everything in his power to ensure the success of the expedition. Nobody could give him a very good character, but as he was known as a pushing fellow and first-rate traveller, besides having made a successful musk-ox hunt in the previous year, I concluded that my best chance lay in going with him. Certainly, with all his faults, I must say that he was thoroughly expert in all the arts of travel with canoes or dog-sleighs, quick in emergencies, and far more courageous than most of the half-breeds of the Great Slave Lake. When I was alone with him I found him easy enough to manage; but his three sons, who accompanied us, are the biggest scoundrels I ever had to travel with, and as they seem to demoralize the old man when they are together, the united family is a bad combination.

Two more days were passed in loading the *Wrigley*, and in discussion among the officers from the two districts, who only meet on this occasion, and have to make the most of the short stay to go over the news of the last year and prospects for the next. Mr. Camsell, who is in charge of Mackenzie River district, was on board, and, although I never actually went within his dominions, was exceedingly kind in giving me supplies from his own outfit, and in doing everything he could do to help me during the year that I spent in the neighbourhood of the Great Slave Lake.

The *Wrigley*, having the rough crossing of the lake to make, is a very different style of boat to the stern-wheelers above, which do all their work in smooth water. She is a screw-boat, drawing seven feet when loaded; and it gives an idea of the great size of the Mackenzie when I mention that a vessel with this draught of water has a clear run of thirteen hundred miles from Fort Smith to Peel's River, a tributary joining the main stream from the west a short distance above its mouth. She has never, I believe, steamed into the Arctic Sea, partly on account of the channel being unknown, and partly owing to the shortness of the season, which necessitates her being constantly at work to supply the forts before the closing of navigation.

After leaving Fort Smith and passing the mouth of Salt River the Slave River widens considerably, and, with a slight current running between low banks and numerous islands, follows a more circuitous course than in its upper reaches. The steamer's course covers a distance of one hundred and eighty miles to the Great Slave Lake, but, in travelling with canoes or dogs, a number of portages are made to cut off bends of the river, and about one-third of the distance is saved.

The granite formation is quickly lost sight of from the water. The sandy banks are covered with a dense growth of willows backed by the pine forest; a gloomy uninviting stretch of country, to which the tall dead trees charred by former fires give a peculiar air of desolation. The soft nature of the sand, and the fact that much of the bank has fallen in through the action of the ice breaking up in the spring, render tracking difficult on this part of the river; the fallen timber leaning over it at all angles, and making it impossible to pass the line. The sluggish nature of the current, however, compensates for this, as its strength can always be overcome by oars or paddles in the bad places. Early on the second day we steamed through the low delta lands at the mouth of the river, and, passing cautiously among the sandy battures lying far off shore, arrived in heavy rain and strong westerly wind at Fort Resolution, situated about ten miles to the westward of the river's mouth. Mr. Mackinlay, who is in charge of the fort, was away; but, as the steamer was delayed for a couple of days by the storm that was blowing, Mr. Camsell gave me very valuable assistance in making preparation for my voyage.

The resources of the fort were at the lowest; no supplies had yet arrived from outside, and the people were entirely dependent on their nets for food : as is usually the case at this time of year, fish were scarce and hard times prevalent. A boat had been fitted out to be sent to the east end of the lake to trade for meat with the Indians hunting there; but after waiting a long time for the steamer, to obtain the ammunition necessary for trading, she was blown ashore and broken up on the night of our arrival. I had intended to take a passage by this boat; but as a party of men had to be sent to Fort Smith to bring down another one, and I was anxious to get among the game with as little delay as possible, I determined to make the journey as well as I could with canoes.

It was now that I made the acquaintance of King Beaulieu's sons, François, José, and Paul, each of them married and father of such a big family that it makes one tremble for the future of the Great Slave Lake country when the next generation has grown up. The original Beaulieu seems to have been a French half-breed brought in by the Hudson's Bay Company among the early *voyageurs* from Red River. He settled at Salt River, where buffalo were numerous at the time, and by an indefinite number of wives raised a large family which is threatening gradually to inundate the North. King's father appears to have been a fighting man, and great stories of his bravery and prowess are told by his sons and grandsons; but his name only appears in the Company's records in connection with various deeds of violence not much to his credit.

All King's family were hanging about the fort in a state of semi-starvation, and I was glad when we eventually started well on in the afternoon of August 19th, with the hope of reaching first some good fishing-ground to supply them with food for immediate want, and afterwards the country of the caribou in the woods to the north of the lake, while beyond that again was the prospect of finding the musk-ox far out in the Barren Ground.

In character a Beaulieu is a mixture of a very simple child and a German Jew; all the lack of reason of the one combined with the greed of the other, and a sort of low cunning more like that of an animal than a human being. He is not a nice man to travel with, as he always keeps a longing eye on his master's possessions, even though he is fully as well-equipped himself, and is untrustworthy if you leave anything in his charge.

To your face he is fairspoken and humble enough, and to hear him talk you would think he had a certain amount of regard for you; but out of sight the promises are forgotten, and he is devising some scheme to annoy you and get something out of you. The only way to treat him is as you would treat a dog; if you are kind to him he takes it as a sign that you are afraid of him, and acts accordingly. With the exception of King there is no fear of violence; but his passion is at times so uncontrollable that he is capable of anything. It is needless to relate all the bother I had with these people, and I shall content myself with saying that the whole time I was with them the camp was the scene of one continuous wrangle; sometimes they would quarrel with me and sometimes among themselves, but we never did anything without having a row.

As far as Fort Resolution the travelling had been almost as easy, although there were many delays, as in civilization; but directly you branch from the Company's main route you are thrown entirely on your own resources, and, owing to the impossibility of carrying enough provision for a prolonged journey in the Barren Ground, the rifle and net are the only means of obtaining food. This is a point to be well considered before undertaking a trip to the country of the musk-ox, as, however well you may be supplied at starting, you are sure to experience some hard times before your object is accomplished.

My only provisions consisted of a couple of sacks of flour and about fifty pounds of bacon, and I might as well have started with none at all. My companions had all the improvidence of the Indian nature, and hated the idea of keeping anything for hard times. There was such a constant begging, not without a certain excuse from hunger, to be allowed to eat flour and bacon, that I was really rather glad when it was all gone, which was actually the case before we left the Great Slave Lake. We had a good supply of tea and tobacco, though it proved after all insufficient, plenty of ammunition for the three Winchester rifles, and powder, shot, and ball for the muzzle-loading weapons of the party; we had also nets and a few hooks and lines, matches, needles, and awls to be used in the manufacture of moccasins and the deer-skin clothes so essential for winter travel; knives of various shapes and sizes, scrapers for dressing skins, and a small stock of the duffel imported by the Company for lining mittens and wrapping up the feet during the intense cold that we were sure to experience during the trip.

Our fleet numbered three large birch-bark canoes, crowded with men, women, and children, amounting in all to over twenty souls, or, to be more practical, mouths. Besides these there were fifteen gaunt and hungry dogs, which had been spending their short summer's rest in starving as a preparation for the hard work and harder blows which were in store for them in the coming winter.

I was of course the only white man in the party, and whatever conversation I held with the three or four half-breeds that I could understand was carried on in the French patois of the North. Among themselves they used the Montaignais dialect of the Chipeweyan language, which is spoken with variations to the northward of the Cree-speaking belt, till its place is taken by the Slavi and Locheaux language of the Mackenzie River; in a couple of months I had picked up enough Montaignais to be able to mix it with French and make myself fairly well understood.

Four deerskin lodges made our encampment. I lived with King, as his camp was always the quietest; in the other lodges there was a continual screaming of children, or yelping of hungry dogs as they felt the cruel blow of axe or paddle, which was the sure result of approaching the savoury-smelling kettle too close. We camped the first night in the delta of the Slave, or, as it is more usually called, the Big River. I distributed a little ammunition, and we killed enough ducks to provide the whole party with a night's provision. The next day a gale of wind was blowing from the lake, and, after following winding muddy channels all the morning, we were obliged to camp again on a point of willows beyond which we should have been exposed to the full violence of the storm, and our overloaded canoes would have had no chance of living in the heavy sea. Here we remained two days, still within twenty miles of the fort. Wild-fowl were numerous, but the great autumn migration had not yet set in, and all the birds that we found had been bred in the muskegs that surrounded us on all sides; they were mostly mallard, widgeon, teal, shoveller, and pintail, the latter being particularly plentiful. Musk-rats swam in all the little creeks and lakes, and, as they are esteemed as an article of food, and their skins are of a trifling value, we killed a great many.

On the third day we paddled along the shore of the lake against a strong head-wind, passing the Isle de Pierre, one of the best fisheries in the neighbourhood, and camped at the Point of Rocks, the first spot on the south side of the lake where the red granite again shows up, and the end of the muskeg country that extends far on each side of the Big River. Here we caught enough whitefish with the nets to enable even the dogs to have a small feed, and, as we killed forty ducks while waiting for the wind to moderate, everybody was satisfied. In the afternoon we put out in a calm to paddle across the open traverse to the first of a group of islands about fifteen miles to the north. This traverse is the terror of the lake for canoes, both in summer on account of the heavy sea which gets up suddenly, and in winter when the drifting snow in stormy weather obscures everything and makes it a difficult matter

Patching a Birch-bark on the Slave River

to keep the course over the ice. On this occasion we got over just in time, and, camping on the nearest island of the group, were delayed for two days by strong north-west winds accompanied by showers of driving rain.

These islands, marked on the map as Simpson's Group, extend for a hundred miles in a north-easterly direction to Fond du Lac, and, if ever explored, will be found to be in immense numbers, varying in size, but all of the same red-granite formation, covered with a scanty growth of pine, birch, and willows. Many of them rise to a considerable height, with the ridges generally running south-west and north-east. A few moose still inhabit the larger islands; but the big herds of caribou from the Barren Ground that used formerly to come here in their wanderings seem to have deserted them of late years. An occasional small pond gives harbourage for a few wild-fowl, while wood-grouse, and in winter ptarmigan, are plentiful. The bare outlying rocks between the islands are the breeding-ground of gulls and terns : divers and a few cormorants give additional life to the lake in summer; but at the first sign of cold weather the water-birds all leave for a more temperate land, and a deathlike silence settles over the frozen channels during the eight months of winter.

The island on which we were encamped, being the most westerly of the group, was exposed to the full force of the gale. The heavy fresh-water seas broke with great violence on the weather shore and on the numerous rocks, some above water and others submerged, that make the navigation of this part of the lake dangerous for anything larger than a canoe. It was no easy matter to get out our nets, even to leeward of the island, and the supply of fish was very scanty; dissatisfaction was prevalent in the camp, and heavy inroads were made on the flour and bacon that would have proved so useful later on. When the weather moderated we started against a strong head-wind, and a hard day's paddling brought us to a spot known as the Inconnu Fishery, situated on an island halfway to Fond du Lac. The Inconnu, or Unknown Fish, is, I believe, entirely restricted to the Mackenzie River country, and its southernmost limits seem to be the rapids at Fort Smith; it was thus named by the early *voyageurs* of the Company, who were unable to classify it, and even to this day there is a great variety of opinion as to what family it is a member of: a long thin fish, not unlike a misshapen salmon, running up to fifteen pounds in weight, with flabby and unpalatable flesh, it is held in very low estimation in comparison with whitefish or trout, and is only appreciated in hard times. At this particular island it will take a bait readily, but I never heard of its doing so in any other part of the lake, although large numbers are caught in the nets. There is some peculiarity in the water which may account for this, as, even in the dead of winter, there is generally an open hole in the ice; and, in passing the Inconnu Fishery, one must keep right ashore to avoid the treacherous spot. Here we were wind-bound again, and indeed for several days made very little headway against the northerly gales that seem almost incessant at this time of year. We had a pleasant spot to camp in every night, but not always enough to eat, and it was the first of September before we sighted the high land on the north side of the lake. This was the first really fine day we had had since leaving the fort, and, taking advantage of it, we left the shelter of the islands, made a bold crossing of the wide stretch of open water, and camped among the scattering pines on the northern mainland. Exactly opposite to us was the narrow entrance to Christie's Bay of the maps, extending some hundred miles to the east and southeast, offering another tempting field for exploration. On the west side of the entrance is a remarkable many-coloured bluff, composed of the soft rock used by the Indians for the manufacture of their stone pipes, which are still in common use.

The range of hills along the north shore, which we now had to coast, average perhaps five hundred feet in height, occasionally reaching a much higher elevation, but without any conspicuous peaks; the land begins to rise at once from the lake, in many places taking the form of a steep cliff. The vegetation is the same as that on the south side of the lake, but more stunted, the pine trees especially showing the increased rigour of the climate; small birch trees are still numerous, and the growth of the hardy willows is almost as strong as at Fort Resolution. Fruit-bearing plants are common. The small muskegs between the ridges of rock are full of a much-prized yellow berry, while blueberry bushes flourish in the dry spots, and a few raspberries are still to be seen; but strawberries, which used to be plentiful on the south shore and among the islands, have disappeared. I noticed here the low trailing plant bearing a woolly red berry, known as Cannicannick by the Indians to the west of the Rocky Mountains, and used by them as tobacco; the Slave Lake Indians sometimes smoke it, but prefer the inner bark of the red willow; the Hudson's Bay negrohead tobacco is in my opinion much improved, as well as economized, by a mixture with either of these substances. Countless streams, the outlet of lakes on the elevated table-land to the north, foam down the deep gulches in the hillside, and confused masses of fallen timber and rocks give evidence of the frequent landslides that take place during the spring thaws.

Again the north wind howled dismally down the lake, and several more days were occupied in reaching Fond du Lac. The enforced delay had a depressing effect upon the whole party, as fish were scarce, and paddling against continual head-winds is always hard work. At last, on Septem-

ber 5th, passing through a narrow arm of the
lake with a perceptible current formed by the pre-
vailing winds, we came in sight of Fond du Lac.
A single house at the head of a snug little bay is
all that is left standing, but the ruins of others,
and a number of rough graves, show that at one
time it was a more populous place. It was formerly an outpost of Fort Resolution, used as a depot for collecting meat, and presided over in a
haphazard manner by King Beaulieu, who is still
rather sore about the abandonment of the post
and his own discharge from the Company's service. The weather now became worse than ever,
snow and hail taking the place of rain and throwing the first white mantle on the hill-tops. It was
evident that such a large party, crippled as we
were with women and children, would never be
able to reach the caribou, in the event of these
animals being far back from the Great Slave
Lake. We had met no Indians, and so had no
means of hearing the news of the caribou, which
forms the one topic of interest among the Dog-
Rib and Yellow Knife tribes who hunt in this
part of the country. Luckily trout and whitefish
were fairly abundant, some of the former reaching such an enormous size that I am afraid to
hazard a guess at their weight, though I afterwards saw one at the fort that turned the scale at
fifty-eight pounds.

CHAPTER III

WE held a big council as to ways and means, and, after much discussion, finally came to the decision that our best chance was to leave the main body of women and children with sufficient men to attend to the nets for them, while the rest of us pushed on to the north with our two biggest canoes, in the hope of falling in with the caribou, and afterwards the musk-ox. We were to leave all the dogs at Fond du Lac, as we expected to send back before the setting in of winter; only two women, King's wife and daughter, were to come with us to dry meat, dress deerskins, and make moccasins. Besides them our crew consisted of King Beaulieu, his sons François, José, Paul, and Baptiste (a boy of twelve), Michel (King's son-in-law), and a small Indian boy who had thrown in his lot with us as the best visible means of getting anything to keep him alive during the autumn. All the provisions that I had brought with me were exhausted, and we had nothing but a dozen small dried whitefish when we left Fond du Lac on September 7th to paddle another thirty miles along the north shore before leaving the lake. Our loads were cut down to the smallest weight possible in order to save time on

King Beaulieu

the portages. I left my Paradox behind as the ammunition was heavy, and trusted entirely to a Winchester rifle; a pair of glasses and a blanket about completed my share of the cargo. I had no instruments for taking observations, no compass, and no watch; and, take it all round, it was a very poorly-equipped expedition. We made a bad start, as, after an hour's travel across a deep bay, we found ourselves storm-bound on a small island, the canoes hauled up on the beach, and such a heavy sea on all sides that we could not get out a net. We spent an uncomfortable night on the island, but the wind moderated a little in the morning and we put out again. After being once driven back to our refuge we managed to reach the mainland, with the canoes half full of water and our blankets and clothes soaked. However, a good fire soon mended matters, and, as we caught enough whitefish to stave off present hunger, contentment reigned in the camp.

The next evening, after another long struggle against the wind, we camped in the small bay at which we intended to make our first portage, and our long journey on the Great Slave Lake was finished. Three ducks, our whole bag for the day, and a kettle of black tea gave us a scanty supper, and, as there was still a little daylight, we each carried a small load to the top of the hill, a distance of two miles, but were disappointed in not seeing any caribou tracks. We thought we had a chance of finding them close to the lake, but as a matter of fact we had several days' journey yet before we fell in with them. It now seemed pretty certain that we were in for a spell of what my companions alluded to as *les misères* till we reached the meat-country, the joys of which formed the chief subject of talk round the camp-fires.

With the first streak of light we began the portage in a driving snowstorm, and long before midday the rest of the cargo and the biggest canoe were landed at the top of the steep climb; the other canoe we abandoned, thinking one was ample for our work in the Barren Ground. We sat down for a smoke at the top of the hill, and took our last view of the Great Slave Lake. Looking southward we could see the far shore and the unknown land beyond rising in terraces to a considerable height, and very similar in appearance to the range we were on. Ahead of us, to the north, lay a broken rocky country sparsely timbered and dotted with lakes, the nearest of which, a couple of miles away, was the end of our portage; a bleak and desolate country, already white with snow and with a film of ice over the smaller ponds. Three hundred miles in the heart of this wilderness, far beyond the line where timber ceases, lies the land of the musk-ox, to which we were about to force our way, depending entirely on our guns for food and for clothing to withstand the intense cold that would soon be upon us. A pair of hawks hovering overhead furnished the only signs of life, and the outlook was by no means cheerful. As I was sitting on a rock meditating upon these things old King came up and said: "Let us finish the portage quickly; it is dinner-time." I quite agreed with him, but put his remark down as a rather unseasonable joke, as I did not think there was a bite to eat among us; but on reaching the lake I was pleasantly surprised to see King fish out a lump of bacon, which he had stowed away some time ago after one of my lectures on improvidence. It was really the last piece, and, although there was no bread (and for the matter of that there was none for the next three months) we all made a good enough meal. The lake was of course named Lac du Lard to commemorate this event.

I think no white man had ever passed through this chain of lakes before, as Sir John Franklin went up by a more westerly route, following the course of the Yellow Knife River, while Hearne and Back both left from the east end of the Great Slave Lake; Stewart and Anderson, when they were searching for survivors of Franklin's last ill-fated expedition, reached the head waters of the Great Fish River by a chain of lakes about eighty miles to the eastward of my present route. If the lakes were known among the Indians by any particular names I enquired their meaning and preserved them; the others I named from incidents in the voyage or from the Company's officers of Athabasca and Mackenzie River districts.

During the afternoon we made four more short portages, passing through the same number of lakes, some of them of a considerable size. We kept a good look-out for the caribou but saw no signs of them, and at dark, after a hard day's work, camped on the east shore of the Lac de Mort. It acquired this name from a disaster that overwhelmed a large encampment of Yellow Knives who were hunting here during one of those epidemics of scarlet fever that have from time to time ravaged the North. Most of the hunters were too ill to walk, and, as game was scarce, the horrors of starvation, combined with disease, almost exterminated the band.

The next two days were occupied in the same manner of travelling towards the north with numerous portages. We could not catch any fish, though we set a net every night, but killed enough ducks to keep us alive without satisfying our ravenous hunger. The weather was still cold, with strong head-winds and frequent snowstorms.

On the third day we caught a big trout and killed a loon and a wolverine, the latter after a most exciting chase on a long point. In the next portage accordingly we made a big feast, although wolverines are only eaten in starving times, as they are looked upon in the light of scavengers and grave-robbers, and *"carcajou*-eater" is a favourite term of contempt. On the present occasion nobody made any objection, and in the circumstances the despised meat tasted remarkably well. Our joy was soon cut short by finding the next lake, which was more sheltered from the wind than the others we had passed through, covered with a sheet of ice sufficiently thick to prevent the passage of a birchbark canoe, while a heavy snowstorm came on at the same time, making matters look more gloomy than ever. King's sons at once expressed their intention of returning to Fond du Lac while the lakes behind them were still open. King, however, here showed great determination, and declared, with an unnecessary amount of strong language, that he had the heart of Beaulieu (the worst sort of heart, by the way), and, when once he had started, would not turn back without seeing the musk-ox. Eventually we persuaded them to come on, and, carrying the canoe, reduced our load to the very smallest amount of necessaries. We then started on foot for an expedition that would have most certainly ended in disaster if we had gone on with it. I noticed that the two women had the heaviest loads to carry, but having myself as much as I cared about for a long distance I made no remarks on the subject. Luckily, after spending a night without eating under the shelter of a bunch of dwarf pines, we discovered the next lake to be almost clear of ice; and carrying our canoe over the four-mile portage we continued our journey as before, pushing on as quickly as possible to reach the Lac du Rocher, where the half-breeds were confident of meeting the caribou, or, at the worst, to camp at a spot well known to them where we might catch fish enough for a temporary support. We had now been in a half-starving condition for several days, and were beginning to lose the strength that we required for portaging and paddling against the continual north wind.

On September 13th we reached the Lac du Rocher, a large irregular sheet of water, so broken up with bays and promontories that it is hard to estimate its size. Camp was made on the south side of the lake, and we set our nets and lines, baited with carefully preserved pieces of white-fish, while others explored the surrounding hills for caribou tracks, but without success. The half-breeds were all much put out by this failure, as they have always found the Lac du Rocher a certainty for caribou at this time of year, and were unable to account for it, except by the theory that the animals had altered the usual course of their autumn migration and were passing to the east of us. There was not a fish in the net when we turned in; but a good trout was caught in the middle of the night, and we all got up and finished the last mouthful. Again we had no breakfast, and the early morning found us discussing various plans in rather a serious manner. The final decision was that Paul and François should push ahead to try and find the caribou, while the rest of us moved the camp to the north end of the lake and worked the fishing till their return; six days were allowed them for their trip, after which each party was to act independently, and we were all to get out of the awkward situation in the best way we could.

Accordingly we took the canoes across the lake as soon as our hunters had started, and put up our deerskin lodge in the shelter of a clump of well-grown pine trees; we tried the hand-lines for hours without any better result than completely numbing our fingers, and towards evening set the net, also without any luck. I took my rifle and walked two or three miles back from the lake, but beyond an Arctic fox, which I missed at long range, saw nothing edible.

There is no better camp than a well-set-up lodge with a good fire crackling in the middle, and in this respect we were comfortable enough, but the shortness of food was telling rapidly. We had made no pretence at eating all day, and since leaving Fond du Lac had subsisted almost entirely on tea and tobacco, while even on the Great Slave Lake provisions had been none too plentiful. We passed the evening smoking, and, as I have found usual in these cases, talking of all the good things we had ever eaten, while eyes shone in the fire-light with the brilliancy peculiar to the early stages of starvation. Outside the lodge the wind was moderated; the northern lights, though it was still early in the year, were flashing brightly across the sky, and far away in the distance we could hear the ominous howling of wolves. Late in the night I awoke, and, on lighting my pipe, was greeted by King with the remark: "Ah! Monsieur, une fois j'ai goûté le pain avec le buerre; le bon Dieu a fait ces deux choses là exprès pour manger ensemble."

Long before daylight we put off in the canoe to visit the net, and to our great joy found five fair-sized trout, quite enough to relieve all anxiety for the day; the weather also had improved, turning much warmer, with the snow rapidly thawing. The half-breeds, who are all Catholics, held a short service, as it was Sunday morning and they are very particular in this respect. Afterwards we all went out hunting, but only two or three ptarmigan, the first we had seen, were killed, and there were still no signs of the caribou. The country here is much less rugged than on first leaving the Great Slave Lake, and the rolling hills are covered with a small plant, halfway between heather and moss, bearing a small black berry, and growing in thick bunches wherever the soil is capable of producing it. This plant, and a wiry black moss which grows in patches on the flat rocks, are much used as fuel in dry weather, if no wood is available; in wet weather they are of course useless. The hollows between the ridges are generally muskegs, thawed out to the depth of a foot, producing a long coarse grass, and in many places a plentiful growth of a dwarf variety of the Labrador tea, an excellent substitute for the product of China. Huge glacial boulders lie scattered in every direction, many of them balanced in an extraordinary manner on the points of smaller stones, which seem to have been of softer substance and gradually worn away. In other spots are patches of broken rocks, covering a large extent of ground and very difficult to travel on, especially when a light coating of snow makes them slippery, and conceals the deep holes in which a leg might easily be snapped; even the caribou, sure-footed as they are, will often make a long detour in preference to taking the risk of a fall among these rocks. Lakes of all sizes and shapes abound on every side, connected by small streams that find their way into the Slave Lake one hundred miles to the southward. Pine timber is now very scarce and mostly small, growing in sheltered spots with long stretches where not a tree is visible. A fairly thick stem starts from the ground and immediately spreads out into a bush with the branches growing downwards, and the top of the tree seldom reaching a height of ten feet. Sometimes, however, even as far out as this, a bunch of really well-grown trees is to be found, probably having the advantages of better soil to spring from. A very few birch sticks, invaluable to the Indian for making snow-shoes, still manage to exist, and patches of scrub willow are frequent. The general appearance of the country and the vegetation, with the exception of the timber, reminded me strongly of the desert of Arnavatn in the interior of Iceland.

A great variety of mosses and lichens flourish

here and in the true Barren Ground outside the tree limit, the *tripe des roches* which has played such a conspicuous part in the story of Arctic exploration being particularly abundant at this spot. The formation of the rocks is still red granite, with a good deal of mica showing in the boulders.

Late in the evening we heard a gun, and, on our replying, four or five shots were fired in rapid succession, the signal of good news; soon afterwards Paul and François came in, each carrying a small load of meat, which we finished promptly. They had fallen in with the caribou about thirty miles on, and reported them to be moving south in great numbers; we had now no hesitation in pushing on to meet them, and were all jubilant at the thought of good times coming. The next day was warm again with south-west wind, and, after passing through the Lac du Corbeau (named from our little Indian, who had acquired the title of *Chasseur du Corbeau* from an unsuccessful hunt he had made after a raven at one of our hungry camps), we portaged into Lake Camsell, a fine sheet of water over twenty miles in length, running more to the east than the other lakes we had passed, full of small islands, and with rather more timber than usual on its shores.

For the first time we could put down our paddles, and, hoisting a large red blanket for a sail, ran in front of the steady fair wind; the water was blue, the sun pleasantly warm, and the snow had almost disappeared. In the afternoon there was a cry of *Et-then, Et-then!* (the caribou), and we saw a solitary bull standing against the sky-line on the top of an island close to the east shore of the lake. As soon as we were out of sight we landed and quickly surrounded him; he made a break for the water, but one of the half-breeds, in hiding behind a rock, dropped him before he put to sea. It was a full-grown bull in prime condition, the velvet not yet shed, but the horns quite hard underneath.

A scene of great activity now commenced. There was no more thought of travelling that night, and, while two men were skinning and cutting up the caribou, the others unloaded and carried ashore the canoe, lit a fire, and got ready the kettles for a feast that was to make up for all the hard times just gone through. There was plenty of meat for everybody to gorge themselves, and we certainly made a night of it, boiling and roasting till we had very nearly finished the whole animal. I could not quite keep up with the others at this first trial of eating powers, but after a couple of weeks among the caribou I was fully able to hold my own. We seemed at length to have found the land of plenty, as ptarmigan were very numerous, just losing the last of their pretty brown plumage and putting on their white dresses to match the snow, which would soon drive them for food and shelter into the thick pine woods round the shores of the Great Slave Lake.

We had to sleep off the effects of over-eating, and it was late in the day before we started down the lake. After two or three hours' sailing at a slow pace we spied a band of caribou, again on an island. With unnecessary haste we made for the land, and, through watching the deer instead of the water, ran the canoe on a sharp submerged rock, tearing an ugly hole in the birch-bark. We all stepped overboard up to the waist, carried the cargo ashore, and, leaving the women to stitch up the canoe with the bark and fibre that is always kept handy when away from the birch woods, started in pursuit of the caribou. The result was that after a great deal of bad shooting we killed sixteen on the island, while the canoe, hastily patched up, with a kettle going steadily to bale out and the women paddling and shouting lustily, succeeded in picking up two more that tried to escape by swimming.

The evening was passed in skinning and cutting up the meat, which was stowed away in rough *caches* of rocks to keep it safe from the wolves and wolverines. These animals are always very plentiful in attendance on the big herds of caribou, and are often the cause of much annoyance to the hunter through stealing meat that he is relying upon for subsistence; in many places where the rocks are small it is impossible to build a *cache* strong enough to keep out the wolverines, which are possessed of wonderful strength for their size.

The following day while Michel, Paul, and myself were walking overland to join the canoe at the end of the lake, we fell in with another band of caribou, and, as the rest of the party landed at an opportune moment, we caught the animals on a long point and made another big slaughter of seventeen, among them some old bulls with very fine heads. A young bull, nearly pure-white in colour, came my way, and I secured him, but unfortunately the skin was afterwards stolen by wolverines. We had now plenty of meat to establish a permanent camp, and set up our lodge at the end of Lake Camsell with the intention of leaving the women and boys to collect and dry the meat and dress the skins, while the men were away on a short hunt after musk-ox before the lakes set fast with ice.

We were now within a short distance of the last woods, if a few bunches of dwarf pines, at intervals of several miles, can be called woods, and were about to push out into the Barren Ground, where, with the exception of an occasional patch of small scrub willow, all timber ceases.

CHAPTER IV

In the various records of Arctic exploration, and especially in those dealing with the Barren Ground, there is frequent mention of deer, reindeer, and caribou, leaving the casual reader in doubt as to how many species of deer inhabit the rocky wilderness between the woods and the Arctic Sea. As a matter of fact, the Barren Ground caribou (which name I prefer, as distinguishing it from the woodland caribou, the only other member of the reindeer tribe existing on the American continent) is the sole representative of the Cervidæ found in this locality.

The chief distinction between this animal and its cousin the woodland caribou, or *caribou des bois fort* in the half-breed parlance, lies in the different size, the latter having by far the advantage in height and weight. I have had no opportunity of weighing specimens of either kind, but should imagine that the woodland must be fully a third the heavier of the two. I cannot agree with some of the natural history books which state that the smaller animals carry the larger horns, as of all the Barren Ground caribou that we killed I never saw any with horns to compare with the giant antlers of the woodland caribou of

Newfoundland or British Columbia; more irregular, if possible, they may be, and perhaps have a greater number of points, but they are far behind in weight, spread, and size of beam. The perfect double plough is more often seen in the smaller specimen, the larger animal being usually provided with only one, or with one plough and a spike. In colour they closely resemble each other, but there is rather more white noticeable in the representative of the Barren Ground, especially in the females, while the texture of the coat, as is to be expected, is finer in the smaller variety. The hoofs have the same curious "snow-shoe" formation in both cases.

The range of the Barren Ground caribou appears to be from the islands in the Arctic Sea to the southern part of Hudson's Bay, while the Mackenzie River is the limit of their western wandering, although not many years ago they are known to have crossed the Slave River in the neighbourhood of Fort Smith. In the summer time they keep to the true Barren Ground, but in the autumn, when their feeding-grounds are covered with snow, they seek the hanging moss in the woods. From what I could gather from the Yellow Knife Indians at the east end of the Great Slave Lake, and from my own personal experience, it was late in October, immediately after the rutting season, that the great bands of caribou, commonly known as *La Foule*, mass up on the edge of the woods, and start for food and shelter afforded by the stronger growth of pines farther southward. A month afterwards the males and females separate, the latter beginning to work their way north again as early as the end of February; they reach the edge of the woods in April, and drop their young far out towards the sea-coast in June, by which time the snow is melting rapidly and the ground showing in patches. The males stay in the woods till May and never reach the coast, but meet the females on their way inland at the end of July; from this time they stay together till the rutting season is over and it is time to seek the woods once more.

The horns are mostly clear of velvet towards the end of September, but some of the females carry it later even than this; the old bulls shed their antlers early in December, and the young ones do the same towards the end of that month, the females being some weeks later. In June both sexes present a very shabby appearance, as the old coats have grown long and white and are falling off in patches; by the end of July the new hair has grown, and the skins are then in their best condition.

The caribou are extremely uncertain in their movements, seldom taking the same course in two consecutive years, and thus affording ground for the universal cry in the North that the caribou are being killed off. I think there is really much truth in the statement that they keep a more easterly route than formerly, as they seldom come in large quantities to the Mackenzie River, where they used to be particularly numerous in winter. This is in a great measure accounted for by the fact that great stretches of the country have been burnt, and so rendered incapable of growing the lichen so dearly beloved by these animals. The same thing applies at Fort Resolution, where, within the last decade, the southern shore of the Great Slave Lake has been burnt and one of the best ranges totally destroyed.

One point that seems to bear out the theory of a more easterly movement is that within the last three years the caribou have appeared in their thousands at York Factory on the west side of Hudson's Bay, where they have not been seen for over thirty years; but I cannot believe, judging from the vast herds that I myself saw, that there is any danger of the caribou being exterminated.

It is absurd to say that the white man is killing them off, as no white man ever fires a shot at them unless they pass very close to a Company's establishment, and the Indians are themselves surely dying out year by year. Nor is it any argument to say that the Indians sometimes starve to death from want of success in hunting, as a glance at Hearne's *Journey to the Northern Ocean in 1771* will show that the same state of affairs prevailed before the Company had penetrated to the Great Slave Lake or Mackenzie River. Starvation will always be one of the features of a Northern Indian's life, owing to his own improvidence; his instinct is to camp close on the tracks of the caribou and move as they move; a permanent house and a winter's supply of meat are an abomination to him.

Since the introduction of firearms the Indian has lost much of his old hunting lore! a snare is almost a thing of the past, but is still occasionally used when ammunition is scarce. It is no hard matter to kill caribou in the open country, for the rolling hills usually give ample cover for a stalk, and even on flat ground they are easily approached at a run, as they will almost invariably circle head to wind and give the hunter a chance to cut them off. But it is with the spear that the vast slaughter in the summer is annually made. The best swimming-places are known and carefully watched, and woe betide a herd of caribou if once surrounded in a lake by the small hunting-canoes. One thrust of the spear, high up in the loins and ranging forward, does the work. There is no idea of sparing life, no matter what the age or sex of the victim may be; the lake is red with blood and covered with sometimes several hundred carcasses, of which fully one-half are thrown away as not fat enough to be eaten by men who may be starving in a month. Surely this should exterminate the game; but, if one remonstrates with the Indians at the waste, the ready answer comes: "Our fathers did this and have taught us to do the same; they did not kill off the caribou, and after we are gone there will be plenty for our children." These animals are easily induced to swim at any particular spot by putting up a line of rocks at right angles to the water, and a line of pine bush planted in the snow across a frozen lake has the same effect; the caribou will not pass it, but following it along fall an easy prey to the hunter lying in ambush at the end of the line. In the winter they are killed in great numbers on the small lakes in the timber, as they seem disinclined to leave the open lake and will often run close up to the gun rather than take to the woods. I have heard this accounted for by the suggestion that they take the report of the gun for a falling tree and are afraid of being struck if they venture off the lake; but I fancy their natural curiosity has a great deal to do with this extraordinary behaviour. It frequently happens that they will run backwards and forwards within range till the last of the band is killed.

The caribou supplies the Indian with nearly all the necessaries of life; it gives him food, clothing, house, and the equivalent of money to spend at the fort. He leaves the trading-post, after one of his yearly visits, with a supply of ammunition, tea, and tobacco, a blanket or two, and, if he has made a good season's hunt, is perhaps lucky enough to have taken one of the Company's duffel *capotes* (about the best form of greatcoat that I have ever seen). He has a wife and family waiting for him somewhere on the shore of the big lake where fish are plentiful, expecting a gaudy dress, a shawl, or a string of beads from the fort, but relying entirely on the caribou for maintenance during the awful cold of the coming winter. The journey up till they fall in with the caribou is usually full of hardships, but once they have reached the hunting-ground and found game a great improvement in affairs takes place; the hunter is busy killing, while the women dry meat and make grease, dress the skins for moccasins, mittens, and gun-covers, and cut *babiche,* which takes the place of string for lacing snow-shoes and many other purposes. For the hair-coats, which everybody, men, women, and children, wear during the cold season, the best skins are those of the young animals killed in July or August, as the hair is short and does not fall off so readily as in coats made from the skin of a full-grown caribou; while the strong sinews lying along the back-bone of an old bull make the very best thread for sewing. Anything that is left over after supplying the whole family finds a ready sale at the fort, where there is always a demand for dried meat, tongue-grease, dressed skins, and *babiche,* so that the Dog-Ribs and Yellow Knives, whose country produces little fur, with the exception of musk-ox robes, are thus enabled to afford some few of the white man's luxuries, tea and tobacco being especially dear to the Indian's heart.

A good hunter kills the caribou with discretion

according to their condition at various seasons of the year. After the females leave the woods in the early spring he has of course only the males to fall back on, and these are usually poor till August, when the bones are full of marrow and the back-fat commences to grow. By the middle of September this back-fat, or *depouille* as it is called in Northern patois, has reached a length of a foot or more forward from the tail, and, as it is sometimes a couple of inches thick and extends right across the back, it is a great prize for the lucky hunter. It is a point of etiquette that when two or more Indians are hunting in company, the *depouille* and tongue belong to the man who did the killing, while the rest of the meat is shared in common.

Towards the end of October, when the rutting season is over, the males are in very poor condition. The females then come into demand, but it is not till the end of the year that they show any back-fat at all, and this is always small in comparison with that of a bull killed in the Fall. The summer months are generally spent by the Indians far out in the Barren Ground, and then, as I have said, they slaughter everything that comes within reach of their spear in the most indiscriminate manner.

Excepting in times of plenty, when the utmost recklessness with provisions is displayed, there are very few parts of the caribou thrown away, and often the actual stomach is the only thing left; the blood is carefully preserved, and some of the intestines are prized as great luxuries. If one does not see the actual preparations for cooking they are good enough, but the favourite dish of all, the young unborn caribou cut from its dead mother, I could never take kindly to, although it is considered a delicacy among the Indians throughout the northern part of Canada. Another morsel held in high esteem is the udder of a milk-giving doe, which is usually roasted on the spot where the animal is killed. Of the external parts the ribs and brisket rank highest, the haunches being generally reserved for dog's food; a roast head is not to be despised, and a well-smoked tongue is beyond all praise. It was the caribou of the Barren Ground that provided the reindeers' tongues formerly exported in such quantities by the Hudson's Bay Company. The general method of cooking everything in the lodge is by boiling, which takes most of the flavour out of the meat, but has the advantage of being easy and economical of firewood.

The marrow is usually eaten raw, and, as there is no blood visible in the bones of a fat animal, it is not such a disgusting habit as it seems to be at first sight, and one readily accustoms oneself to the fashion. Everybody who has travelled in the North has experienced the same craving for grease as the cold becomes more intense. In the case of a white man the enforced absence of flour and all vegetable food may be an additional cause

for this feeling; but it is a fact that you can cheer-
fully gnaw a solid block of grease or raw fat that
it would make you almost sick to look at in a land
of temperate climate and civilized methods of living.

The Indian is by no means the only enemy of
the caribou. Along the shore of the Arctic Sea
live straggling bands of Esquimaux who kill great
quantities of these persecuted animals, although
employing more primitive methods than their
southern neighbours; it is done, moreover, at the
most fatal season of the year, just as the females
have arrived at the coast and are dropping their
young. Then there are the ever-hungry wolves
and wolverines that hang with such pertinacity
on the travelling herds and rely upon them entirely for subsistence. It is rarely that a caribou
once singled out can escape. The wolves hunt
in bands and seldom leave the track they have
selected; the chase lasts for many hours, till the
victim, wearied by the incessant running, leaves
the band and his fate is sealed; he has a little
the best of the pace at first but not the staying
power, and is soon pulled to the ground. Many
a time I witnessed these courses, and once disturbed half a dozen wolves just as they commenced their feast on a caribou in which life was
hardly extinct, and I took the tongue and *depouille* for my share of the hunt.

I only saw wolves of two colours, white and
black, during my stay in the North, although I

heard much talk of grey wolves. There was some sort of disease, resembling mange, among them in the winter of 1889-90, which had the effect of taking off all their hair, and, judging from the number of dead that were lying about, must have considerably thinned their numbers. They do not seem to be dangerous to human beings except when starving; but the Indians have stories of crazy wolves that run into the lodges, kill the children, and play general havoc. I know that they do at times get bold under stress of hunger, as my own hauling dogs were set upon and eaten by them while harnessed to the sleigh close to the house at Fond du Lac; nothing remained but the sleigh, and a string of bells that must have proved less tempting than the rest of the harness.

I scarcely credit the statement I have often heard made, that the wolverines will kill a full-grown caribou, although it is possible that they may attack the young ones. They follow the herds more for the pickings they can get from the feasts of the wolves, and are content with showing their fighting powers on hares and ptarmigan; if meat is not to be had they will eat berries freely, and their flesh is then not so bad as after they have had a long course of meat. The *carcajou* possesses great strength and cunning in removing rocks and breaking into a *cache;* it climbs with great agility, and has a mean trick of throwing down a marten-trap from behind and taking out the bait, and is generally credited by

A Dead White Wolf

the Indian with more wiles than the devil himself. It is an animal common enough in many parts of Canada, but is rarely seen in the woods on account of its retiring habits. In the Barren Ground, however, I had many opportunities of watching them through the glasses as they worked at the carcass of a caribou or musk-ox, and was much struck by the enormous power exercised by so small an animal; in travelling it seems to use only one pace, the *lope* of the Western prairies, which it is said to be able to keep up for an indefinite time.

Another great source of annoyance to the caribou are the two sorts of gadfly which use these animals as a hatching-ground for their eggs. The biggest kind, which seem the most numerous, deposit their eggs on the back, and, as they hatch out the grubs, bore through the skin and prey on the surrounding flesh. They begin to show in October, and grow bigger through the winter till the following spring, the number of holes in many cases rendering the skin absolutely useless for dressing. The other kind of fly lays its eggs in the nostril, with the result that in the months of May and June a nest of writhing grubs, slimmer and more lively than the grubs under the skin, appears at the root of the tongue; at this time of year the caribou may be often seen to stop and shake their heads violently, with their horns close to the ground, evidently greatly troubled by these grubs. Of the latter kind the Indians who travelled with me in the summer have a great horror, warning me to be very careful not to eat them, as they have an idea they would surely grow in a man's throat; and whenever we killed an animal, the first operation was to cut off its head and remove these unpleasant objects. By the beginning of August all the grubs have dropped off and the holes healed up, while the new coat has grown and the skins are then in their best condition.

I could not hear of any attempt ever having been made to domesticate the caribou, though there is no good reason why they should not be trained to do the same work as the reindeer of Northern Europe. If this were brought about it would do away with the greatest difficulty of winter travel, the trouble about dog's food, which cripples any attempt to make a long journey except where game is very plentiful; wherever there was green timber and hanging moss the caribou might find its own supper, and would always come in better for food than a thin dog in times of starvation.

The caribou afford a wide scope for the superstitions so ingrained in the Indian nature, and the wildest tales without the least foundation are firmly believed in. One widely-spread fancy is that they will entirely forsake a country if anyone throws a stick or stone at them, and their disappearance from the neighbourhood of Fort Resolution is accounted for by the fact of a boy, who had no gun, joining in the chase when the caribou were passing in big numbers, and clubbing one to death with a stick; this belief holds good also down the Mackenzie River, as does the idea that these animals on some occasions vanish either into the air or under the ground. The Indians say that sometimes when following close on a herd they arrive at a spot where the tracks suddenly cease and the hunter is left to wonder and starve. It is very unlucky to let the dogs eat any part of the head, and the remaining bones are always burnt or put up in a tree out of reach, the dogs going hungry, unless there happens to be some other kind of meat handy. Another rather more sensible superstition, presumably invented by the men, is that no woman must eat the gristle of the nose (a much-esteemed delicacy), or she will infallibly grow a beard.

Such are examples of the endless traditions told of the caribou, which will always form the chief topic of conversation in the scattered lodges of the Dog-Ribs and Yellow Knives.

CHAPTER V

On the 17th of September we left our camp at the north end of Lake Camsell for a short expedition in search of musk-ox, which we expected to find within fifty miles of the edge of the woods. By this time we had all fattened up, and entirely recovered from the effects of the short rations we had had to put up with before we fell in with the caribou.

My crew consisted at starting of King, Paul, François, Michel, and José; but as the two latter speedily showed signs of discontent I made no objection to their turning back, and despatched them to Fond du Lac to get ready the dog-sleighs, snow-shoes, and everything necessary for winter travel. As a matter of fact they did absolutely nothing except squander a relay of provisions and ammunition that had been sent on by the trading-boat from the fort to meet me at Fond du Lac. I was not sorry to see the last of them, as four of us were quite enough to work the canoe, and a small party naturally stands in less danger of starvation than a big one; moreover, they were certainly the most quarrelsome men in the camp, which is saying a good deal, as we had all done our fair share in that way since leaving the fort.

We started without any meat, expecting to find caribou everywhere, and in this respect we had great luck all the time we were out; but we were not so well off for shelter. We had brought only one lodge from Fond du Lac, which was of course left for the women, while we took the chance of what weather might come, hunting the lee-side of a big rock towards evening, and often finding ourselves covered with an extra blanket of snow (*le couvert du bon Dieu,* as King called it) in the morning.

The plan of campaign was to reach the musk-ox by canoe and bring back as many robes as we could carry before the winter set in; or, failing this, to kill and *cache* caribou along our line of travel, so that we should have meat to help us reach the musk-ox with dog-sleighs after the heavy snow had fallen and all the caribou had passed into the woods.

I named the first lake that we portaged into King Lake, a narrow sheet of water some five miles in length, and here we were storm-bound all day by a northerly gale, the force of the wind being so great that we could not move the canoe to windward, although the water was smooth enough. The weather improving in the morning, we paddled down the lake and passed into a small stream running out of its north end. A couple of miles down stream, with a portage over a small cascade (the thirty-fourth and last portage that we made with the big canoe), brought us to a huge lake running in a south-east and north-west direction, said to be the longest of all the lakes in this part of the country, and by the Indians' account four good days' travel, or over one hundred miles in length; the part that I saw is certainly over fifty miles, and is said to be not half the total distance. The lake is narrow in most places, and cut up by long points into numerous bays; there are a great many islands, particularly at the north-east end, similar in appearance to the main shore, which is just like the country I have described at the Lac du Rocher, except that at the end of the big lake the hills reach a greater elevation, and present more the aspect of a regular range, than in any other part of the Barren Ground that I saw.

The position of Mackay Lake, as I named it after Dr. Mackay of the Athabasca district, is worthy of remark, as it is the best starting-point from which to work the most important streams of both watersheds. It lies very nearly on the height of land between the Great Slave Lake and the Arctic Ocean; its west end must be but a short portage from the Yellow Knife River, while from its eastern extremity runs out the large stream, named by Anderson the Outram, but more generally known as Lockhart's River, from the fact of its falling into the Great Slave Lake at Lockhart's house, which was established for the relief of Stewart and Anderson when they went in search of the missing Franklin Expedition.

The Great Fish, or Back's River, which they descended on that occasion, heads within half a mile of the north bay of Aylmer Lake, lying next below Mackay Lake, on Lockhart's River. Fifteen miles to the north is another large sheet of water known to my companions as the Lac de Gras, through which the Coppermine River runs on its course direct to the Arctic Sea.

The point at which we fell on Lake Mackay is about the edge of the woods, and here we camped for the last time with pine timber, finding a small hunting-canoe which some of the Beaulieus had left during the previous autumn. This we decided to take with us, and it proved extremely useful later on in crossing the Coppermine.

On Sunday, September 22nd, with a fresh fair wind and our blanket pulling strong, we ran for several hours in a north-east direction; the little canoe which we carried athwartship made the steering difficult, as her bow and stern kept striking the tops of the big waves that were running after us, but we met with no accident except the carrying away of our mast.

We were continually in sight of large bands of caribou, but they seemed to take little notice of the extraordinary apparition. Towards evening we saw a herd on a long point projecting far out from the south shore of the lake, and, thinking it would be a good place to make a *cache*, landed inside them and walked down the point in line. We had the animals completely hemmed in, and, when they charged through us, nine dropped to quick shooting at short range.   There was little fuel of any kind on the spot, and we had to eat our meat almost raw, as is the fashion of the Barren Ground on these occasions.   In the morning we ferried all the carcasses to a convenient island close to the point, put them in *cache* among the rocks, and proceeded down the lake, camping at sundown at the head of a small bay near its northeast end.

The weather now changed, and once more the north wind came howling across the open country straight from the Arctic Sea, and a steady continuous frost set in.   We hauled up the big canoe and set out on foot, taking with us only our rifles and ammunition, a blanket apiece, and a couple of small kettles, besides the little canoe, which proved an awkward load to carry against the strong head-wind.   We must have walked about twenty miles, occasionally making use of a lake for the canoe, when we reached the south shore of the Lac de Gras, much disappointed in seeing no musk-ox or caribou all day.

The Lac de Gras is much broader than Lake Mackay, and rounder in shape, although at one spot it is nearly cut in half by points stretching out from each side.   The Coppermine River runs in at the east and out at the west end, and the distance is not great to the site of Fort Enterprise, Sir John Franklin's wintering place in 1820, and the scene of the awful disasters which befell his first overland expedition.

We were now hard up for provisions again, and the first daylight found us hunting for something to eat. Two of us walked along the shore, while the others paddled the canoe, but we could find neither musk-ox nor caribou; at midday we met and changed places, King and myself making rather a bold crossing in the shaky little canoe, while Paul and François walked round. On approaching the north shore of the lake we noticed a raven rise and throw himself on his back in the air, uttering the curious gurgling note which always seems to imply satisfaction. King exclaimed, "See the raven putting down his load! there is something to eat there"; and true enough there was, for we found the carcasses of eight musk-ox, killed, as we afterwards heard, a month before by a party of Yellow Knives, who had driven the animals into the water and massacred the whole band. Half a dozen gulls flapped away heavily, and we caught sight of a wolverine sneaking off as we came near. Neither of us much fancied the appearance of the feast that lay before us, but we had eaten nothing for some time, and one is not particular in such cases, especially as it is never certain when the next meal will turn up. We robbed from the wolverines and ravens, and, signalling to Paul and François, made a meal of the half-putrid flesh in a little patch of willow scrub that happened to be close at hand. It is

never pleasant to find the game you are hunting
killed by somebody else, but in this instance it
was a relief to know that we had a supply of
meat, such as it was, to fall back upon in case
we came to grief later on.

After supper we crossed the Coppermine, a big
deep stream even here, with a current of a mile
and a half an hour, running out of another lake
which stretched northward and eastward as far
as we could see. Here we left the small canoe
to cross with on our return, and walked on late
into the night, hoping to find some more willows,
but eventually made a wretchedly cold camp without fire on a long promontory, to which we always after alluded as Le Point de Misère. A
light snowstorm made us still more uncomfortable, and it was well on in the next afternon before we found willows enough to make a fire,
sighting almost immediately afterwards a big
band of caribou. We killed eight, and, as all the
small lakes were firmly frozen over by this time,
were able to make the safest form of *cache* by
breaking the ice and throwing the meat into shoal
water, which would at once begin to freeze and
defy all the efforts of the wolverines. Two
months afterwards we chopped out this meat,
and found it fresh and palatable, although the
outside was discoloured by its long soaking.
When we had finished our *cache* we lit a comparatively big fire in a bunch of well-grown willows,
and spent the rest of the day in eating and mend-

ing our moccasins, which were all badly worn out by the rough walking of the last few days. We had left our main camp badly provided in this respect, as the women had not had sufficient time to dress any skins before we started, and in consequence we were all troubled with sore feet during our wanderings in search of the musk-ox.

Curiously enough, now we did not want them, the ptarmigan appeared again in great quantities, although we had not seen any since leaving our big canoe. The only other birds remaining were a few hawks, owls, gulls, and ravens; the wildfowl had all left, and as a matter of fact we had come across very few since leaving the Great Slave Lake. About this time, too, we killed the first Arctic hare, an animal by no means to be despised, as it is fully as big as an English hare and will at a pinch provide a meal for a small party; at this time of year they are completely white, with the exception of the tips of the ears which are black; they are usually tame, and, being very conspicuous before the snow covers the ground, afford an excellent mark for the rifle.

On this day we crossed a peculiar ridge composed of fine gravel and sand, resembling at a distance a high railway embankment. It is a well-known landmark for the Indians, and is said by them to stretch, with few interruptions from the east end of the Athabasca Lake to the east end of Great Bear Lake.

September 27th was a red-letter day, marking

the death of the first musk-ox. Soon after leaving camp we came to a rough piece of country, full of patches of the broken rocks that I have already described, and, mounting a small hill, saw a single old bull walking directly towards us at a distance of three hundred yards. We lay down in the snow, and I had a capital chance of watching him through the glasses as he picked his way quietly over the slippery rocks, a sight which went far to repay all the trouble we had taken in penetrating this land of desolation. In crossing an occasional piece of level ground he walked with a curious rolling motion, probably accounted for by the waving of the long hair on the flanks; this hair reaches almost to the ground, and gives the legs such an exaggerated appearance of shortness that, at first sight, one would declare the animal to be incapable of any rapid motion. The shaggy head was carried high, and when he finally pulled up at sight of us, within forty yards, with his neck slightly arched and a gleam of sunshine lighting up the huge white boss formed by the junction of the horns, he presented a most formidable appearance. His fate was not long in doubt, as my first shot settled him, and the main object of my trip was accomplished; whatever might happen after this, I could always congratulate myself on having killed a musk-ox, and this made up for a great deal of the misery that we afterwards had to undergo.

Although not absolutely prime, this animal was

a fine specimen of an old bull, with the yellow marking on the back clearly defined, and as good a head as any I saw during my stay in the musk-ox country. We took the whole skin, with head, horns, and hoofs, and *cached* it among the rocks, where I am sorry to say it lies to this day; I intended to pick it up in the course of our winter hunt, but unfortunately we were caught in a snowstorm on the Lac de Gras, and were unable to find the *cache.* In the evening we scattered over the country, hoping to find a band of musk-ox, but another bull, killed by Paul, was the only one seen.

On the following day the frost was much keener; the smaller lakes and the sheltered bays in the big one were set fast, and we began to realise that the sooner we started back the better chance we had of getting across Mackay Lake with the canoe, and avoiding the long detour to cross Lockhart's River, which was sure to remain open much longer than the lakes. The winter was coming on quickly, and we were badly provided with clothes to withstand its severity; our moccasins were in rags, and everybody showed signs of being footsore. By rough reckoning we were about on the 65th degree of latitude, and it seemed too reckless to push on any further towards the North, as already we were separated from the nearest timber by a hundred miles of treeless waste; even if we found a band of musk-ox, we should be forced to come out again with dogs to haul in the robes, as our big canoe was now too far back for us to think of carrying any great weight with us. Although we had not made a successful hunt, our trouble was not all thrown away, as enough meat *caches* had been made to insure us a fair chance of getting out into the same country on the first deep snow.

Nobody liked to be the first to talk about turning back, but on reaching the top of a low range of hills and seeing a flat desolate stretch of country lying to the north of us, with the lakes frozen up and no sign of animals or firewood, King turned to me and said: "It is not far from here that the white men died from cold and starvation at this time of year; let us go back before the snow gets deep and we are not able to travel." The old man looked particularly tough at this moment; none of our faces were very clean, but his was the more remarkable, as the blood of the last caribou that we killed had splashed in it, and, running down his beard, had mixed with his frozen breath and appeared in the form of long red icicles hanging from his chin. I think he knew what was in my mind and had an idea that I was laughing at him, for suddenly his quick temper got the better of him and he broke into one of those wild volleys of blasphemy that I had heard him give way to so often, and, turning on his heel, said that I could do as I liked, but he was going to make the best of his way back to the lodge. The walk back in front of the wind was not nearly so bad as it had been coming out head to it; and in many places we could travel straight over the ice, and, by cutting across the bays instead of walking round, save a considerable distance. Whenever we got this chance we put our loads on a handful of willow-brush and dragged them after us, finding it far easier than carrying them on our shoulders.

Another night we spent without fire on the Point de Misère, and on October 3rd crossed the Coppermine amidst running ice, and there abandoned the little canoe. On the south side of the river we fell in with the biggest band of caribou we had yet seen, numbering fully three hundred; but as we had no need of any more meat *caches* on the Lac de Gras, we only killed enough for present use.

This crossing of the Coppermine, by the way, is an important spot in the history of the Dog-Ribs and Yellow Knives. It has always been a favourite swimming-place for the caribou, and many a struggle took place for the possession of this hunting-ground in the old days when there was continual warfare between the two tribes. At the present day it is a breach of etiquette for any Indians to camp here, as it is supposed that if the caribou are once headed back at this point they will not come south of Mackay Lake. This rule had evidently been broken lately, as we found signs of a recent encampment, and King considered that this amply accounted for our not finding the caribou before we reached the Lac du Rocher.

After two more days' hard travelling we arrived at our big canoe, and had the satisfaction of finding some meat, that we had left there, untouched by the wolverines; but the bay was frozen solid, and there was no open water within two miles. Beyond the points of the bay we could see the white-capped waves running, but we knew that at the first spell of calm weather the whole lake would set fast.

I now saw an example of the readiness of idea which King possessed in devising shifts and expedients to get out of difficulties. Of course he had had fifty years' experience in northern travel, but he was certainly, in my opinion, far above the average of the many other half-breeds and Indians who had been my companions in more or less difficult journeys in various parts of Canada. Before I thoroughly understood his scheme we commenced operations, by lashing together all the poles and paddles into a rough sort of ice-raft; on the top of this we placed the loads that we had carried so many miles, forming a smooth bed, two feet above the level of the ice, on which to rest the canoe. The bay had evidently frozen and broken up once, and the second freezing had left a rough surface; many of the floes were piled on top of each other, while the rest had been turned on edge, and it was necessary to keep the canoe clear of these sharp edges, which would have ripped the tender birch-bark like a knife. One man ran ahead, trying the strength of the ice with an axe, while the others hauled on the raft, and our method of progression was so satisfactory that just before dark, after much ominous cracking of the ice but no disaster, we camped on the east point of the bay close to the edge of open water. The half-breeds showed great knowledge of ice, and, with an occasional tap of the axe, picked out the safest route without making a mistake.

The canoe propped on her side gave us the best shelter we had had for many a night, and, finding willows enough for a fire, we all felt jubilant at the idea of reaching the first clump of pines on the following day, besides getting an opportunity to rest our feet, which by this time were in a very bad condition. In this, however, we were doomed to disappointment.

At the first sign of daylight we launched the canoe, and, breaking our way out through the young ice, were soon paddling in a heavy beam sea, with every splash of water freezing on us, and many stops to knock the ice from our paddles. After two or three hours of this work the wind died out, and, as we approached a group of small islands that cut the lake up into numerous channels, we saw a thin sheet of ice across the whole width. All hope of passing with the canoe was given up, and we headed for the south shore while a heavy snowstorm made it difficult to keep the course; the surface water was rapidly thickening into ice, and the sharp needles began to scrape unpleasantly along the sides of our frail vessel. We were none too soon in reaching the land, and had to carry the canoe over the thick ice near the shore. Here we turned her over carefully, and putting the poles, paddles, and all necessaries underneath, abandoned her to be buried under the snow till I might want her again the next summer. Late in the following June we found her, none the worse for her long exposure to the rigour of a winter in the Barren Ground, but even then there was no sign of open water in Mackay Lake.

We had now to continue our journey on foot; but by keeping to the shore of the lake, and sometimes making use of the ice in crossing a bay, we only camped twice before reaching the pine timber. Late on the third day we came to the bank of an ugly, quick-flowing stream, and saw a large bunch of pines on the far side. Waist-deep we made a ford among the running ice, and were soon drying ourselves by a blazing fire of pine-wood.

The whole of life is said to go by comparison, and although a few pine-trees in a wilderness of snow might seem the height of desolation to a man lately used to the luxuries of the civilized world, it appeared to us like a glimpse of heaven after the exposure of the last few weeks. It really was a pleasant spot, and one which has impressed itself on my memory more than any other camp that we made during this trip. A band of caribou, passing close by, provided us with supper, while a big pack of ptarmigan held possession of the little pine-trees, and kept up a constant expostulation at the intrusion of the scarcely known human beings. Hunger and danger were behind us just at present, and we felt in the best of tempers as we lay down for a long sleep on sweet-smelling pine-brush.

Shortly after leaving camp in the morning another band of caribou appeared, and, as the lodge was now not far ahead, we killed about a dozen, and put them in *cache* for later use. We then walked steadily on all day, and in the evening came in sight of Lake Camsell, over which the sun was setting in full northern splendour, throwing a wonderful purple light across the thin film of ice that coated the water. It was late in the night, and it was not till we had fired several gun-shots at intervals, that we heard an answering signal, and found that the women had set up the lodge in the next bunch of pines, as they had exhausted all the firewood close to the old camp.

Meat was abundant, for the caribou had been passing, and many had been killed by the women and boys. Bales of dried meat formed a solid wall round the lodge, varied here and there by a bladder of grease or a skin-bag full of pounded meat, while bunches of tongues and back-fats were hanging from the cross-poles to smoke. The scene reminded me of the old fairy stories in which the hero used to discover houses, with walls of sugar and roofs of gingerbread, full of all the good things imaginable, while any member of the Beaulieu family would make a respectable ogre to guard such treasures. Of course the lodge was dirty and infested with the vermin from which these people are never free; but there was an air of warmth and plenty about it very agreeable after the hand-to-mouth existence we had been leading.

On looking back at this expedition I cannot help thinking that we were lucky in getting through it without more trouble; it was just the wrong time of year to be travelling, too late for open water and too early for dogs to have been of any service, even if we had had them with us. One of the heavy snowstorms that, judging from Sir John Franklin's experience, are common in the end of September and beginning of October, would have made the walking much more laborious, as even the little snow that was on the ground delayed us considerably. Another source of danger was the numerous falls among the broken rocks; but though we all came down heavily at times, and, once or twice, with big loads of meat on our backs, no damage was done. The caribou kept turning up most opportunely, and we had no real hardships from want of food. Fuel was nearly always insufficient, but we only

had two fireless camps, both on the Point de
Misère. In many places we used black moss in
addition to whatever willow scrub we could collect, and so long as the weather was dry found
it quite good enough for boiling a kettle, but
when the snow fell it was perfectly useless. This
absence of a fire to sit by at night is the most
unpleasant feature in travelling the Barren
Ground.

CHAPTER VI

THE day after our arrival was Sunday, a fine, calm day with bright sunshine, of which we took advantage to wash our scanty stock of clothing and generally pull ourselves together. Cleanliness of the body is not looked upon with much favour by the half-breeds, but Sunday morning was always celebrated in the lodge by the washing of faces and a plentiful application of grease to the hair. After this operation was over we held a consultation as to the best way of carrying on our hunt of the musk-ox, which had so far not proved successful. The same old wrangling and abuse of each other ensued, and finally the following decision was arrived at. Paul and François were to go back to Fond du Lac, so soon as their feet were in a fit condition to travel; they were to occupy themselves in getting ready the dog-sleighs, and to return on the first deep snow to the spot where we had killed the caribou on the day that we reached the lodge. If any of the Indians, of whom I had seen absolutely nothing so far, were going to the musk-ox, arrangements should be made with them to come all together, so that we might have the benefit of as many sleighs as possible to haul wood. All our dried meat was to be put in *cache* at Lake Camsell, and the camp moved to a clump of pines that we had noticed the day before. King and myself were to remain with the women, to kill meat enough to enable us to start well supplied for the musk-ox country.

We built a rough scaffold with the longest poles obtainable, and stowed all the meat as high above the ground as possible. Then we pulled down the lodge, and, after a couple of days' walk with heavy loads, camped on the south side of a ridge, from the summit of which we had a commanding view of Lake Mackay and the surrounding country. There was little chance of many caribou passing without being observed, as there were usually several pairs of sharp eyes on the look-out.

As this was to be our home for a month or so, we took care to pick out a good spot and set up the lodge in the most approved fashion, taking advantage of the little shelter that the stunted pines could afford.

A mile or two to the east lay the northern end of a large sheet of water, running about forty miles in a southerly direction, known to the Indians as "The Lake of the Enemy," and formerly the home of that terrible Evil Spirit supposed to haunt the Barren Ground. It is hard to get a full description of the Enemy, as, although many people have seen it, they are at once afflicted with insanity, and are incapable of giving an accurate account of their experience; but one must not dare to express unbelief in the existence of the Enemy any more than in that of the Giant Musk-Ox, fully ten times the size of the biggest bull ever seen, whose track many Indians say they have come across far out in the Barren Ground.

King and myself spent most of our time prowling about in search of caribou, but for the first fortnight few came and we were only just able to keep ourselves in fresh meat, although there was soon plenty of dried meat from the animals we had *cached* at this spot a week before. I now saw what an advantage it is to take women on a hunting-trip of this kind, and certainly King's wife and daughter were both well up in the household duties of the country. If we killed anything, we only had to cut up and *cache* the meat, and the women and small boys would carry it in. On returning to camp we could throw ourselves down on a pile of caribou skins and smoke our pipes in comfort, but the women's work was never finished. The rib bones have all to be picked out, and the *plat côte* hung up in the smoke to dry; the meat of haunches and shoulders must be cut up in thin strips for the same purpose, and the bones have to be collected, pounded down, and boiled for the grease which is in such demand during the cold weather about to commence. But the greatest labour of all lies in dressing the skins, cutting off the hair, scraping away every particle of flesh and fat, and afterwards tanning them into soft leather for moccasins, which are themselves no easy task to make. Many skins, too, have to be made into parchment or carefully cut into *babiche* for the lacing of snowshoes, and again, there are hair-coats to be made for each member of the party. In an ordinary Indian lodge the women have to put up with ill-usage as well as hard work; but most of the half-breeds know enough to treat them fairly; and King, except in his moments of passion, when he did not stop at any cruelty, treated his womenkind very well.

One of our first expeditions was to hunt birch for making the frames of snowshoes, which might be needed at any time, and King soon had a pair ready for lacing; he was very clever with the crooked knife, the universal tool of the North, but the stunted birch is hard to bend to the proper shape, and requires constant watching during the process of warping.

The evenings were generally spent in long discussions over our pipes, for tobacco was still holding out, and the old man was keen to hear about the doings of the white man in the Grand Pays, as the half-breeds indefinitely term the whole of the outside world. The ignorance existing among these people is extraordinary, considering how much time they spend at the forts, and how many officers of the Hudson's Bay Company they have a chance to talk to, besides the missionaries of both faiths. It is a different matter with the Indians, as they seldom come to the fort, and cannot hold much conversation with the Whites without an interpreter. It was difficult, for instance, to persuade King that the Hudson's Bay Company does not rule the whole world, or that there are countries that have no fur-bearing animals, which in the North furnish the only means of making a living for the poor man. He was much interested in stories of the Queen, although he could never believe that Her Majesty held such a high rank as the Governor of the Company, and quite refused to acknowledge her as his sovereign. "No," he said; "she may be your Queen, as she gives you everything you want, good rifles and plenty of ammunition, and you say that you eat flour at every meal in your own country. If she were my Queen, surely she would send me sometimes half a sack of flour, a little tea, or perhaps a little sugar, and then I should say she was indeed my Queen. As it is I would rather believe Mr. Reid of Fort Province, who told me once that the earth went round and the sun stood still; but I myself have seen the sun rise in the morning and set at night for many years. It is wrong of you White Men, who know how to read and write, to tell lies to poor men who live by the muzzle of their guns."

Another matter over which his mind was greatly exercised was the last North-West Rebellion under Louis Riel. He was convinced that during this rising the half-breeds and Indians had declared war upon the Hudson's Bay Company, and gained a decisive victory besides much glorious plunder; and he asked why such an outbreak should not succeed on the Great Slave Lake, where there was only one man in charge of a fort. He had many questions too to ask about the various good things that we eat and drink in England, and criticised severely the habit of eating three regular meals a day, which he described as eating by the clock instead of by the stomach, a much more greedy habit than that of gorging when meat is plentiful and starving at other times. On several occasions during our travels together I had reason to expostulate with him on the carelessness he displayed with provisions, but without making the least impression. "What is this improvidence?" he would say. "I do not like that word. When we have meat why should we not eat *plein ventre* to make up for the time when we are sure to starve again?" He could never realise that starvation might be partially avoided by a little care.

Often King would spin me a long story as we lay round the fire in the lodge; usually some tradition handed down from the time when all the animals and birds could converse together; what the wolf said to the wolverine when they went on a hunting-trip in company, and how the ptarmigan invited the loon to dine with him in a clump of willows in the Barren Ground, while there was a big stock of giant stories, with heroes much resembling those of the favourite nursery tales of one's childhood. Again he would come down to more recent times and describe the battles of the Dog-Ribs and Yellow Knives, which seem to have been carried on in the same sneaking fashion that has always distinguished the warfare among the tribes of Canadian Indians; there was no open fighting, and all the victories were won by a successful approach on an unsuspecting and usually sleeping encampment of the enemy, the first grey of dawn being the favourite time of attack.

The following story of the Deluge, as believed by the Yellow Knives, I copied down from King's recital; it appears to be a curious mixture of old tradition with some details from the Biblical version as taught to the Northern Indians on the arrival of the first priests in the country.

Many years ago, so long ago in fact that as yet no man had appeared in the country of the Slave Lake, the animals, birds, and fishes lived in peace and friendship, supporting themselves by the abundant produce of the soil. But one winter the snow fell far more heavily than usual; perpetual darkness set in, and when the spring should have come the snow, instead of melting away, grew deeper and deeper. This state of affairs lasted many months, and it became hard for the animals to make a living; many died of want, and at last it was decided in grand council to send a deputation to Heaven to enquire into the cause of the strange events, and in this deputation every kind of animal, bird, and fish was represented. They seem to have had no difficulty in reaching the sky, and passing through a trap-door into a land of sunshine and plenty. Guarding the door stood a deerskin lodge resembling the lodges now in use among the Yellow Knives; it was the home of the black bear, an animal then unknown on the earth. The old bear had gone to a lake close at hand to spear caribou from a canoe, but three cubs were left in the lodge to take care of some mysterious bundles that were hung up on the cross-poles; the cubs refused to say what these bundles contained and appeared very anxious for the return of the old bear.

Now the idea of spearing caribou did not find favour with the deputation from below, and as the canoe was seen lying on the shore of the lake, the mouse was despatched to gnaw through the paddle, and as he had nearly accomplished this feat the bear came running down in pursuit of a band of caribou that had put off from the far shore. When he was close up to his intended victims and was working his best, the paddle suddenly broke, the canoe capsized, and the bear disappeared beneath the water. Then the animals, birds, and fishes grew bold, and pulling down the bundles, found that they contained the sun, moon, and stars belonging to the earth; these they threw down through the trap-door to lighten the world and melt the snow, which by this time covered the tops of the tallest pine-trees.

The descent from Heaven was not made without some small accidents. The beaver split his tail and the blood splashed over the lynx, so that ever afterwards till the present day the beaver's tail is flat and the lynx is spotted; the moose flattened his nose, and many other casualties occurred which account for the peculiarities of various animals, and the little bears came tumbling down with the rest.

And now the snow began to melt so quickly that the earth was covered with water, but the fish found for the first time that they could swim, and carried their friends that could not on their backs, while the ducks set to work to pull up the land from beneath the water.

But it was still hard to make a living, so the raven, then the most beautiful of birds, was sent to see if he could find any place where dry land was showing; but coming across the carcass of a caribou he feasted upon it, although the raven had never before eaten anything but berries and the leaves of the willow. For this offence he was transformed into the hideous bird that we know, and to this day is despised of every living thing; even omnivorous man will not eat of the raven's flesh unless under pressure of starvation. The ptarmigan was then sent out and returned bearing in his beak a branch of willow as a message of hope; in remembrance of this good action the ptarmigan turns white when the snow begins to fall in the Barren Ground, and thus warns the animals that winter is at hand.

But the old life had passed away and the peace that had reigned among all living things was disturbed. The fish, as the water subsided, found that they could no longer live on the land, and the birds took to flying long distances. Every animal chose the country that suited it best, and gradually the art of conversation was lost. About this time too, in a vague and indefinite manner about which tradition says little, the first human being appeared on the shore of the Great Slave Lake.

The weather continued fine without severe frost till the middle of October, the snow was still light on the ground, but the lakes all set fast. On the night of the fourteenth a storm arose equal in violence to a Dakota blizzard and continued till the following evening, by which time there were a couple of feet of snow on the ground. It was impossible to keep the drift from coming into the lodge, and as soon as the storm was over we had to throw down our shelter and clear away the banks that had accumulated inside. This was distinctly the coming of winter and there was no more sign of a thaw; the cold kept growing severer, especially on clear days, but I had no thermometer to mark its intensity. The daylight was shortening rapidly and the sun shone with little warmth.

With the increasing depth of snow there was a noticeable migration of life from the Barren Ground. Ptarmigan came literally in thousands, while the tracks of wolves, wolverines, and Arctic foxes made a continuous network in the snow. Scattered bands of caribou were almost always in sight from the top of the ridge behind the camp, and increased in numbers till the morning of October 20th, when little Baptiste, who had gone for firewood, woke us up before daylight with the cry of *La foule! La foule!* and even in the lodge we could hear the curious clatter made by a band of travelling caribou. *La foule* had really come, and during its passage of six days I was able to realise what an extraordinary number of these animals still roam in the Barren Ground. From the ridge we had a splendid view of the migration; all the south side of Mackay Lake was alive with moving beasts, while the ice seemed to be dotted all over with black islands, and still away on the north shore, with the aid of the glasses, we could see them coming like regiments on the march. In every direction we could hear the grunting noise that the caribou always make when travelling; the snow was broken into broad roads, and I found it useless to try to estimate the number that passed within a few miles of our encampment. We were just on the western edge of their passage, and after-

The Indians Driving Caribou

wards heard that a band of Dog-Ribs, hunting
some forty miles to the west, were at this very
time in the last straits of starvation, only saving
their lives by a hasty retreat into the woods,
where they were lucky enough to kill sufficient
meat to stave off disaster. This is a common
danger in the autumn, as the caribou coming in
from the Barren Ground join together in one
vast herd and do not scatter much till they reach
the thick timber. It turned out very well for us,
however, and there is really no limit to the number we might have killed if we had been in need
of them; but it was too far out to make a permanent winter's camp, and hauling such a long
distance with dogs is unsatisfactory, as most of
the meat would be consumed on the way. We
killed therefore only so many as we could use,
and had some luxurious living during the rest of
our stay in this camp. The caribou, as is usually
the case when they are in large numbers, were
very tame, and on several occasions I found myself right in the middle of a band with a splendid
chance to pick out any that seemed in good condition. The rutting season was just over, and as
the bulls had lost all their fat and their meat was
too strong to eat, only does were killed. A good
deal of experience is necessary to tell the fat ones,
but the half-breeds can tell age and sex pretty
well by the growth of the horns; often King told
me which to shoot at, and it was seldom that he
made a mistake in his choice.

This passage of the caribou is the most remarkable thing that I have ever seen in the course of many expeditions among the big game of America. The buffalo were for the most part killed out before my time, but, notwithstanding all the tall stories that are told of their numbers, I cannot believe that the herds on the prairie ever surpassed in size *La foule* of the caribou.

Soon after the migration had passed, José Beaulieu arrived from Fond du Lac in company with an Indian, having made the journey on foot in eight days. Things had apparently gone all wrong there; they had been starving, and had of course taken everything of mine that they could lay hands on, both provisions and ammunition. They had then quarrelled over the division of the spoil, but as the caribou turned up within two days of the house contentment was now reigning. José had brought a little tea and tobacco, of which we were now badly in need, and a long string of grievances against his brothers at Fond du Lac. He had done nothing to help me in any way, although he had promised to have everything ready for the first snow, and seemed rather surprised that I did not take much interest in his wrongs. He got even with me, however, on his way back, by breaking into a *cache,* that I had made before reaching the Lac du Rocher, and stealing the tobacco that I was relying on for our next trip in the Barren Ground.

José reported the woods to the south of us to

be full of caribou, and a big band of Yellow Knives camped at the Lac de Mort, some of whom were talking of coming for a musk-ox hunt, if I could give them ammunition. I sent word to the chief that I could supply three or four of them, and ordered Paul and Michel to come on with the dogs as soon as possible. The snow was by this time quite deep enough for travelling, and any delay meant an increased severity in the weather, while in any case it would be late in the year before we got back to Fond du Lac.

After José left we relapsed into our lazy existence of eating and sleeping, having no more excuse for hunting; occasionally we made a short trip on snowshoes to examine some of our *caches* and bring in a little meat, and once went for a three days' expedition to our meat on the island in Mackay Lake, and made a more secure *cache* by putting the carcasses of the caribou under the ice. At other times we amused ourselves by setting snares for ptarmigan, which were in great numbers, or by hauling a load of wood across a small lake in front of the lodge, as we had used up all the fuel within easy reach. On the shore of this lake was a fine specimen of the balanced rocks so common all over the open country; an enormous boulder many tons in weight, so neatly set on the three sharp points of an underlying rock that it could be easily shaken but not dislodged; the lake is known among the Indians as the "Lake of the Hanging Rock." We might have done some successful trapping for wolves, wolverines, and foxes, but had unfortunately left all our steel traps at Fond du Lac in order to travel as lightly as possible in the portages.

Quickly and without incident the short days slipped away until on the tenth of November, as I was returning to camp, I heard a gunshot to the southward of us. Instantly all was excitement, and we had barely time to answer the signal before a large party of men and eight dog-sleighs came in sight over the ridge. At first I could recognise no one, as the day had been very cold and their faces were covered with hoar frost, which makes it hard to distinguish one man from another; but they turned out to be Paul, François, and Michel, besides several Indians, among whom was Zinto, the chief of the Yellow Knives, who had come some hundred miles from his hunting-camp on purpose to pay me a visit.

A small supply of tea and tobacco had come up, but not nearly enough for our wants, and I could see that we should have to do without these luxuries just at the time when we most required them; there was also a little flour, and we had a big feast of flour and grease the same evening; all the new arrivals came into the lodge, and sixteen people and fully as many dogs slept inside that night. After supper I handed round a small plug of black tobacco to each man, as is the invariable custom of the officer in charge of a fort

on the arrival of a band of Indians; and when
the pipes were lit Zinto gave me to understand
that he had a few remarks to make to me. He
would have been a fine-looking specimen of a
Yellow Knife but for a habit of blinking his eyes,
which gave him a rather owlish expression; he
was possessed with a great idea of a chief's importance, but I found him a pretty good fellow
during the many dealings that I afterwards had
with him. King acted as interpreter, and I fancy
rather cut down the speech in length, but this was
the gist of it. "Zinto was very pleased to see a
white man on his hunting-ground. He had
known several at the forts, but had never before
seen one among the caribou. Many years ago his
father had told him stories of some white men
who had wandered across the Barren Ground and
reached the sea-coast; they had all endured much
hardship, and many had died from cold and starvation; he did not know why they came to such a
country, when by all accounts they were so much
better off at home, but suppose there was some
good reason which an Indian could not understand. For his own part he liked the Whites; all
that he valued came from their country, and he
had always been well treated by the Company.
He was willing to help me as much as he could
now that I had ventured so far into his hunting-
ground, but the musk-ox hunt in snow-time was
hard; only the bravest of his young men went,
and last year was the first time they had made

the attempt. The Dog-Ribs who traded at Fort Rae often went, but they had an easier country, as the musk-ox were nearer the woods. There would be much walking to do, and the cold would be great; however, if I meant to go he would order his young men to look after me, and on no account to leave me if from starvation or any other cause I could not keep up. I was to have the first choice of the meat in the kettle and the best place in the lodge to lie down. He hoped we should have a successful hunt, and, although he knew that we were short of such things, he could not help asking for a little tea and tobacco to give him courage for his journey back to the camp. If he received this he should have a still higher opinion of the white man and his heart would be glad."

I replied that I was much gratified at seeing the chief of the Yellow Knives in my camp, and was sorry that I could not give him a more imposing reception on the present occasion; I had heard much to his credit from King Beaulieu and from the Company's officer in charge of Athabasca district; he was spoken of as a good chief and friendly towards the Whites. I had come from far across the big water on purpose to see the country of the Yellow Knives, and was anxious to know how they lived, and how they hunted the various kinds of animals upon which they depended for subsistence. For this purpose I now proposed going for a musk-ox hunt, and was glad to see that some of his tribe were prepared to accompany me. I could let them have enough ammunition for the trip, and would share with them the meat *caches* that we had made along our line of travel, and also the tea and tobacco while it lasted. Much interest was felt in my country with regard to the Yellow Knives, and I hoped to be able to give a good account of their treatment to a stranger when I returned home. If his young men behaved well while they were out with me they should all receive presents when they reached the fort.

Here the effect of my oration was rather spoilt by the Beaulieus breaking in to ask what presents they were to receive. Had they not been faithful so long, and gone so much out of their way to help me? and then the misery they had gone through in the Barren Ground on the last musk-ox hunt! Now followed a tremendous quarrel among themselves, mostly, I believe, about the stealing they had been doing at Fond du Lac, and whether the value of the articles they had taken should be deducted from the wages I had agreed to pay them before starting. After the discordant clamour had subsided a little, Zinto replied that he was satisfied, and thanked me for the small present of tea and tobacco which I could not well refuse; we then discussed all the various plans for the forthcoming hunt, and sat up feasting till late in the night.

Something in the proceedings of the evening

must have displeased King, as he suddenly astonished us all by saying that he would not go with
us. What the grievance was I never found out,
but he was obstinate on the point. I had been
relying on him for interpreter, and was rather
annoyed at his refusal to go, especially as François, the best French speaker in the outfit, declared his intention of returning straight to Fond
du Lac. Michel too was wavering, but finally decided to go, as Paul, who behaved very well on
this occasion, steadily declared that he was quite
willing to accompany me, and would carry out
the promise that he had made at Fort Resolution
to go the whole trip. These two then and myself,
together with the five Indians, Noel, William,
Peter, Saltatha, and Marlo (brother of Zinto),
and twenty-four dogs hauling six sleighs made
up the party that eventually started for the Barren Ground about midday on Sunday, November 11th.

King maintained his ill-temper till the hour of
departure, saying that he did not want so many
men and dogs in his lodge eating up the provisions that he had worked so hard to earn, and
that the sooner we started the better he would be
pleased. He used some particularly offensive
language to me, but relented at the last moment
and gave me his own hair-coat and a new pair of
snow-shoes, of which I was badly in want. He
also promised to do his best in the way of leaving
meat *caches* along the course that we should fol-

low on our return from the musk-ox country. I
was rather sorry to leave the old fellow after all,
as on the whole we had been pretty good friends
while we lived together, and he certainly had
great influence over the Indians which might
have been useful during our difficult journey.

CHAPTER VII

THAT night we made an open camp in a bunch
of pines on the south side of Lake Mackay, at
which point we intended to load wood for use in
the Barren Ground. We were much better found
in all respects than on the last occasion, and having dogs with us should not be obliged to carry
anything ourselves. We used the ordinary travelling sleighs of the North; two smooth pieces of
birch, some seven feet in length, with the front
ends curled completely over and joined together
with cross slats secured with *babiche* into a total
width of sixteen inches. A ground-lashing is
passed along through holes in the outside edge of
the sleigh, and to this is fastened a rough deer-
skin wrapper in which the load is stowed as neatly
as possible and the wrapper laced on the top, so
that in case of a capsize, which frequently happens, nothing can fall out. The traces are hitched
on to loops in the front end of the sleigh, and
four dogs put in the caribou-skin harness one in
front of the other. The company officers have
imported leather dog-harness with buckles for
their own use between the forts; but I think for
handling in really cold weather the caribou-skin,
or better still moose-skin, with thongs instead of
buckles, is preferable.

Our twenty-four dogs rejoiced in endless varieties of names, English, French, and Indian, some popular names introduced by the Whites being freely given without reference to sex or colour. For instance, in my own sleigh the foregoer, a big yellow bitch, answered to the name of Napoleon, whilst just behind her came a black bushy-tailed dog La Reine; we had three Drap Fins, from their resemblance to the fine black cloth so dearly beloved by the half-breeds and Indians, two Chocolates of different colours, besides Cavour, Chandelle, Diable, Lion, Blucher, Royal, Bismarck, and a host of unpronounceable Indian names.

We were all dressed alike in coats of caribou-skin with the hair outside and hoods fastened up closely under the chin, and these we hardly took off day or night for the five weeks that we were out. Our hands were thrust into moose-skin mittens lined with duffel and hung round the neck by highly ornamented plaited woollen strings, or in the case of a man of little wealth with a more humble piece of *babiche,* but most of my companions managed to show a little colour in this respect. We rolled our feet in duffel and cased them in huge moccasins, of which we all had two or three pair; and as we were very careful in drying them every night before sleeping to get rid of all dampness caused by perspiration there was not a single case of frozen feet during the whole journey, although the big cold of an

Arctic winter had now fairly set in. We used small snow-shoes about three feet in length, as most of the travelling would be on the frozen lakes where the snow is always drifting, and, consequently, pretty hard. One man, or in case of softer snow two, went ahead to break the road and the dogs followed in their tracks, or, if they showed any disinclination to start, were most unmercifully clubbed and cursed by name till they did so.

A big deer-skin lodge and a sufficient number of carefully trimmed poles had been brought up from Fond du Lac, as it would have been impossible to endure the cold and almost perpetual wind without shelter of any kind, but they had the disadvantage of greatly increasing the weight of our load. King had given us a little dried meat, but only enough for a couple of days for such a large outfit; the dogs alone required at least fifty pounds a day to keep them in good condition. We had the meat *caches* ahead, and hoped to fall in with the musk-ox before we ran out of provisions entirely. The danger of course lay in not finding these animals when we got far out, as the caribou had almost all passed into the woods and we could not hope to see any after the first few days. Our ammunition was rather limited, but with care we had enough to keep the muzzle-loading weapons supplied, and Paul and myself had a fair amount of cartridges for our Winchester rifles. We were obliged to wrap deer-skins round the levers and the parts of the barrel that our hands touched to avoid contact with the iron, which sticks to the bare skin in cold weather and causes a painful burn.

The next day was spent in cutting wood into short lengths and loading it on to the sleighs. In the morning Marlo was very ill from the surfeit of flour he had had in King's camp, but was well enough to travel a short distance in the afternoon, and we pitched our lodge in the snow, clear of all timber. Here I had my first experience of a winter camp in the Barren Ground.

A spot being chosen where the snow is light and the ground clear of rocks, a ring of the requisite size is marked out. Snow-shoes are taken off and used as shovels for throwing away the snow from the inside of this ring, making a wall varying in height according to the depth of snowfall. Outside this circle the sleighs are turned on edge, the poles planted behind them, and the deer-skin lodge spread round, forming as comfortable a camp as can be expected in such a country. The wood allowed for supper is carefully split and a fire lighted, the kettle hanging over it from three small sticks carried for the purpose; the lumps of meat for dog's food are spread round the fire till sufficiently thawed, when a lively scene commences outside the lodge, every man feeding his own dogs and watching them to see there is no foul play. By the time this is over the melted snow in the kettle is boiling, and every

man gets his piece of meat in much the same
manner as the dogs. I always had the privilege
of first choice, but in the dense clouds of smoke
that usually filled the lodge it was by no means
easy to take the full advantage of it. We drank
tea while it held out, and then fell back on the
greasy snow-water that the meat was boiled in.
There was always a good proportion of caribou
hair in everything we ate or drank, varying afterwards to the coarse black hair of the musk-ox,
which was far more objectionable.

As soon as supper was over and our moccasins
dry the fire was allowed to go out, to economize
wood, and each man rolled himself up in his
blanket, lay down on the frozen ground, and
slept as well as he might till it was time to travel
again. Directly all was quiet the dogs forced
their way in and commenced a free fight over us
for any scraps or bones they could find lying
about; finally they curled themselves up for the
night without paying much attention to our comfort. A warm dog is not a bad thing to lie against
or to put at your feet, but these hauling dogs
seem to prefer to lie right on top of your body,
and as most of them are a considerable weight
a good night's rest is an impossibility. Any attempt to kick or shove them off produced a general row, and a moving foot was often mistaken
in the darkness for a hostile dog and treated as
such; Paul received one rather bad bite on his
toes, but the rest of us all got off with slight nips.

Making Camp

We had to be careful to put everything edible, in the way of moccasins, mittens, and even snow-shoes, under us, as these are things that few dogs can resist, and there is nothing more annoying than to find all the *babiche* eaten out of your snow-shoes in the morning. When the hungry time came later on the dogs began to eat the lodge, and would soon have let us houseless but for one man always keeping watch at night.

One is accustomed to hear of men sleeping in fluffy woollen bags in the Arctic regions, but I found that a deer-skin coat and one blanket were sufficient to keep me warm except on the very coldest nights. I had told Michel particularly to bring another blanket that I had left behind at Fond du Lac, and abused him roundly when I found he had come without it. It seems that an Indian had arrived at the house with a load of dried meat and grease, and was in want of a blanket; Michel, to use his own expression, took pity on him and gave him my blanket in exchange for the grease. He doubtless considered this a pious act of charity, but had rather spoilt it by consuming the grease himself; and on my asking him why, if he felt so sorry for the Indian, he had not given him one of his own blankets, or at least kept the grease for me, he replied: "I have only two blankets and I have a wife; you have no wife, so one blanket is enough for you; besides, I love grease, and it is hard for me to see it and not eat it."

In the middle of the night Saltatha, always the earliest, got up and drove out the dogs, lit the fire, and prepared another meal, exactly similar to our supper of the evening. Usually we harnessed up many hours before daylight and travelled, with only an occasional ten-minutes' rest, till the sun had been long down and there was just enough daylight left to make camp; dinner was completely cut out of our day as being too heavy a strain on our firewood. There was no attempt at washing made by any of the party during the whole time that we were out, and indeed it would have been an impossibility, as our small fires were only just sufficient to melt the snow for cooking purposes.

In clear weather the nights were of wonderful brilliancy, and after we had been out a couple of weeks the moon was big enough to add a little light, and of course kept steadily improving in this respect; but the starlight alone illumined the waste of snow sufficiently to see landmarks far ahead. Generally the Aurora was flashing in its full glory, and if there was no wind the travelling was pleasant enough. At the first sign of dawn, and thence till the sun rose, the cold always became more severe, and if a light head-wind happened to get up at the same time there were sure to be some frozen noses and chins in the outfit. The hair on our faces, even to the eyebrows and eyelashes, was always coated with rime, giving everybody a peculiarly stupid expression; my beard was usually a mass of ice, and I had great difficulty in thawing it out by our small fires, although it proved a grand protection from frost-bite. I think I was the only one that escaped being bitten in the chin, but my nose, cheeks, and forehead were touched several times.

The sunrise was often very beautiful, and the effects of long duration, as the sun is close to the horizon a considerable time before he shows above it, while the dense blue blackness in the north and west gives the impression that the night is still lingering there. Often a sun-dog is the first thing to appear, and more or less of these attendants accompany the sun during his short stay above the horizon. The driving snow, which obliterates everything in blowing weather, often spoils the evening effects; but once or twice I saw the sun set over a frozen lake, tinting the snow with various shades of red, and throwing a beauty over the wilderness that it is useless for me to attempt to describe.

A thick fog hung over everything during the whole of the second day out from the woods, and of course made it extremely difficult to find the meat *cache* in Lake Mackay; at dark we camped on the first land that we came to, but had no very accurate idea of our position. Luckily the weather cleared towards morning, and we made out the island on which we had stored the carcasses of the caribou killed on September

22nd. We had some trouble in punching a hole with our only ice-chisel and hauling out a solid lump of meat and ice some five feet thick and many feet in circumference; but the Indians were much cheered at the sight of so much provision, and declared themselves ready to go out to the sea-coast if necessary. The short day was nearly over by the time we had got the meat, so we camped for the night on the island; but before daylight we were off again, and when the sun set had nearly reached the end of the lake and made a wood *cache* on a conspicuous point for our return journey. The next day was thick again, and we were lucky in finding the bay in which we had left the big canoe during our last expedition. A very curious thing, illustrating the difficulty of recognising objects in these fogs, happened just as we were leaving the ice. We saw an animal, apparently at some distance, bounding along the horizon at a most remarkable pace; all down the line there were cries of *Er-jerer* (musk-ox), *Et-then, Le loup!* guns were snatched from the sleighs, and even the dogs charged at a gallop in pursuit of the strange animal. After a rush of ten yards the quarry disappeared; the first man had put his foot on it, and it turned out to be one of the small mice so common in the Barren Ground. What it was doing out on the lake at this time of year, instead of being comfortably curled up under ground, I cannot say; but it certainly gave me the impression that if these fogs continued we should run a good chance of coming to grief through losing our way.

At sunrise the weather cleared, and we found a small band of caribou at the beginning of the twenty-mile portage to the Lac de Gras. After we had killed three and fed the dogs, we began our overland work. The snow was much softer here, with many large rocks showing through, and some steep hills made travelling hard for the dogs. Night caught us about half-way between the two lakes, and the north wind freshened up into a tempest such as I have never seen surpassed by the blizzards of the western prairies. Fortunately we found a fairly sheltered place for the lodge or it must have been swept away; as it was the deer-skin flapped with a noise like that of a sail blown to pieces at sea; two of our lodge-poles were carried away, and we were in momentary expectation of being left without shelter to the mercy of the storm; the driving snow forced itself in, and men and dogs were only recognisable by the white mounds which marked their position. For thirty hours we lay like this till the wind abated at midnight, when we started again towards the north, and continued walking till we had crossed the big bay of the Lac de Gras into which the Coppermine River runs. We camped a little short of our second meat *cache* on the Point de Misère, and on the following day, although the fog had settled down again, Paul, by a very good piece of piloting, discovered the small lake in which we had *cached* the meat. We were getting pretty hard up again by this time, and the Indians, with the exception of Saltatha whose good spirits never failed, were showing signs of sulkiness. This new supply, however, gave them fresh courage, and we were all confident of finding the musk-ox before we got to the end of the six caribou that we picked up here. We experienced the same difficulty in breaking the ice, and as we spent much valuable time in getting out the meat, made but a poor day's journey. On the following day we passed the most northerly point that we had reached in the autumn, and were now pushing on into a country that none of us had ever seen before.

At the spot where we had left the Lac de Gras we had noticed a few small willow sticks showing above the snow, which afterwards proved very useful. Following a small stream we reached another large lake, stretching in a north-easterly direction, and camped at the far end of it in a heavy snowstorm that had been going on all day. During this time we were keeping a sharp lookout for musk-ox; but we could find no tracks, and as the weather continued thick had no opportunity of seeing animals at a distance. Two more days we travelled on in this manner, making long journeys with our meat nearly finished and our wood-supply growing rapidly less; for there had been more delay, from various reasons, than we had anticipated, and we had been careful to avoid *caching* wood for our return journey as we might be unable to follow the same course. The shape of the hills here changes in a most distinct manner. The usual undulations give way to sharp scattered buttes, composed of sand and taking very remarkable forms, a solitary conical mound being a common feature in the scenery. Small lakes were still numerous, and for a considerable distance we followed a large stream, evidently one of the head waters of the Coppermine, here running in a south-east direction.

On November 20th we dropped on to a lake some twelve miles in breadth, and crossed to the north shore in falling snow. We had been on short rations, men and dogs, for some time, and our last mouthful was eaten for supper this night. When we made camp a few miles beyond the lake the outlook therefore was by no means cheerful. The continual thick weather spoilt our chance of finding the musk-ox, and we were now too far away from the woods to have much chance of reaching them without meat. Of course we could always have eaten the dogs, but then we should have been unable to haul our wood, which in the Barren Ground is almost as necessary as food. As we felt certain that we were well in the musk-ox country we decided to spend the next day in hunting at all risks, and by good luck the morning broke clear and calm. Michel and myself remained in camp to look after the dogs, which had now become so ravenous that they required constant watching to keep them from eating the lodge, harness, and everything else that they could get at. The others went in couples in different directions with the agreement that if anyone discovered a band of musk-ox they should return at once to wait for the rest of the party to come in, when we were all to start with the dogs in pursuit. There was no breakfast, and all the hunters were off before daylight, evidently fully aware that the success of our expedition, if not our chance of supporting life, was centred in the result of the day's proceedings; and it was certainly a great relief when Paul and Noel appeared towards mid-day and reported a large band of musk-ox undisturbed a short distance to the north. Peter and Marlo returned soon afterwards, having found another band in a more westerly direction. I distributed a pipeful of the now very precious tobacco, while we waited for William and Saltatha, and discussed the plan of attack. I was rather surprised at Noel's asking Paul to tell me that I might have some of the musk-ox, as he was pleased at receiving the tobacco. I was about to reply that I had come far, and been to a great deal of trouble, on purpose to kill some of these animals, and I should think it rather extraordinary if I were not allowed to do so, when Paul explained that it was a custom among the Yellow Knives to consider a band of musk-ox as the property of the discoverer, and only his personal friends were granted the privilege of killing them without payment of some kind.   Sometimes an Indian would go through all the hardships of a hunt, and then have to give up nearly all his robes because he had not been lucky enough to discover a band and was out of favour with his more fortunate companions; so I told Noel I was very grateful for his kindness, and made him believe himself a remarkably good Indian.   By this time it was getting late, and as the wind had risen the snow was beginning to drift.   There was much grumbling at the delay, and in spite of my remonstrances at breaking up our agreement to wait for William and Saltatha, the dogs were harnessed, the lodge pulled down, and the sleighs loaded.   I pointed out that the snow was drifting badly and that the other two would not be able to follow our tracks; but was told that it was only white men who were stupid in the snow, so I made no further objection.   After travelling about three miles through some rough hills, we caught an indistinct view of the musk-ox, fully a hundred in number, standing on a side-hill from which most of the snow had drifted away; and then followed a wonderful scene such as I believe no white man has ever looked on before.   I noticed the Indians throwing off their mitten-strings, and on enquiring the reason I was told that the musk-ox would often charge at a bright colour, particularly red; this story must, I think, have originated from the Whites in connection with the old red-rag theory, and been applied by the Indians to the musk-ox. I refused to part with my strings, as they are useful in keeping the mittens from falling in the snow when the hand is taken out to shoot, but I was given a wide berth while the hunt was going on. Everybody started at a run, but the dogs, which had been let out of harness, were ahead of us, and the first thing that I made out clearly through the driving snow was a dense black mass galloping right at us; the band had proved too big for the dogs to hold, and most of the musk-ox had broken away. I do not think they knew anything about men or had the least intention of charging us, but they passed within ten yards, and so frightened my companions that I was the only man to fire at them, rolling over a couple. The dogs, however, were still holding a small lot at bay, and these we slaughtered without any more trouble than killing cattle in a yard. There is an idea prevalent in the North that on these occasions the old musk-ox form into a regular square, with the young in the centre for better protection against the dogs, which they imagine to be wolves; but on the two occasions when I saw a band held in this manner, the animals were standing in a confused mass, shifting their position to make a short run at a too impetuous dog, and with the young ones as often as not in the front of the line. There was some rather reckless shooting going on, and I was glad to leave the scene of slaughter with Marlo in pursuit of stragglers. Marlo, in common with the other Indians, had a great horror of musk-ox at close quarters, and I was much amused at seeing him stand off at seventy yards and miss an animal which a broken back had rendered incapable of rising. He said afterwards that the musk-ox were not like other animals; they were very cunning, could understand what a man was saying and play many tricks to deceive him; it was not safe to go too near, and he would never allow me to walk up within a few yards to put in a finishing shot. After killing off the cripples, we started back to the place where we had left the sleighs, and, night having added its darkness to the drifting snow, we had the greatest difficulty in finding camp. Marlo confessed he was lost, and we were thinking what it was best to do for the night when we heard the ring of an axe with which somebody was splitting wood in the lodge; the others, with the exception of William and Saltatha, were all in, but there seemed little chance of these two reaching camp that night. We had eaten nothing for a long time, so we celebrated our success with a big feast of meat, while the dogs helped themselves from the twenty carcasses that were lying about. They gave us very little trouble in the lodge, as we saw nothing of them till we skinned the musk-ox next day, when two or three round white heaps of snow would

uncurl themselves on the lee-side of a half-eaten
body. I questioned the Indians about the two
missing men, and they were unanimous that unless the night got colder they were in no danger
of freezing to death; they were sorry that they
had not waited, and would go at the first sign
of daylight to see if they were in the old camp.
Peter and Noel accordingly started very early in
the morning, and found the men lying close together under the snow at the old camp; they had
returned at dark, and as our tracks had drifted up
there was not the least chance of finding us.
They were slightly frost-bitten in the face and
hands, but as soon as they had got over their first
numbness were able to walk to camp, where they
soon forgot their natural indignation at the mean
trick we had played them in the joys of warmth
and food. We were obliged to be a little extrava-
gant in our wood to make up for the hard times
of the night before, and Saltatha soon recovered his liveliness; he was far away the best Indian that I met in the North, always cheerful and
ready for work, and afterwards, in the summer,
the only one of the Yellow Knives brave enough
to volunteer for an expedition down the Great
Fish River. A hard life he leads, always in pov-
erty, a butt and a servant to all the other Indians,
who are immeasurably his inferiors for any useful purpose. Although a capital hunter, they
swindle him out of everything he makes, and
take the utmost advantage of the little fellow's

good-nature; he seems to have no sense in this respect, and will jump readily at any bargain that is offered him. He is just the man for an expedition in the Barren Ground, as when once he has given his word to go he can be relied upon to carry out his promise, which is more than I can say for the rest of his tribe, who only wait to rebel and desert till a time when they think you can least do without them.

We spent most of the day in skinning the musk-ox, which, by the way, is not a pleasant undertaking in cold weather; the skin is naturally hard to get off, and on this occasion the carcasses had grown cold during the night, and the difficulty was greater than usual. The robes were in splendid condition; the undergrowth, which resembles a sheep's fleece and is shed in summer, was now thick and firm, while the long permanent hair had obtained the black glossiness distinctive of a prime fur. We cut up all the meat that the dogs had left us, and loading it on the sleighs with the robes, moved camp about five miles to the west to be ready to go in search of the other band which Peter and Marlo had discovered. We calculated that we should be able to haul forty-five robes, besides meat enough for our journey, back to the woods, and at present we had only half a load.

While the men were planting the lodge I climbed to the top of a high butte to have a look at the surrounding country; the hill was so steep

that I had to take off my snow-shoes to struggle
to the summit, and was rewarded for my trouble
by a good view of probably the most complete
desolation that exists upon the face of the earth.
There is nothing striking or grand in the scenery,
no big mountains or waterfalls, but a monotonous snow-covered waste, without tree or scrub,
rarely trodden by the foot of the wandering Indian. A deathly stillness hangs over all, and the
oppressive loneliness weighs upon the spectator
till he is glad to shout aloud to break the awful
spell of solitude. Such is the land of the musk-
ox in snowtime; here this strange animal finds
abundance of its favourite lichens, and defies
the cold that has driven every other living thing
to the woods for shelter.

CHAPTER VIII

EARLY on the following morning we left camp with the light sleighs, and at sunrise were close to the place where the second band had been discovered. We were a long time in finding them, as the fog had settled down again, but at last made out a band of sixty on a high ridge between two small lakes in a very easy place to approach. Directly after we sighted them Paul's sleigh, which was ahead, capsized over a rock, and his rifle, which was lashed on the top of it, exploded with a loud report. The bullet must have passed close to some of us, as on examination the rifle appeared to be bearing right down the line, and it was lucky that nobody was killed or crippled; a wounded man would have had little chance of getting back to the woods alive. The musk-ox took not the slightest notice of the report, although we were within a couple of hundred yards of them, and we soon had eighteen rounded up, the main body breaking away as they had done before. A sickening slaughter, without the least pretence of sport to recommend it, now took place till the last one was killed, and we were busy skinning till dark.

I took some of the best heads, but most of them

were afterwards thrown away by the Indians to
lighten the load on the sleighs. The animals
that we killed in this band were of various ages,
and it was interesting to note the growth of the
horns in different specimens. They begin in both
sexes with a plain straight shoot, exactly like
the horns of a domestic calf, and it is then impossible to tell the male from the female by the
head alone. In the second year they begin to
broaden out, and the bull's horns become much
whiter and project straighter from the head than
the cow's, which are beginning already to show
the downward bend. At the end of the third
year the cow's horns are fully developed, and I
do not think they grow much after that age;
with the bulls, however, the horns are only just
beginning to spread out at the base, and it is not
till the sixth year that the solid boss extends right
across the forehead, the point of junction being
marked by a slight crack into which the skin has
been squeezed during the growth of the horns.
A curious fact is noticeable in the horns of the
young bulls before the boss has begun to form;
they are quite soft and porous at the base, and
can easily be cut with a knife; when once the
boss has grown, the horn is as hard as a rock.
I made careful inquiries of the Indians on these
points, and they told me that, except in the case
of very young or very old animals, they could always tell the age of the musk-ox by a glance at
their horns.

We had the greatest difficulty in finding our way back to the lodge, and it was late before we turned in, everybody agreeing that we had done enough, and ought to make our best way back to the timber before our firewood was exhausted. The loads would be quite as heavy as they had been coming out, for we now had the weight of robes and meat to make up for the wood we had used. We had, roughly, three hundred and fifty miles to travel to reach Fond du Lac, but intended to take the last part of the journey easily after we fell in with the caribou. I should like to have known our exact position on the map, and the distance from the sea-coast at Bathurst Inlet, but of course had no chance of making even an approximate calculation; the Indians had no local knowledge, as they were entirely beyond any country they knew. Our only luxuries, tea and tobacco, were now finished, and I found that the want of tobacco was the most trying hardship on the whole trip: one pipeful as you roll up in your blanket for the night imparts a certain amount of comfort, and makes you take a more cheerful view of life; but when even this cannot be obtained there is a perpetual craving for a smoke, and the best of tempers is liable to suffer from the deprivation. After we had boiled our last handful of tea-leaves three times over, Saltatha ate them with great gusto, and in future we drank the water in which the meat was boiled. I did not miss the tea nearly so much as the tobacco, and soon began to like the hot greasy *bouillon* well enough to struggle for my full share.

We were late off next morning, and could not make a good day's journey, as the snow was soft till we got on the large lake, and we were further delayed in the evening by finding another band of musk-ox. The Indians said they could carry half a dozen robes more, and insisted, against my wishes, on killing this number; the consequence was that we had to camp for the night, and the dogs were more overloaded than ever; they were able, however, to eat to their hearts' content, and there was very little left of the six musk-ox in the morning. Two long days' travel took us back to the point on the Lac de Gras where we had seen the willows above the snow, and as the dogs were showing signs of fatigue and their feet were much cut about by the sharp snow-needles sticking between their toes, we decided on taking a day's rest. We managed to pull up enough small willows to keep a bit of a fire going most of the day, and if we had had tobacco should all have enjoyed ourselves immensely. It was a bright clear day, without wind and terribly cold. I climbed to the top of a hill in the afternoon to see if I could make out the west end of the lake, but an intervening hill made it impossible to get a clear view, and I could form no idea of its length. On this day I felt the top of my tongue cold in breathing, and my companions, who were well accustomed to low temperatures, all re-marked the extreme severity of the cold.

It must have been about midnight when I heard Saltatha splitting wood, and the well-known cry of *Ho lève, lève, il faut partir!* Look-ing out of my blanket I felt the snow falling in my face through a big hole that the dogs had eaten in the lodge, and said that it was no use moving, as we should never be able to find our way across the broad traverse that lay ahead. I was laughed at as usual, and after a breakfast of boiled meat we started out into the darkness. I soon saw there was little chance of picking up the skin of the musk-ox that we had *cached* in September, as, although the intention was to fol-low the shore of the lake till we came to the *cache,* we lost sight of land immediately with ab-solutely nothing to guide us on our course. There was no wind, and such a thick downfall of snow that matters did not improve much when the blackness turned into grey with daylight.

I have often heard it stated that the gift of finding their way is given to Indians under all conditions by a sort of instinct that the white man does not possess, but I never saw children more hopelessly lost than these men accustomed all their lives to Barren Ground travel. I have seen it happen to half-breeds and Indians many times, and have come to the conclusion that no man without a compass can keep his course in falling snow, unless there is wind to guide him.

It is always advisable to put ashore at once, or, better still, not to leave your camp in the morning, as then you know your point of departure on the first signs of a break in the weather. On this occasion the usual thing happened; we walked all day, changing our roadbreaker every hour or so, while the men behind shouted contrary directions when they thought he was off his course. Luckily we found land just at dark, and camped immediately. A great discussion ensued as to our position, and opinions varied greatly about the direction of the north star; but we could do nothing till the weather improved, and even then, unless it grew very clear, or the sun came out, we might not know which course to take, as landmarks are few and far between. Fuel could not last more than three nights with the strictest economy.

The wind rose in the evening, and the snow ceased falling, but began to drift heavily. In the night there was a tremendous uproar. I was awakened by hearing the universal Indian chant *(Hi hi he, Ho hi he)*, and much clapping of hands, while the dogs were howling dismally far out on the ice, evidently thinking they were meant to hunt something, but disappointed at not being able to find anything to tear to pieces. I looked out to see what was going on, and found everybody sitting in the snow shouting; Saltatha had discovered a single star, and the noise I had heard was the applause supposed to bring out one of the principal constellations, so that we might get an idea of our direction. The heavens certainly did clear, and when daylight broke and the wind moderated we made out our position easily enough. In fourteen hours' walk we had come perhaps five miles straight, having made a huge circle to the right and fallen on an island close to the shore that we had left in the morning. There was still the whole width of the lake to cross, but when we camped late in the portage between the two big lakes I thought we had got out of the scrape very well. There was no apparent reason why the snowstorm should have stopped, and a continuation of it must have brought us serious trouble.

The next day was worse than ever. A gale from the south in our teeth and drifting snow made it cruel work to face the storm; but we had to go, as feul was rapidly vanishing, and we had already burnt some of our lodge-poles, and we hoped to reach a small wood-*cache* that night. We could find the way, as we had the wind to guide us; but the snow was soft, and the dogs were hardly able now to drag the sleighs over the rough hills; one of the poorest froze in harness and had to be abandoned. Our blankets, which we usually wrapped round our head and shoulders when facing the wind, now came in for dog-cloths, and certainly saved some more of the dogs from being disabled by frost-bite; but as the snow melted between their backs and the blankets, the latter got wet and afterwards froze till they would stand like a board, and were then a most uncomfortable form of bedding. The slow pace at which we were forced to travel made it much worse, and we all found our faces slightly frozen. At dark we camped nearly at the end of the portage, although we did not know it till morning, and reluctantly cut up another couple of lodge-poles for firewood, besides a small box in which I had been carrying my journal and ammunition.

The wind lightened during the night, and backing into the east came fair on Lake Mackay. We found our wood-*cache* all right, and set out on the sixty-mile walk that still lay between us and the first pine-timber. The travelling on the lake was better than in the portage, and well on in the night we put ashore on the island where we had stored our first meat during the autumn musk-ox hunt. The dogs were too tired to go any further without rest, or we should have pushed on all night. Our last lodge-pole was burnt to cook a kettleful of meat for breakfast on December 1st, and before daylight we were off, with no thought of camping till we could make fire. The sun at this time only stayed above the horizon for a couple of hours, and had sunk beneath the snow before we made out far ahead the high ridge under which the first clump of pines lay. We were badly scattered along the track, and some of the dogs, and the men too for that matter, had great difficulty in keeping up pace enough to make the blood circulate; it was six hours later, and we were all pretty well used up, when we saw the little pines standing out against the sky line.

What a glorious camp we had that night! The bright glare of two big fires lit up the snow-laden branches of the dwarf pines till they glittered like so many Christmas-trees; overhead the full moon shone down on us, and every star glowed like a lamp hung in the sky; at times the Northern Lights would flash out, but the brilliancy of the moon seemed too strong for even this wondrous fire to rival. It was pleasant to lie once again on the yielding pine-brush instead of the hard snow, and to stretch our legs at full length as we could never stretch them in the lodge; pleasant, too, to look back at the long struggle we had gone through, and to contrast our present condition with that of the last month. Our experiences had been hard and not without their share of danger, and we could now congratulate ourselves on having brought our hunt to a most satisfactory conclusion. I had fully succeeded in carrying out the object of my expedition, and could look forward to a period of ever-increasing comfort, culminating in the luxury of life at a Hudson's Bay Fort within a few weeks. I had intended to winter at the edge of the Barren Ground, but was forced to give up the idea, as I had seen too much of the Beaulieus to care about living any longer with them. The fact that meat was scarce again did not trouble me, as I was by this time accustomed to empty larders and had fallen into the happy Indian method of trusting that something would turn up; besides, we were pretty sure to run across the caribou within the next few days. The want of tobacco was the worst grievance that I had, but the prospect of obtaining this was getting brighter after each day's travel.

Very late at night Saltatha turned up with a badly frozen nose and chin. One of his dogs had given out and been abandoned, and he had been pushing the sleigh for many hours; he had almost given up trying to bring in his load when he saw the blaze of the fires far off and his courage came back. The sun was up before anyone turned out, but the dogs were better for the rest, and a short day took us into a big bunch of pines on King Lake, within an easy day of a small meat *cache* that I had made while we were camped at the Lake of the Enemy. I had my doubts about finding the place, as none of the others knew where it was, but was lucky enough to hit it off; and we took out the meat of two caribou, after breaking an axe to pieces in our endeavours to chop away the ice which had formed between the rocks from the melting of the snow during a warm spell in the beginning of October.

The same night we camped at the scaffold on

which we had stored all the dried meat that the women had made while we were away on the first musk-ox hunt. King was to have taken most of it, leaving us sufficient for a couple of days' supply, and a note in the syllabic characters introduced into the North by the priests informed us that he had kept his promise. There were plenty of signs that he had done so; but the wolverines had been before us, and a few shreds of meat lying at the foot of the stage told the story plainly enough. This was rather a disappointment, and matters looked worse when we had travelled the whole length of Lake Camsell at our best speed. Here again we expected to find a *cache,* as some meat had been left when we killed the first caribou in the autumn, but the wolverines had taken it. This is a common incident in Northern travel, but never fails to draw forth hearty execrations on the head of the hated *carcajou.*

There was much talk of abandoning loads and making a rush to reach the caribou or a Yellow Knife encampment which was supposed to lie some distance ahead of us; but I opposed this scheme strongly, and for once managed to get my own way. The weather was fine, and we cared little for the cold, as we could always make a fire in case of freezing. Without eating much we pushed on rapidly for two days, crossing the Lac du Rocher, the scene of our starvation in September, and finally on the third morning found a band of caribou, of which we killed enough to relieve all immediate anxiety. By this time we were among thick timber and following closely our canoe-route of three months ago.

In the early hours of December 7th we came to a line of pine-brush planted across a small lake, and soon afterwards fell on the tracks of fresh snow-shoes; before daylight, at the end of a long portage over a thickly wooded hill, we dropped into an encampment of a dozen lodges. It turned to be Zinto's camp, and all my Indians found their wives and families awaiting them here. There were great rejoicings over our arrival, as we had been so long on the hunt that a good deal of anxiety was felt for the safety of husbands and brothers. Zinto invited me into his lodge, gave me a feast of pounded meat and grease, a cup of tea, and, better still, a small plug of black tobacco; this seemed too good to leave, and as we had travelled many hours in the night I decided to spend the rest of the day here.

The camp was very prettily situated on a small flat a few feet above the edge of a frozen lake; and when the sun rose over the hill, lighting up the brown deer-skin lodges with their columns of blue smoke rising straight up in the frosty air, the snow-laden pine-trees, and the silver-barked birches, the whole scene seemed a realization of one of Fenimore Cooper's descriptions of an Indian camp in winter.

Much talking had to be got through, and the

story of our musk-ox hunt was told many times over. I was the object of great interest, and was closely questioned as to my experiences in the Barren Ground and the contrast between life there and in my own country. After Zinto had satisfied himself on these points he broached more abtruse subjects, insisting on knowing my opinion with regard to the differences of the Protestant and Roman Catholic faiths, and seeming pleased to hear that he was by no means the first man who had found this point hard to fully understand. Many other things there were about which he desired information; but I am afraid some of my answers conveyed little meaning to him, as I was myself rather hazy about many of the topics of conversation, and had only Michel, who was the worst Frenchman of all, for interpreter, Paul having gone off to see his wife who was camped a few miles to the east. But when Zinto got on to trading he was quite at home, and before leaving I had to give him an order for many beaver-skins (the medium of trade in the North), to be paid at Fort Resolution. He was very good in providing me with everything I wanted for my journey, and gave me a new pair of snow-shoes and a sleigh, besides lending a dog to replace one that had fallen lame; meat he was short of, but he had heard that the Beaulieus had been killing caribou, so that I was likely to find *caches* by the way; a track was broken to Fond du Lac, and we ought to get there easily in three days. Zinto thought the Great Slave Lake would be entirely frozen over and fit to travel on by this time, as lately the sky had been clear in the south; when there is any open water a perpetual mist rises from it and lies like a huge fog-bank over the lake.

A happy indolent life the Yellow Knives lead when the caribou are thick on their pleasant hunting-ground round the shores of the Great Slave Lake, and most of the hard times that they have to put up with are due to their own improvidence. This is their great failing; they will not look ahead or make preparation for the time when the caribou are scare, preferring to live from hand to mouth, and too lazy to bother their heads about the future. They are rather a fine race of men, above the average of the Canadian Indian, and, as they have had little chance of mixing with the Whites, have maintained their characteristic manners till this day; they are probably little changed since the time when the Hudson's Bay Company first established a trading-post on the Big Lake a hundred years ago. When the priests came into the country the Yellow Knives readily embraced the Roman Catholic religion, and are very particular in observing all the outward signs of that faith, but I doubt if their profession of Christianity has done much to improve their character. They are a curious mixture of good and bad, simplicity and cunning; with no very great knowledge of common honesty, thoroughly untrust-

worthy, and possessed with an insatiable greed
for anything that takes their fancy, but with no
word in their language to express thanks or grati-
tude. To a white man they are humility itself,
looking upon him, by their own account, as their
father, and so considering him bound to provide
them with everything they want, even to his last
pair of trowsers or pipeful of tobacco; refuse
them anything when you are dependent upon their
services on a journey, and they will leave you in
the woods; for their own part, if they have ammunition they are always at home. In another
way they are generous enough, and take great
pride in showing hospitality. Go into one of their
lodges, and a blanket is spread for you in the seat
of honour farthest away from the flap that does
duty for a door; a meal is instantly provided, no
matter if it takes the last piece of meat in the
camp, and the precious tea and tobacco are offered
you in lavish quantities. The Yellow Knives are
a timid, peaceable race, shrinking from bloodshed
and deeds of violence, and it is seldom that quar-
rels between the men got beyond wrestling and
hair-pulling. The women are, as a rule, not quite
so hideous as the squaws of the Blackfeet and
Crees; they are lax in morals, and accustomed to
being treated more as slaves than wives in the
civilized interpretation of the word. They do all
the hard work of the camp, besides carrying the
heaviest loads on the march; and in too many
cases are rewarded with the worst of the meat

and the blows of an over-exacting husband. Early marriages are fashionable, as a man is useless without a wife to dry his meat and make moccasins for him. The great object of a Yellow Knife beauty is to secure a good hunter for a husband; the man who can shoot straight, and is known to be skilful in approaching the caribou, is always a prize in the matrimonial market and need have little fear of a refusal, especially as the husband is supposed to hunt for his father-in-law after marriage, and the old man will use all his influence to arrange the match. Superstition still reigns supreme among these people; any mischance is put down to "bad medicine," and reasons are always forthcoming to account for its presence. There are several miracle-workers and foreseers of the future in the tribe, who are said to perform very wonderful things, but I found them extremely shy of showing off their accomplishments when I asked for an exhibition. Like all other Indians who live the wild life that they were intended to live, the Yellow Knives are dirty to the last degree. They are careful about combing and greasing their hair, and are lavish in the use of soap, if they can get it, for face and hands, but their bodies are a sanctuary for the disgusting vermin that always infest them; they seem to have no idea of getting rid of these objectionable insects, but talk about its being a good or bad season for them in the same way that they speak of mosquitos.

From every point of view, then, the Indian of the Great Slave Lake is not a pleasant companion, nor a man to be relied upon in case of emergency. Nobody has yet discovered the right way to manage him. His mind runs on different principles from that of a white man, and till the science of thought-reading is much more fully developed, the working of his brain will always be a mystery to the fur-trader and traveller.

At sunrise the following morning I left Zinto's camp, with Michel and Marlo, bound for Fond du Lac, all the other musk-ox hunters going back to domestic happiness. The weather was still bright and cold, and the days perceptibly longer as we travelled south. We were again short of meat, as all the Indians were in the same plight, and although we saw a band of caribou shortly after starting, we were unable to get a shot at them. Towards evening we found a small *cache* of meat hung in a tree, and knowing that it must belong to some of the Beaulieus I had no compunction in taking it. Here we left our canoe-route, and passing to the westward of the Lac de Mort headed straight for the house at Fond du Lac. The woods were well grown and signs of life abundant; the tracks of wolves, wolverines, foxes, and an occasional marten, frequently crossed the road, and ptarmigan were continually flying up under the leader's feet. Here, too, I saw again my old friend the Whisky Jack, as he is called throughout the North, a grey and white bird the size of a thrush, with a most confiding disposition and an inordinate love of fat meat; he sits on the nearest tree while the camp is being made, comes in boldly, inspects the larder, and helps himself with very little fear of man. If it is a starving camp he chortles in contempt and flies away, having a very low opinion of people who travel without provisions; but if meat be plentiful he spends the night there, and comes in for rich pickings in the morning when the camp is struck. This bird is common throughout the wilder parts of Canada, and has acquired many names in different places; in the mountains of British Columbia he is the Hudson's Bay bird or grease bird, and far away to the East the moose bird, caribou bird, Rupert's bird, and camp-robber.

On the afternoon of the second day we met the Indian Etitchula, who had left the fort with us in August and had been hanging on more or less to our party ever since. He was on his way back to King Beaulieu's Camp, two days' travel to the north-east, having made a trip to Fond du Lac to make a raid on my tea and tobacco, and see if there was any news of us, as King was greatly alarmed at our prolonged absence. We relieved him of a little tea, but he had not been able to get any tobacco out of François, who had roundly asserted that it all belonged to him; he also gave us a couple of whitefish, which proved a very acceptable change from our long course of straight meat. Late the same evening we made our last camp on the high land close to the edge of the mountains within five miles of the house; we could easily have got in that night, but I much preferred a quiet camp under the stars to the company of the gang of Beaulieus who were sure to be at Fond du Lac.

One word of caution against using the compressed tea imported by the Hudson's Bay Company into the North as a substitute for tobacco; it is very good to drink, but if you smoke it you pay the penalty by a most painful irritation in the throat, which is made worse by breathing the intensely cold air. We all tried it that night, and all swore never to do so again, although I have often smoked the ordinary uncompressed tea without disastrous results and with a certain amount of satisfaction.

We were off in good time on the morning of December 10th, and were soon sitting on the sleighs, rushing down the steep incline, with frequent spills from bumping against trees; this was the only piece of riding I had during the whole five weeks' travel. The first signs of the *petit jour* were just showing as we pulled up at the house, and François quickly produced the tobacco he had refused Etitchula. I think for a few minutes they were really glad to see us back safe, but soon the old complaints began. Times had been hard, although the women and children all looked fat enough to belie this statement; José had been catching whitefish, but had refused to give any to François; while the latter, according to José, had been very mean in distribution of my effects, eating flour every day himself but giving none away. They had gone through nearly everything between them, and moreover did not seem the least bit ashamed of their conduct. As my dogs were all used up, I decided to leave them here, and made arrangements with François to bring his own train on to the fort with me. It seemed that notwithstanding the hard times he had sufficient meat and fish stored away for our trip, and there were still a few pounds of flour left, so that we should live in luxury all the way in.

I spent the day shooting a few ptarmigan, indulging in much tobacco, and listening to the petitions of the various ill-used members of the family. José was particularly amusing; he had been the most useless man of the lot, never even venturing into the Barren Ground, but spending most of his time at Fond du Lac, shooting away my ammunition and playing havoc with tea and tobacco, besides robbing the *cache* at the Lac du Rocher. Now he was full of love for me, and gave me a list of things that he wanted in addition to his wages, as a reward for all that he had done and was ready to do for me. Among other items, he wanted my rifle and hunting-glasses, and remarked that my Paradox gun, which had been lying here all the time, would be very useful for him at the goose-hunt in the following spring.

Fortunately none of the Beaulieus know how to put together a breech-loading gun, so the Paradox and its ammunition had been left in peace to do me good service in the summer. I think the Paradox is the most useful gun yet invented for purposes of exploration, as it does away with the necessity of carrying a separate weapon for shot and ball, and shoots very true with either; but there seems no reason why the patent should not be applied to a 20-bore. For procuring food in a really rough country, where a man has to carry his own ammunition, the ball-cartridges for a 12-bore are needlessly heavy, and the charge of shot is too great for the close range shooting which is usually done on these occasions.

CHAPTER IX

At Fond du Lac I slept for the first time since we left the fort under a roof, but on account of the awful squalor of the house I should have much preferred the usual open camp in the snow. Daylight found us under way again, François and myself, with a small boy to run ahead of the dogs; as we were travelling light I expected to be able to ride the last half of the journey, but for the first two days the fish for dogs' food made our load too heavy to travel at a fast pace. I left all the musk-ox and caribou heads and skins that I had managed to save, to come in with Michel and Marlo when they made the usual journey to the fort for New Year's day, on which occasion the Indians from all quarters bring in their furs to trade, and receive a small feast of flour and sugar, an event not to be missed on any account, even though wives and families may be left to starve in the woods and the famished dogs drop with fatigue along the track.

There was no news as to the state of the ice, as we were the first people to attempt the crossing of the lake this winter. It is usually not safe for travel till the middle of December, so we coasted along the north shore, increasing the distance, but getting greater safety by doing so. We took things easily, making early starts and putting ashore frequently for a cup of tea; it was a great improvement on the canoe-travelling which had delayed us so much in the autumn. At sundown every night we picked out a sheltered spot among the tall pine-trees where firewood was plentiful, threw away the snow with our snowshoes, and put down a thick mat of pine-brush; then a huge fire was lit and enough wood cut for the night, the fish thawed for the dogs, and supper cooked for the men. We had bread at every meal, which is in itself a luxury after four months of straight meat; the day ended with tobacco, and we rolled ourselves in our blankets to sleep, till the position of the Great Bear told us it was time to be on the march once more. People who live in civilization find it hard to believe that men in these northern latitudes habitually sleep out under the stars, with the thermometer standing at 30°, 40°, and even 60° below zero; yet it is those same people of civilization who suffer from colds in the head, lung-diseases, and a variety of ailments unknown to the *voyageur,* whose only dangers are starvation and the risk of accidents incidental to travelling in rough countries.

On the second day we passed a couple of houses occupied by an Indian, Capot Blanc, with whom I afterwards became great friends; he had left for the fort a couple of days before, but the ice was reported to be dangerous in the Grand Traverse. Another Indian, Thomas, a brother of Marlo and Zinto, was ready to start, and joined in with us for the rest of the journey; he had only two dogs, but with a light load managed to keep up easily enough. The ice among the islands was pretty good, but the snow was soft and deep, and it was not till our fourth night out from Fond du Lac that we camped on the last outlying island, ready to take the Traverse. About eighteen miles away to the south, without any chance to put ashore till we reached it, lay the Ile de Pierre, and we were to make for a half-breed's house that lay within a mile of it on the main shore of the lake. It had been arranged that I was to ride in pomp across this piece, so, after a good breakfast about three o'clock, I turned into the sleigh and soon dropped off to sleep to the music of sleigh-bells and a volley of French oaths with which François encouraged his dogs every few minutes. At this time the stars were shining brightly, and there was not a breath of wind. I must have slept for a couple of hours when François awoke me with the information that we were lost. Turning out of my warm berth I found a gale of wind blowing, with snow falling and drifting heavily; I could hardly make out the men in the darkness, though they were all standing within a few yards of me. Of course I had not the slightest idea where we were, or the direction in which we had been travelling. François seemed undecided, but Thomas was quite sure that by keeping the wind abeam we should hit off the Ile de Pierre. We put him ahead, and he proved perfectly right in his direction; for after four hours' steady walk we made out the land, the weather clearing a little at daybreak. We had headed a little too far to the west, but were soon inside the half-breed's cabin, where we found plenty of fish for the dogs, and so decided to spend the day there, as the wind had freshened up again and the drifting snow made travelling unpleasant. We did not know what a narrow escape we had had till the owner of the house came in, after making an attempt to visit his nets. He reported the ice broken up to the west by the violence of the gale, and had we kept a little more in that direction we might easily have walked into open water in the darkness and made a disastrous ending to our expedition.

Our course the next day lay over shoal water, mostly inside sankbanks and through narrow channels of the delta of the Slave River. We crossed the main stream on good ice, and following the shore of the lake for ten miles, rattled into the fort about two o'clock, within ten minutes of the arrival of the outward-bound packet from Mackenzie River. Luckily enough it had been delayed one day by the storm that had overtaken us in the Grand Traverse, and I had an opportunity of sending out letters by the dog-sleigh that was to leave the same night. For true hospitality

there is nothing in the world to beat the welcome
back to a Hudson's Bay post in the North after
one has made a long journey in the wilds; no
need to trouble your head with the idea that you
may not be wanted, or that you will eat too much
of the ever insufficient supplies sent in from the
outside world to the officer in charge. Why is it
that the less a man has, and the harder things
are to obtain, the more ready he is to divide?
It does not seem to work in civilization, but it is
certainly so in rough countries, and especially
with the Hudson's Bay Company's officers in the
Far North. Perhaps it is because they have all
seen hardships and privations in the Company's
service and know the value of a helping hand
given in the time of need; men who have suffered
themselves have always more feeling for the sufferings of others than people who have lived only
on the soft side of life.

I don't think I ever enjoyed a meal so much as
that first dinner at Fort Resolution, after a most
necessary wash. A year later I dragged myself
into a small trading-post at the foot of the Rocky
Mountains after many days' total starvation, but
had then got beyond the capacity of enjoying anything. On the present occasion I was able to
thoroughly appreciate the change from my four
months' experience in the Barren Ground. How
strange it semed once more to sit at a table, on a
chair, like a white man, and eat white man's food
with a knife and fork, after the long course of

Skins in the Post Storeroom

Taking the Post Dogs for Exercise

·

squatting in the filth of a smoky lodge, rending a piece of half-raw meat snatched from the dirty kettle. Then, too, I could speak again in my own language, and there was a warm room to sit in, books to read, and all the ordinary comforts of life, with the knowledge that so long as I stayed in the house I had my own place, while the wind and the snow had theirs outside.

There was no scarcity at the fort this year, although the autumn fishing had not been successful. The Fond du Lac boat had brought in a good supply of dried meat, and there was a better stock of flour than is usually to be found at a northern fort. Mr. Mackinlay, too, had got in a fair supply of luxuries from Winnipeg, and, as Mrs. Mackinlay was an excellent manager, we always lived as well as one should wish to live anywhere.

Fort Resolution is a fair sample of a trading-post in the North. It is situated on the south side of a bay, the entrance to which is sheltered by a group of islands, the largest known as Mission Island, from the Roman Catholic mission established there in charge of Father Dupire. The original site was on an outlying island known as Moose Island, but the present position on the mainland has been found more practicable. The buildings consist of the master's house, a comfortable log-building flanked on each side by a large store, one used for provisions and the other as a fur and trading store; these were originally within a stockade and formed the fort proper, but the peaceful nature of the Indians has removed all need for defensive works. Outside is a small row of log-houses, occupied by the engaged servants, freemen, and a couple of pensioners too old to make their living in the woods. Close at hand are the buildings belonging to the Protestant Mission, while the willows and bush-growth of a densely-wooded level country hem in the small patch of cleared ground on which the settlement stands; here potatoes and a few other vegetables are raised, and in a favourable season produce very fair crops. There are a yoke of work-cattle for hauling wood and a couple of milch cows are kept, as hay is easily procured in the numerous swamps which are scattered through the woods in every direction. The only high land to be seen is a conspicuous bluff marking the entrance to the Little Buffalo River some ten miles along the lake shore, this stream heads in to the south, and as it breaks up earlier in the spring than the Little Slave River it is used at that time of year as a route to Fort Smith, one overland portage being made, to drop on to the main stream a short distance below the fort.

Looking out over the vast expanse of frozen lake on still, bright days some very beautiful and curious mirage effects can often be seen. Everything takes an unnatural and frequently inverted form; islands so far away as to be below the horizon are seen suspended in the air, and it is impossible to recognise a point or bunch of trees with which you are perfectly familiar in ordinary circumstances.

There are four engaged servants at the fort; a white man, Murdo Mackay, native of the Hebrides, who was serving a five years' contract with the Company, and three half-breeds, by far the best of whom was Michel Mandeville, who has held the position of interpreter at Fort Resolution for several years. Except at the time of the Fall fishery, an engaged servant's work is light—cutting and hauling enough firewood to keep the fort supplied, visiting the nets and lines, and an occasional trip with the packet, or to get trading-goods from another fort.

Christmas passed away quietly, but there was stir enough when the Indians came in for New Year and the trading began. The old system of barter is still carried on, with the beaver-skin for a standard. An Indian's pile of fur is counted, and he is told how many skins' worth of goods he has to receive; then he is taken into the store and the door solemnly locked, as it is found impossible to trade at all with more than one at a time. It seems very simple; the Indian knows exactly how many skins he has to take, and the value in skins of every common article. But, to begin with, he wants everything he sees, and the whole stock would hardly satisfy him, and it is a long time, with many changes of opinion, before he has spent the proceeds of his hunt. Then arises the question of his debt, and he tries to take the largest amount possible on credit for his spring hunt; the trader cannot refuse absolutely to make any advances, as there are some things essentially necessary to the Indian's life in the woods, but the debts are kept in proportion to the man's character. After he has finished his trade, he shows his purchases to his friends, and, acting on their advice, usually comes back to effect some change, and the game begins all over again; sometimes a whole day is passed in laying out a hundred skins, roughly fifty dollars according to our method of calculation. Before the Indian leaves the fort he always comes in and does a little begging while saying good-bye to his master.

I had a very bad time of it settling up with the Beaulieus. Promises that I had made under stress of circumstances had to be redeemed, but it was hopeless to try and satisfy them; although they had each received far more than had been originally agreed upon, they continued grumbling till they left the fort. On New Year's day a big ball was given to the half-breeds, while the Indians were provided with the materials for a feast, and held a dance of their own in one of the empty houses. It was the poorest display imaginable; many of the Canadian tribes have really effective dancing, but the Yellow Knives appear to have a very elementary idea of graceful movement. Their only figure is to waddle round in a circle, holding each other's hands, keeping up a monotonous chant, and spitting freely into the middle of the ring. In the big house Red River jigs and reels were kept up with unflagging energy till daylight.

As soon as everything had quieted down and the Indians had gone back to their hunting-ground, Mackinlay and myself started on an expedition after the caribou to try and kill some fresh meat for the fort. We took Michel, the interpreter, with us, and Pierre Beaulieu, a brother of King's; and a resident of Mission Island joined us with his two sons, as there was news of the caribou being at no great distance on the far side of the lake. It was now the dead of winter, the season of the *gra' frète,* and we had two remarkably cold days' travel to reach the north shore of the Great Slave Lake. We struck into the woods, not far to the eastward of the Gros Cap, the point forming the eastern extremity of the long narrow arm leading to Fort Rae. We each had a sleigh of dogs, and were able to ride most of the time on a good road broken by a band of Indians hunting in the neighbourhood. Two long days over small lakes and through the thick pine woods, in a country much resembling that of Fond du Lac but of lower elevation, brought us among the caribou, but they were not in very large numbers.

We had everything we could want to make life pleasant in the woods, abundance of tea and tobacco, meat if we killed it, and no hardships; the cold was severe of course, but there was plenty of firewood, and it was our own fault if we could not keep ourselves warm. Three days we spent in hunting, and, although we did not kill very much, there was a little meat to take back; we never really found the caribou in any quantity, or we should have made a big killing and *cached* the meat, to be hauled later on when the days grew longer. A rattling three days' journey took us back to the fort, as old Pierre, who is one of the most rushing travellers I ever met, hustled us along to save using his meat on the way home; he had no intention of feeding his dogs from his load for more than two nights when he had fish to give them at home. This trouble about dogs' food is the great drawback to winter travelling in the North; a dog, to keep him in good order, requires two whitefish, weighing each perhaps three pounds, every night. This adds so much to the load that a ten days' journey is about the longest one can undertake with full rations all round, unless it be in a part of the country where game is plentiful or fish can be caught *en route.*

After the caribou hunt, we amused ourselves about the fort; sometimes going in search of ptarmigan, which are usually to be found among the willows close to the edge of the lake; and sometimes paying Father Dupire a visit on his island, a couple of miles away, to hear some of his interesting experiences during a residence of many years among the Indians. Close at hand lay the Protestant Mission, where there was always a welcome, and, with these attractions and a fair supply of books, time did not hang at all heavily till early in February the winter packet from the outside world arrived. I received a big bundle of letters, the first that reached me since June, but it happened that none of the newspapers for the fort turned up, and we were left in ignorance of what had happened in the Grand Pays.

So many travellers have written about this great Northern Packet and the wonderful journey that it makes that it is unnecessary for me to say much about it. On its arrival at Fort Resolution it presents the appearance of an ordinary dog-sleigh, with a man ahead of the dogs, which are driven by a half-breed, with plenty of ribbons and beads on leggings and moccasins, capable of running his forty miles a day with ease, and possessed of a full command of the more expressive part of the French language.

Dr. Mackay, who was on his yearly round of visits to inspect the outlying posts in his district, came down from Fort Chipeweyan with the packet, and we had a long talk respecting a summer trip to the Barren Ground which I proposed making.

My intention was to leave the fort on the last ice in the spring and travel with the dogs to the spot where we had left our big canoe in the autumn, there to await the breaking up of the lakes and to descend the Great Fish River with the first open winter. I had no special object in reaching the sea-coast, as a birch-bark canoe is not the right sort of craft for work among salt-water ice; and it was more to see what the Barren Ground was like in summer, and to notice the habits of the birds and animals, than for the sake of geographical discovery, that I wished to make the expedition.

The Great Fish River has been twice descended before, but of course both Back's and Anderson's parties were compelled by the shortness of the summers to confine their exploration to the immediate neighbourhood of the river; and I thought that, by spending more time at the head-waters than they had been able to do, I should get a good idea of the nature of the country and an insight into the Indian summer life among the caribou. The difficulty was to obtain a crew; but Dr. Mackay very kindly consented to Mackinlay's accompanying me, and also lent me the two engaged servants, Murdo Mackay and Moise Mandeville, brother of Michel Mandeville the interpreter, but not half such a good fellow. We hoped to be able to engage the services of some of the Indians to guide us to the head of the river, but they have such a dread of the Esquimaux, who hunt farther down the stream, that we hardly expected any of the Yellow Knives to accompany us beyond that point. Long ago there

was always war between the Indians and the Esquimaux, and Hearne's description of the massa-
cre at the Bloody Falls on the Coppermine gives
a good idea of the hatred that existed between
these tribes. For many years they have not met,
and although the Esquimaux seen by Anderson
on the Great Fish River appear peaceful enough,
the Yellow Knives hunting at the head of the
river are in constant fear of meeting them.

Zinto, the chief, and another Indian, Syene,
arrived at the fort soon after Dr. Mackay left,
and we consulted them as to the best route to
follow, and whether we could depend upon their
tribe for any help. They told us that there was
no difficulty in reaching the head-waters of the
river, as the Indians were in the habit of coming
there every summer, but beyond was an unknown
country; they both remembered Anderson's expedition, and were full of stories about the difficulties of navigation, the numerous portages and
the likelihood of starvation, but knew nothing
from personal experience. We failed lamentably
in the attempt to discover when the ice in the
river usually broke up. Syene told us that it was
in the moon when the dogs lie on their backs in
the sun, and Zinto volunteered the information
that it was soon after the leaves begin to shoot
on the little willows in the Barren Ground; but
we could not work it out into any particular
month. Both promised to make dried meat and
pemmican for us if they fell in with the caribou,

and to leave *caches* in the last bunch of pine-trees. Next day they left for their camp, two hundred miles away in the woods, to await the first signs of warmer weather to start for the spring musk-ox hunt. Zinto was to come to the fort about the 1st of May, and personally conduct us to the places where he had piled up the meat of many caribou for our use.

CHAPTER X

ABOUT the middle of February, 1890, little
François, an Indian living at the mouth of Buffalo River, arrived with the news that during a
hunting-trip he had made to the southward he
had seen the tracks of a band of wood buffalo
and intended to go in pursuit of them after this
visit to the fort.

Mackinlay and myself both wanted an excuse
to be in the woods again, and the next day saw us
plodding across the bay on snow-shoes to the
comfortable little shanty, under the high bluff,
which forms the most conspicuous landmark
within sight of Fort Resolution. The establishment was presided over by an old lady, formerly
cook at one of the forts, and kept with a cleanliness not always to be found in a white man's
dwelling. The following morning we started
with two sleigh-loads of fish for the dogs and
provisions and blankets for ourselves. François
brought his wife and little girl, besides a rather
crazy boy, given to epileptic fits, but a good worker in the intervals between his attacks. We followed the river for a mile or two, then turned
into the woods on the west bank, and, crossing a
lake of some size, headed in a south-west direc-

tion through the thick pine-forest, occasionally picking up a marten from a line of traps set by little François, for we were following the track that he had made on his last trip, or finding a rabbit hung by the neck in one of his wife's snares; very cunning these old women are in all things concerning the stomach, and if there are many rabbit-tracks to be seen in the snow there is little danger of going without supper.

On the second day we crossed a large prairie dotted with lakes, formerly the home of many beavers, and still bearing evidence of their labours in the long banks which served as dams and the huge mounds which were once their houses. The beavers have all gone long ago, and the ladies who wore the pretty fur-trimmed jackets in far-away England, and the husbands who grumbled at their price, are gone too; but the beavers have left the most impression on the face of the earth. Wonderful moulders of geography they are; a stream dammed up in a level country forms a huge lake where the forest stood, the trees fall as their roots rot in standing water, and, if the dam be not attended to by the workers, a fertile grass-covered prairie takes the place of the lake. From the Liard River and Great Slave Lake, to the Peace River on the east side of the Rocky Mountains, extends the greatest beaver country in the world. It is known by Indian report alone, as no white man ever penetrates far into the wilderness of pine-forest and morass;

many streams head away into the interior of this unknown land, but the white man has only seen their mouths, as he passes up or down the main waterways of the North. It is true that the Company's men have ascended Hay River, a large stream falling into the Great Slave Lake, and by making an overland portage, have dropped on the Peace River at Fort Vermillion; but they have always made hurried voyages and have had no opportunity of exploring much new ground.

Scattered over this huge extent of country are still a few bands of buffalo. Sometimes they are heard of at Forts Smith and Vermillion, sometimes at Fort St. John close up to the big mountains on Peace River, and occasionally at Fort Nelson on the south branch of the Liard. It is impossible to say anything about their numbers, as the country they inhabit is so large, and the Indians, who are few in number, usually keep to the same hunting-ground. These animals go by the name of wood buffalo, and most people are of opinion that they are a distinct race from the old prairie buffalo so numerous in bygone days; but I am inclined to think that the very slight difference in appearance is easily accounted for by climatic influences, variety of food, and the better shelter of the woods. Here too the giant moose and the woodland caribou have their home, and even in the short journey that I made into this district the tracks in the snow told a tale of plenty. Many black bears' skins are brought out every year, and towards the mountains the formidable grizzly is often encountered by the fearful hunter. Nor are the small fur-bearing animals wanting; foxes—red, cross, and a few silver—seek their living on the prairie, while wolverines, fisher, mink, marten, and lynx may be trapped in the woods, and a few otters frequent the streams and lakes. In the summer ducks, geese, and many other water-birds have their nests in the muskegs, and two or three varieties of the tree grouse are always to be found. "The hunter's Paradise!" says the sporting reader; "let us go and have a hunt there." But now for the other side of the picture. In the summer it is practically impossible to travel, as it is a swampy country not to be crossed with horses, and the lakes are too far apart to be available as a canoe-route, while the mosquitos are intolerable. Only when the snow has fallen, and all water is held fast in the grip of winter, has one a chance of exploring this Land of Promise with dogs, sleighs, and snow-shoes; but, by this time, the summer life has all flown far away southward, and, though I think one would be fairly safe in pushing on, there is always a chance of coming across a large tract of gameless country, and finding a difficulty in obtaining provisions.

After three days' good travel we reached the end of François' road, and long before daylight on the following morning were away to try and find the buffalo tracks. We had a long day's walk over a perfect hunting-ground, crossing several open ridges with sufficient elevation to give us a view of the surrounding country. Prairie and timber were about in equal proportion, and the eye could follow the windings of a large stream that falls into the Little Buffalo River close to the Fort Smith portage; its water are strongly impregnated with sulphur, and do not readily freeze; in fact this stream, although it has little current, remains open during a considerable part of its course even in the coldest weather. About noon we found the track that we had been looking for, easily distinguishable from the many tracks of moose and woodland caribou that we had crossed; little François made a capital approach, and after a couple of hours' walk we sighted a band of eight buffalo feeding in a small wood-surrounded swamp. There are few spots on the American continent to-day where one can see buffalo in their wild state, but the Indian gave us no time to watch them, and completely spoilt the chance of clean shooting by letting off his gun too soon; we only wanted to kill one, as we could not haul any more meat, and it is really a pity to kill animals so nearly extinct as these. As it turned out there were several snap-shots fired as they ran into the woods, and two tracks of blood in the snow showed that we had done too much shooting, although it was not till late in the second day that we secured a cow that had travelled many miles before lying down.

By the way, it is as well when going for a hunting expedition in the North to leave at home all the old-fashioned notions of shooting-etiquette. If you see a man in a good position for a shot, run up, jostle his elbow, and let your gun off; if an animal falls, swear you killed it, and claim the back-fat and tongue no matter whether you fired or not; never admit that you are not quite sure which animal you shot at. It is only by strict attention to these rules that a white man can get a fair division of plunder when shooting with half-breed Indians.

The other buffalo, on whose track there was little blood, had not separated from the band, although we followed it for a whole day, and, as this was a sure sign of its having been only slightly wounded, perhaps not much damage was done; a badly struck animal will always leave its companions and lie down.

There was much rejoicing when late on the third night the result of our hunt was hauled into our pleasant camp in a clump of thick pine-timber, The little girl patted and played with the meat as an English child would with a doll, and eventually dropped off to sleep with the raw brisket for a pillow; while Pierre, the boy, after a huge feast was seized with such a violent fit that for a long time I was afraid it would prove his last. The others took no notice of him beyond putting down a log to keep him from rolling in the fire, and in the morning he seemed perfectly well and

hungry as ever for buffalo-meat. With heavily-
laden sleighs we started back for the fort, but a
wind-storm had drifted up our track over the
prairie, and the dogs had hard work to drag their
loads. In one of our steel traps were the remains
of a cross fox that a wolverine had eaten, and
beyond a few more martens our fur-hunting was
unsuccessful. It took us four days to reach little
François' house at the mouth of the river, and
another half-day to get to the fort, where we
found everything quiet, as usual in the monotony
of the long winter. February was nearly over,
and the "moon of the big wind" was doing its
best to keep up its reputation. Day after day the
north wind howled over the lake, drifting the
snow into a vast ridge on the lee shore and making it no easy matter to find the trout-lines, which
had now to be set four or five miles out at sea,
the fish moving into deep water as the cold gets
more intense and the ice thicker. The thermometer hanging against the wall of the house ranged
between *minus* 30 and *minus* 45 degrees Fahrenheit, and this state of affairs continued until I left
the fort for another hunt with little François.
We spent three weeks happily enough in the
woods, doing a little trapping, and getting enough
moose and caribou-meat to keep the dogs and
ourselves in good condition. Our course lay the
same way as on the last hunt, to take advantage
of the road and visit the line of traps; but we
pushed further on till we came across the tracks

of a party of Indians hunting from Fort Smith.
We saw no sign of buffalo, and as François' wife
damaged her leg rather badly we were obliged to
haul her back on the sleigh, and this accident put
an end to our trip. Away far in the forest beyond the influence of the great frozen lake we
found the first indications of the coming spring.
By the end of the first week in April the snow
was falling under our snow-shoes in the middle
of the day, and the sun, which now had a long
course to run, shone with considerable power; the
pine-trees threw out the delicious scent so suggestive of Nature's awakening after her long
snow-wrapped sleep, and a puff of warm south
wind, sighing through the poplars, whispered a
message of hope from a more favoured land. But
winter made a final struggle, and it was not till
the 25th of April that the collapse came. Then
the snow in the woods around the fort melted
away rapidly, and the bare ground showed in
patches. On May 1st water was standing in
pools over the ice in the bay, the snow had disappeared except in the drifts, a light rain was
falling, and the first goose was killed from the
door of the master's house; small bands of wild-
fowl were passing frequently, and cranes were
calling in the swamps to the southward; daylight
lingered in the sky all night, but there was always a sharp frost while the sun was down.

It was time to shake off our luxurious habits
and push out again for the North to take full ad-

vantage of the short summer of the Barren Ground. The fort seemed to wake up with the spring, and there was bustle and activity everywhere. The furs had to be spread out to dry before they could be baled up; fish had to be thrown out of the provision-store as they thawed, and the dogs were happy for once. There was talk of ploughing and planting the potato-crop; Indians kept dropping in with small bundles of fur, to trade for ammunition for the goose-hunt, which would soon be in full swing; canoes were patched up and made tight in readiness for the first open water. But there was a rumour that the expedition to the Great Fish River would fall through, as no crew could be found, and some discontented spirits had been trying to persuade the Indians against going with us; the half-breeds were all full of excuses, and for a time it looked bad for us. Mackinlay was of course keen enough for the trip, and so was Murdo Mackay, the Scotch engaged servant; and luckily David, an Esquimau boy from Peel's River, who had been left at Fort Resolution for the winter to learn English from the Protestant missionary there, was willing to come with us, and, although not a first-rate traveller, might be very useful as interpreter if we fell in with any of his countrymen. Moise Mandeville was more obstinate and had the greatest horror of the expedition, but he finally agreed to come in the capacity of steersman and as Montaignais' interpreter. We were still without a guide. Zinto, despite his promises, had not put in an appearance, and there was as yet no news of him. Meanwhile preparations went on; dogs were got together, new snow-shoes provided for each member of the party, and all available pounded meat and grease converted into pemmican as the most portable form of provisions; four sacks of flour were forwarded to Fond du Lac to await our arrival, and the women round the fort were busy making moccasins for men and dogs, as the latter have to be shod in spring-travelling, to prevent their feet being cut to pieces on the rough needle-ice that appears after the snow has melted off the lakes. We also took a light canvas lodge in place of the heavier deer-skins, and found it a great saving in weight, especially after rain; dressed deer-skins hold water like a sponge, and where firewood is scarce are extremely hard to dry.

On May 4th Mr. Clark arrived from Fort Smith to take charge of Resolution during Mackinlay's absence. The slushy state of the snow made travelling hard, but the Fort Smith people had managed to bring us a welcome supply of tea, tobacco, ammunition, and a few matches; none of these necessary articles were to be had at Resolution, as the unusually heavy fur-trade had left the store empty. We collected all the touch-wood we could get hold of, and each took a flint and steel, while Dr. Mackay sent us a burning-glass, a compass, and a watch from Chipeweyan, besides half a dozen pair of spectacles to keep off snow-blindness, from which an unprotected eye is sure to suffer. There was also a small stock of axes, knives, and beads, presents for the Esquimaux in case we fell in with them. Arrangements were made for the fort boat to meet us at the old site of Lockhart's house, at the north-east end of the Great Slave Lake, on August 1st, to bring us across the lake, as I wished to start for the South in time to get back to civilization before the rivers and lakes were set fast by the coming winter.

The day after Mr. Clark's arrival a couple of Indians came in from Fond du Lac. Zinto had not yet arrived there, but was expected any day; he had no meat for us, and caribou were reported scarce on the road we proposed taking; most of the Yellow Knives would be at Fond du Lac to meet us if they found food enough for present use. Pierre Lockhart, an Indian who had come to the fort, immediately engaged with us as guide to the Great Fish River, saying that whatever the other men might do he would be faithful to the end of the journey, even if we wanted him to go to the sea-coast: needless to say he was the very first to desert on the appearance of hard times.

It was a goodly procession that left Fort Resolution on the afternoon of May 7th, for every sleigh was pressed into service to help us over the bad ice that lay between the fort and the big river, and all the goose-hunters had been waiting till we started to move their families to the favourite feeding-grounds. Across the first bay there was fully a foot of water, with a crust of ice caused by the last night's frost; this top crust had to be broken, and the dogs waded up to their bellies, with the sleighs floating behind them: bitterly cold for the feet and hard to avoid a fall, which meant a thorough drenching in the icy water. On reaching the delta and passing into the narrow channels at the mouth of the big river the ice was much better, as the water had run off through the cracks; the crossing of the main stream looked dangerous, but, by carefully picking our way and sounding the ice with an axe, we got across without accident and camped in a bunch of willows on the far side. The fires were kept up late that night and much talking was done, as to-morrow we had to say good-bye to our companions, and many instructions were given to wives, mothers, and children with reference to their good behaviour during our absence. The red glow of sunset stayed in the sky till it mingled with the brightness of the coming day; often a whirr of wings told of a flock of wildfowl passing overhead, and a few geese that had arrived from the south kept up a continual *honking* as they searched for a patch of open water to alight on. But the frost was sharp in the night, and on breaking camp at four o'clock we found the crust of surface-ice in the next bay strong enough in most

places to bear our sleighs, which were now reduced to two in number and much more heavily
loaded than on the previous day. Sometimes a
man would break through, and, floundering on the
bottom ice, would bruise his shins and feet in a
desperate manner, and we were all badly knocked
about when we put ashore at Tête Noire's House,
five miles beyond the Ile de Pierre, ready to take
the big traverse on the following day. A couple
of hours out from the land brought us again to
dry snow, as the change of climate is very sudden after leaving the south shore of the lake.
Crossing the big traverse was ordinary winter
travelling, although the snow was soft in the
strong sunshine; we made use of the frost at
night and generally rested during the heat of the
day. Between the islands snow-shoes were necessary, and, although spectacles were constantly
worn, some of the men began to show signs of
snow-blindness; occasionally we found a bare
rock to camp on, but more generally made the old
winter form of encampment on the snow. It was
not till the sixth day after leaving the fort that
we pulled into Fond du Lac, and found nearly
the whole tribe of Yellow Knives awaiting us
with King Beaulieu and his family at their head;
there were five and twenty lodges, and in every
one we heard the old story of *Berula* (no meat);
they had tried fishing without success, and hoped
the white masters would give them a little flour
and pemmican. Why had they not pushed on to

some of the sure fisheries in the big lake when they found the caribou fail? They wished to talk with us, they said, and so had stayed and starved at Fond du Lac till we came. What did they want to speak to us about? Only this, that an Indian's life is hard, and he has at all times need of a little tea and tobacco to give him courage; they had heard we were taking much tea and tobacco, besides other presents, to the Esquimaux. In vain did we tell them that we had not enough for own use; there was no peace till pipes were going in every lodge.

Zinto had not put up any meat for us. At one time he had killed a good many caribou, but he had met with a band of Dog-Ribs from Fort Rae and the two tribes had camped together; the chief of the Yellow Knives was bound in honour to give a feast to his guests, and after the meat that was meant for us had been used for this purpose they fell to gambling. The unfortunate Zinto lost all his ammunition, so that he had no chance to kill any more caribou, much as he would have liked to help the white men in their undertaking.

The snow was lying deep in the woods and as yet no breath of spring had visited Fond du Lac, although at Fort Resolution, not more than one hundred miles to the south, the buds were by this time shooting on the birch and willow trees, and the ground had been bare for two weeks; no wildfowl had arrived, and the Indians were of opinion that such a late spring had never been

Dog-rib Powwow at Fort Resolution

Group of Dog-rib Indians

known, advising us strongly not to attempt to force our way into the Barren Ground till there was some indication of better weather. It seemed to us, though, that we should never be in a better position to start than now, as any delay meant waste of provisions, and we hoped to find caribou before we began to starve. Several days we spent in talking to the Indians before we came to any satisfactory conclusion, and we had the greatest trouble in persuading any of them to come with us. Finally it was settled that Capot Blanc, Saltatha, Syene, and Marlo, with their wives and families, should start with us, and on reaching the head of the Great Fish River should wait there and hunt while we made the descent of the stream. Capot Blanc behaved very well at all the consultations, speaking up for the white men whenever an opportunity offered, but the interpretation was unsatisfactory; Moise refused this duty in the presence of the Beaulieus, and the latter, so far as we could make out, used all their influence with the Indians to damage our chances of making a successful expedition. David, the Esquimau, rather complicated matters by falling in love with King's daughter, but he made no objection to starting, and soon forgot all about her in the excitement of the journey. On the last evening that we spent at Fond du Lac a Dog-Rib arrived with his family from the Barren Ground in a wretched state of starvation. He had come in by the route

that we proposed to take, and gave a very unsatisfactory report of the country: the cold was
still severe, and he had met with no game since
leaving the musk-ox a couple of weeks before;
one of his children had died of starvation and he
was forced to bury her under the snow at the Lac
de Mort; the rest had barely escaped with life.
Of course we gave them enough flour and pemmican to take them to a well-known fishery twenty miles on, but our provisions were going very
fast. Most of the Yellow Knives had already
moved away to the fishery, and the encampment
was entirely deserted when we pulled down our
lodges on the morning of May 21st. Paul Beaulieu was to have caught us up to show us some
meat-*caches* that he had made in the winter, and
we had engaged an Indian, Carquoss, to fish for
his wife while he was away; but we saw neither
Paul nor his *caches*. Carquoss, however, joined
us later on, and explained that he had given up
fishing because we had not left him any tea and
the other Indians had laughed at him.

A miserable-looking outfit we were as we
plodded for two days along the north shore of the
lake, against a strong head-wind and driving
snowstorms. Seven trains of starving dogs
hauled their loads in a melancholy procession,
and over twenty people walked in the narrow road
made by the passage of the sleighs; by far too
large a party for any rapid travelling, and badly
handicapped by women and children. On the

third day we turned up the mountain, and followed the course of a stream coming in on the north shore; we mounted by a series of frozen cascades, many of them so steep that we were obliged to use ropes to help the dogs, and towards evening camped at the far end of the first lake on the plateau. This day's work was not got through without a good deal of growling, as everybody was kept on short rations to make the most of our provisions; three days' full allowance for human beings alone, to say nothing of the thirty dogs, would have put an end to our supplies.

From this lake the country was level, and the women were quite able to manage the dog-sleighs, while the men scoured the country on either side of the track in search of caribou or ptarmigan. The birds were fairly plentiful, but of course at this season were all paired, and there was no chance of making a slaughter at a single shot, as one can do in the fall of the year when the birds are in big packs; this shooting at separate birds was a serious strain on our ammunition, but the ptarmigan helped us out till we fell in with the caribou. It was almost a certainty to find these birds in every bunch of pines, and they kept up such a constant crowing round the camp at night that they had a poor chance of escaping the hungry man's gun. After the snow has melted the male bird gets pugnacious and runs up to meet the hunter, with his feathers puffed out, offering a fair mark for a stone; but before this happened we disdained ptarmigan, and would only kill the fattest-looking caribou. We eked out a precarious existence in this manner for a week, making short days' journeys, as the dogs could not travel fast or far. Pierre Lockhart deserted one morning when breakfast was particularly scanty, and taking his gun and blanket started back for Fond du Lac; we were depending on him for guide, but it was rather a relief when he went, as he was inclined to steal food, and had several disgusting habits that made his absence from the lodge rather acceptable than otherwise. Marlo's brother-in-law disappeared about the same time, but we thought they had gone off together and did not trouble ourselves further about them.

On the last day of May, acting on Capot Blanc's advice, we forked from our canoe-route, and took a more easterly course, to fall on the chain of lakes by which Anderson and Stewart had reached the Great Fish River. We hoped to find caribou in this direction, and on the same day that we made this change in our course the indefatigable Saltatha, having made a much longer round than the rest of us, came into camp late at night with a load of caribou-meat on his back; he had seen snow-shoe tracks to the east, but falling in with the caribou had turned back to the camp without following the tracks.

Sunday, June 1st, brought a distinct change in the weather; a mild south-west wind was melting the snow rapidly, and several flocks of geese and

ducks passed to the north. A few geese were
called up to the camp and killed from the doors
of the lodges; the Indians imitate to perfection
the cry of any bird, and at this time of year the
geese are easy to call, as they are always in search
of open water, and seem not a bit surprised to
hear their friends calling to them from a group
of deer-skin lodges. In the morning we sent two
men to bring in the rest of Saltatha's meat, with
orders to investigate the tracks, and see if there
was another encampment of Indians to the east,
as none of the caribou hunters had intended to
leave the Great Slave Lake till the thaw 'came.
Our peaceful Sunday was greatly disturbed by a
royal row in one of the lodges, and we sent for
Capot Blanc to ask him what the trouble was.
The old fellow was glad enough to get into our
lodge away from the clamour, and explained the
cause of the disturbance in his even low-pitched
voice, so pleasantly contrasted with the Yellow
Knife Billingsgate that was being freely used
outside. "It is the women," he said; "the wife of
Syene has called the wife of Saltatha by a bad
name, because she would not give her some meat;
the wife of Saltatha has taken the wife of Syene
by the hair and beaten her in the face with a
snow-shoe till her nose bleeds very much; the
men have tried to separate them, but that only
makes things worse. It is always like this in our
camps when we starve. If the men are alone

they are quiet; but when there are women there is no peace. Is it so also in your country?"

Late in the night the men who had gone to fetch the meat came back, hauling on the sleigh Marlo's brother-in-law José, whom they had found lying in the snow, without fire, in a bunch of dwarf pines; the snow-shoe tracks were his, and but for the lucky chance of Saltatha's killing the caribou in that direction he must have perished in a day or two, as he was too weak to travel. He had left us to hunt ptarmigan, and lost himself eight days ago, and, as we supposed he had deserted with Pierre, we had taken no trouble to look for him. He was one of the unlucky ones, believed to have seen "the Enemy" in his youth, and it certainly says little for his wits that he was unable to follow the tracks of such a large party. José had used up what little ammunition he started with on the first day, and since then had eaten nothing; he was without matches or touchwood to make fire, and as the weather had been cold he must have suffered greatly. We fed him up to the best of our ability, and he recovered rapidly when meat was abundant in the camp.

CHAPTER XI

On the following day we made an easy day's travel to the east, and most of us succeeded in killing caribou while the women drove the dogs. From this time, all through the summer till we again reached the Great Slave Lake late in August, we had no difficulty about provisions; although there was many a time when we could not say where we might find our next meal, something always turned up, and we were never a single day without eating during the whole journey. I really believe it is a mistake to try to carry enough food for a summer's work in the Barren Ground, as the difficulty of transport is so great, and after the caribou are once found there is no danger of starvation.

We were now travelling with the bull caribou, which had just left the thick woods, and made easy marches from lake to lake in an north-east direction; the weather became cold again for the last time, and June 7th was like a bad winter's day with a strong north wind and snowstorms. Then the summer came suddenly, and on the 11th we were obliged to camp on a high gravel ridge to await *le grand dégel*, which rendered travelling impossible, till the deep water had run off the ice.

Although we had been so far taking it very easily, a rest was of great service, as many of the party were suffering from acute snow-blindness caused by the everlasting glare of the sun on the treeless waste; there was no dark object to rest the eyes upon for a moment, and besides the actual pain the constant inflammation injured the sight and made rifle-shooting very uncertain. The Indians smeared their faces with blood and wood-ashes, and the white men were further protected with spectacles; but these efforts were only partially successful in keeping off the glare. I was lucky in getting off quite free myself, but should imagine that it must be a most painful affliction.

Along the foot of the sandy ridge, which closely resembled the one I had seen the autumn before at Lac de Gras, were many small lakes partially thawed, and here the snow geese, or white "wavies," were resting in thousands, waiting till the warm weather should have melted the snow from their feeding-ground along the sea-coast. We could have made enormous bags of them, as they were tame and disinclined to leave the open water; but we were sparing with our ammunition, as we might want it badly later on. Great numbers were killed, however, and their prime condition told of the good feeding-ground they had left far southward. There were also plenty of large Canada geese, but the grey wavy, or laughing goose, the best of all for eating, is much scarcer. Of the more edible ducks the pin-tail seems to be the only one that comes so far beyond the Great Slave Lake, but long-tailed ducks and golden eyes were in great numbers along this sandy ridge. Of the loons, the red-throated variety was by far the most numerous, and the Pacific or Adam's diver was fairly common, but the great northern diver, although plentiful on the Great Slave Lake, does not appear to visit the Barren Ground.

While we were waiting here, another band of Indians from Fond du Lac caught us up, and our camp assumed still larger proportions; but as we were fairly among the game it did not much matter. With the new arrivals were two blind men, Pierre and Antoine Fat, who preferred a wandering life to the support they would doubtless have been given at the fort. Both were good fishermen, and would spend hours sitting on the ice at the edge of an open hole with the greatest patience, and later on made heavy catches of trout. Pierre would often walk with the hunters to get his share of the meat; Capot Blanc was usually his guide, but seldom did more than trail a stick after him and the blind man followed the sound; when a caribou was killed, Pierre was led up to it, and in spite of his blindness would do the butcher's work cleanly and well.

The snow melted away rapidly; the hillsides were running with small streams, the ground showed up in ever increasing patches, and a thick mist, which the Indians say always appears at the time of the big thaw, hung over everything. On June 16th we found that most of the water had run off through the cracks in the ice, and resumed our journey, after solemnly burning some thirty pairs of used-up snow-shoes. At first walking without them seemed hard to me, as I had used them continually since the previous October, and we all found that our feet were made sore by walking on the rough ice; unfortunately the skins of the caribou that we killed were so riddled by grubs that they were unfit to dress for leather, and we were always short of moccasins. We still travelled along easily, as the river would not break up for a fortnight at the earliest, and our best plan was to move with the caribou, which seemed to be keeping up with the edge of the snow much in the same manner as ourselves. The portages between the lakes were often three or four miles in length, and, as the snow had gone, we were obliged to carry the heavy loads on our backs; firewood was getting scarce, and I came to the conclusion that our old canoe-route was by far the best way to reach the Barren Ground in summer or in winter. A few warm days made a great difference in the appearance of the country. Leaves began to sprout on the little willows, and the grass showed green on the hillsides; sober-hued flowers, growing close to the ground, came out in bloom, and a few butterflies flapped in the hot sunshine, while we were still walking on eight feet of solid ice. Mosquitos appeared in myriads:

in the daytime there was usually a breeze to blow
them away, and the nights were too cold for
them; but in the calm mornings and evenings
they made the most of their chance to annoy us.

On June 25th we planted our lodges on a high
ridge overlooking Lake Mackay. It has always
been the fashion of the Yellow Knives to camp
in an elevated position, in order to have command
of the surrounding country in looking out for the
caribou, or, in the olden times, for a band of hostile Indians. Right across the lake we could see
the bay in which we had left our big canoe during our first attempt to find the musk-ox, and the
hills forming the height of land between the Great
Slave Lake and the Arctic Sea; on our right lay
Lockhart's River and the huge Aylmer Lake,
which we were about to cross. Blind Pierre knew
the whole picture as well as any of us; on my
way back to camp at sundown I found him sitting on a boulder smoking, for we always rather
favoured him in the matter of tobacco; his face
was turned to the north-east, and he was evidently taking in all the details of the landscape,
without the sense of sight. *"Tetchenula, Tetchen
Yarsula, Tetchen Taote* (no wood, not a little
wood, no wood at all)," he said, as he waved his
hands towards Aylmer Lake; then, with a sweep
of his arm, he traced correctly the course of
Lockhart's River, with a rapid downward motion,
to denote its abrupt termination in a series of
rapids and waterfalls as it joins the Great Slave

Lake. Poor old fellow, it must be hard for him not to see the country he loves so well; but he is happy, after his fashion, in the summer-time when the caribou are thick.

From this point we sent Moise with three Indians and our own dogs to bring up the big canoe from the south shore of Lake Mackay, where I had left her in the beginning of last October. Many little hunting-canoes had been picked up along the track from Fond du Lac, and now every sleigh carried a canoe athwartships; these proved useful enough in crossing the small lake in the course of Lockhart's River, as on arriving at the far side we found open water between us and the land, and had to use the canoes to ferry our cargo to the shore, the dogs swimming with the empty sleighs in tow, while some enterprising spirits, who conceived the idea of floating ashore on blocks of ice, came in for a ducking. The ice on Aylmer Lake was still solid, but extremely rough, causing great damage to our moccasins. We kept near the north shore, with sometimes a long traverse across a deep bay; at the head of every bay a stream ran into the lake, and the open water at its mouth was always a sure find for trout; forty or fifty large fish were often caught in a day with hook and line at these places, and, as we could always kill caribou, even the dogs were getting fat in this land of plenty. Soon we began to see scraps of musk-ox hair on the large boulders where these animals had been rubbing, and on the second day's travel along Aylmer Lake David had an adventure with an old bull. David was by far the keenest hunter in the outfit, but up till now had not succeeded in killing anything bigger than a goose, and it was an exciting moment for him when he got within range of a musk-ox. He had heard strange stories about these animals when a small boy among his own countrymen at the mouth of the Mackenzie River, and it was not without a little trembling that he fired one of his scanty stock of bullets. The beast was wounded but would not die, and David, standing off at a safe distance, soon exhausted all his bullets; he then proceeded to load his gun with round stones, and finally with handfuls of gravel; his last charge of powder was used to fire the ramrod, but another half hour elapsed before the musk-ox expired. As this was the first one that had been killed on this trip, the proud hunter was made a good deal of when he came into camp with the best of the highly-flavoured meat.

On the evening of July 1st we made the encampment at the head of the most northerly bay of Aylmer Lake, named Sandy Bay by Back, from the conspicuous sand-ridges that here form the divide between the lake and the Great Fish River, a distance of three quarters of a mile. The ice was still firm in Aylmer Lake, but there was a little difficulty in getting ashore through a narrow belt of open water, and the head-reaches of

the river were clear. We were inspecting the
stream, to see what chance there was of being
able to run the canoe through the numerous
rapids, when Noel, one of the Indians who had
been with me on the winter hunt, came up with
the news that he had spied a large band of musk-
ox feeding a couple of miles down the river. The
women were badly in need of their hides for making moccasins, as the caribou-skins were still in
poor condition, so a hunt was arranged in a fashion that I had not seen before. Most of the guns
crossed the river, and a spot was selected for the
slaughter just where the stream broadened out
into a small lake; at right angles to the river
mounds of stone and moss were put up at a few
yards' distance from each other, ornamented with
coats, belts, and gun-covers, and behind the outside mound Capot Blanc took up his position. A
steep hill ran parallel with the stream about two
hundred yards away, and along this guns were
posted at intervals, with the intention of heading
the musk-ox towards the water. Noel and Marlo,
supposed to be the two best runners, were to
make a long round and start the band in our
direction; I was stationed with three other guns
among some broken rocks on the south side of
the river, just opposite the barrier; and orders
were given that no shot should be fired till the
musk-ox took to the water.

It was a most interesting scene, and I would
not willingly have changed places with any of

the loyal Canadians who were at this time cele-
brating the anniversary of Dominion Day, with
much rye whisky, a thousand miles to the southward. I had plenty of time to admire the surrounding landscape, and the sunset that lit up the
snow-drifts on each side of the river; when suddenly over the opposite ridge appeared the horns
of a band of caribou, and for a moment the leader
was outlined against the sky as he paused to look
at the strange preparations going on in the valley
below. Behind me a ptarmigan, perched on a
rock, crowed defiance; but there was no other
sound, except the rush of water and the occasional grinding of an ice-pan dislodged from some
small lake in the course of the stream. Fully an
hour we sat among the rocks, and were beginning to think that the hunt had miscarried, when
we heard a distant shouting far down the valley,
and the next moment caught sight of a scurrying
black mass crossing a spur of the hill close to the
river's bank. The men posted along the ridge
took up the cry as the musk-ox passed them, and
joined in the chase; soon the animals came to the
barrier, and pulled up short at the apparition,
while, to increase their alarm, the hoary head of
Capot Blanc arose from behind a mound of rocks
right in front of them. This was the critical
moment, and they would certainly have taken to
the water and been at the mercy of their pursuers
but for an untimely shot that caused them to
break, and I was not sorry to see that several of

the band escaped. I had had a splendid view till now, as the musk-ox halted within twenty yards of me, but we were forced to lie low when the shooting began, as bullets were rattling freely among the rocks in which we were hiding. We did no shooting on our side of the river, except to finish off a couple that took to the water; seven were killed in all, six cows, and a calf about a month old; there were no bulls in the band, and from what I afterwards saw they seemed to keep separate from the cows during the summer. A solitary old bull is often met with at this time of year.

When the hunt was over, I inquired the meaning of the shouting that had been kept up so continually throughout the drive, and was informed that this was necessary to let the musk-ox know which way to run. At starting they had shouted, "Oh, musk-ox, there is a barrier planted for you down there, where the river joins the little lake; when you reach it take to the water, there are men with guns on both sides, and so we shall kill you all"; when the men are out of breath, they shout to the musk-ox to stop, and, after they have rested, to go on again. These animals are said to understand every word of the Yellow Knife language, though it seems strange that they do not make use of the information they receive to avoid danger instead of obeying orders. The partial failure of the hunt was attributed to the fact that Moise had called across the river to me in French, and the musk-ox had not been able to understand this strange language.

The sun had risen again when we got back to camp, and there we found the big canoe, not a bit damaged by her long rest under the snow or her adventurous journey on the dog-sleigh. The day was spent in getting in the meat and skins, and early the next morning we carried the canoe across the portage and launched her on the waters of the Great Fish River. The cargo was all sent overland to a lake some six miles down the stream; sleighs were abandoned, as there was now no snow to haul on, but the dogs' work was by no means over, the only difference being that they had to carry loads on their backs instead of dragging a sleigh; rough deer-skin pack-harness was made, and the loads secured in a manner worthy of a Mexican mule-packer. We came to grief with the canoe at the third rapid, and should have done much better to have made the portage to the lake, instead of trying to navigate the difficult stream. A long delay was necessary to effect repairs, and there were so many portages over ice-blocks along the edge of the lake, when we reached it, that the sun was high on the following morning before we camped. The same work continued for several days, the Indians toiling overland heavily loaded, and our own party struggling with the ice in a chain of lakes through which the river runs. On the edge of one of these lakes we stopped for dinner on the spot where Stewart and

Anderson separated from their Indian guides before descending the river in 1856. The rough stone fireplaces, by which they had economised fuel, were still standing, and Capot Blanc, seated on one of them, gave us a long lecture on the events that had taken place during their expedition, as he had heard the story from his father. More than thirty years had elapsed since the last party of Whites camped by the side of the Great Fish River, and thirty years again before them Back the discoverer had pushed out into the unknown land. Why has all exploration in the Barren Ground ceased? No more is known of the country than was discovered by Franklin and Back sixty years ago in their short summer journeys, and the expeditions sent out in search of the former in the 'Fifties. There are many thousands of square miles on which the foot of white man has never stepped. The Canadian Government has an efficient body of surveyors and geologists at its command, and it is curious that no attention is paid to one of the most interesting fields for exploration.

On July 6th, after slow and tiresome travelling, we reached the north end of a large sheet of water named by Back Musk-ox Lake, and finding enough willow-scrub for firewood, determined here to await the breaking up of the ice in the lake. Judging by the Indian's account the season was fully three weeks later than usual, and, as I wished to be back at Fort Resolution in time to

save the open water up Peace River before winter set in, there was a poor chance of our being
able to penetrate far into the country of the Esquimaux. Musk-ox Lake runs pretty nearly due
north and south, and is fifteen miles in length,
averaging about two miles in width. Our camp
was just at the point where the river runs out,
and a short distance above is the best swimming-
place for the caribou known to the Indians. In
some years immense slaughters are made here,
but on the present occasion the caribou did not
cross in their usual numbers, so that our companions had no chance to put up the dried meat that
we expected to get for our cruise down stream,
and we could only kill enough for the present
support of such a large encampment. Across the
lake is a hill of insignificant height, known as
the Musk-ox Mountain, a good landmark, and a
favourite haunt for the animals from which it
takes its name.

This is the northerly limit of the Yellow
Knives' hunting-ground. Northwards is the land
of the dreaded Esquimaux, and many rumours
were brought into the camp of a strange track
seen on soft ground, of men standing far off on
the sky-line, and a blue cloud of smoke arising
far down the valley of the river. The Indians
were convinced that their old enemies were continually close to them, despite the fact that it
would be an impossibility for canoes to have yet
ascended the stream on account of the ice. We

afterwards discovered that there was a debateable ground, fully sixty miles in width, between Musk-ox Lake and the highest point that the Esquimaux reach.

There is here a very striking change in the appearance of the country. The old red granite formation gives way almost entirely to ironstone, split up into slabs and piled into such peculiar shapes that one might imagine giants had been building castles over the rolling hills. Some of the slabs were turned on edge and formed perfect turrets towering many feet into the air, and in many places were heaps of shiny black sand, resembling coal-dust, piled up into conical mounds almost too steep to climb. Wherever vegetation had a chance to grow it was much more luxuriant than one could suppose possible in such a climate. The stunted willows, not two feet in height, were thickly clothed with bright green leaves; there was abundance of grass, and in many spots the pretty little Arctic flowers formed a bright carpet along the foot of a slowly melting snowdrift.

Capot Blanc and myself made an expedition into the roughest part of this country, to the north-east of Musk-ox Lake, but we found travelling very hard, as we had to climb continually over broken masses of ironstone. This is another well-known haunt of "the Enemy," and Capot Blanc attributed to his malign influence the disaster that prevented our further exploration in this direction. We reached a stream of no

great size, one of the tributaries of the Great Fish
River, and attempted to wade across to the opposite bank, selecting the head of a small rapid
for the purpose, as the water appeared to be shal-
lower there.   On reaching the centre of the current our legs were swept from under us, and
we were immediately running the rapid at the
imminent risk of breaking our heads against a
rock.   We both reached the still water at the
foot of the rapid with nothing worse than a few
bruises, and moreover held on to our guns, but of
course our ammunition was spoilt, and we were
obliged to make the best of our way back to
camp.   Capot Blanc afterwards told me that he
thought the Enemy had made the water strong,
to keep us from coming into his country, and it
would be flying in the face of Providence to
make another attempt.   It would be interesting to
know how far this ironstone formation extends;
and, as the journey to Musk-ox Lake and back to
the fort might easily be made by canoe during
the summer, the trip would amply repay the geolo-
gist and botanist for their trouble.

Many other little expeditions we made in
various directions, sometimes watching the birds,
and sometimes in pursuit of caribou or musk-ox.
One hunt in particular I remember, which took
place appropriately enough on the top of Musk-ox
Mountain.   We had made out the moving black
spots through the glasses from the lodge, and, as
there was still a demand for hides from the

women and meat was being used in great quantities, we paddled across the lake through a narrow channel in the ice. The sun went down while we were climbing the ascent, and a long wait was necessary, as the animals were feeding towards us on the flat top of the mountain and there was no cover to enable us to make a nearer approach. The mosquitos buzzed merrily round us while we lay behind the rock and watched the grotesque motions of the calves as they played with each other, little suspecting that danger was so close. Presently the band moved within easy range and we opened fire with four guns. Seven were killed, and Mackinlay caught a calf that stayed by the body of its dead mother, a fluffy, long-haired little beast; I was sorry that we could not keep it alive, but it would have been impossible to carry it in a birch-bark canoe. Cruel work, this shooting in the summer-time, but it was necessary to keep the camp in meat even though mother and young had to be sacrificed. I had a long run after a cripple, and eventually killed it on the shore of a large lake in a valley eastward of the mountain. The sun was high when I found the rest of the hunters eating marrow-bones in front of a big fire, in a clump of well-grown willows close to the canoe, and we took a load of wood back to the camp, sending over the women for the meat and skins later in the day.

The weather during this time was variable in

the extreme; two or three hot days would be followed by a snowstorm, and once we were visited by a hurricane that did much damage to lodge-poles, and caused us to shift camp hurriedly to the lee-side of a steep cliff hanging over the river. July 10th was exceptionally hot in the morning, with the mosquitos at their worst; in the middle of the day there was a thunderstorm, and at five o'clock the ground was covered with snow. The ice now began to show signs of rotting, and the channel of open water round the weather edge of the lake grew rapidly broader.

We had many talks with the Indians about the chances of our being able to get together a crew; but they had no enthusiasm about the voyage, and wanted nothing better than to keep us hanging about the head of the river, providing them with ammunition. Saltatha was the only one of the band who volunteered to go, and he insisted on having another Indian with him, as he was not used to the ways of white men, and would feel safer if he had one of his own tribe with him in case of accidents; but he hoped we should not go farther than the big lake (Beechey Lake) which he had heard us talking about, for it was getting late in the year, and when the ice is long in melting winter comes again soon. At last it was arranged that Saltatha and Noel were to come in our canoe, while Marlo and Carquoss accompanied us with a small hunting-canoe, to carry a little ammunition in case we lost our cargo by

capsizing in a rapid; we should then have a chance
of making a living, and be able to cross the tributary stream if we had to return on foot.   On
our part we agreed to turn back from Beechey
Lake, reserving the privilege of taking the little
canoe overland from there to Bathurst Inlet.   As
caribou were scarce, the rest of the Indians were
to work their way back towards the Great Slave
Lake, except Capot Blanc, who was to stay on
the divide at Aylmer Lake, if he could kill enough
meat to keep his family, and there await our return.

The evening before we started, Syene, who was
a Medicine Man, sent a message to our lodge that
he was going to foretell the result of our expedition down the river, so we went over to hear what
was in store for us.   His lodge was full of Indians, but they made room for us, and we sat
down on a blanket on the side of the fire farthest
from the door.   Syene held a drum made of
tighty-stretched deer-skin parchment, which he
punched continually with a caribou's thigh-bone,
keeping up a melancholy chant, and singing a sen-
tence or two every few minutes.   "It is not that I
can see anything myself," he said, "but it is an
unborn child that is speaking to me." Mrs. Syene,
who was sitting close to the Medicine Man,
clasped her hands and groaned, as if in great
pain, by way of giving assent to this statement.
"The child sees the canoe of the big masters running down the strong water of a rapid; below the

rapid is a long point, and seven lodges of the Esquimaux are planted on the point. There is blood on the snow-drift; it is the blood of a white man. One man is walking on the bank of a river; he walks like a starving man, and the child knows not if he is white or Indian. Now all is dark, and the child has ceased speaking."

Not a very cheerful prophecy, and it was hard to make out how far the Indians believed in the Medicine Man; but our crew were rather downhearted about it, although, as is usual all the world over, the people who were not going the journey themselves took a philosophical view of the whole affair.

*

CHAPTER XII

ON Thursday, July 17th, at two o'clock in the afternoon, we struck camp and started on a four-mile portage to the next lake down stream, as the river-bed was too full of large boulders to navigate the strong current with safety. It was hard work carrying the cargo and canoe through the mosquito-stricken ironstone country, and we did not camp till midnight. Here another bad omen was observed. Mackinlay and I had gone ahead, after carrying over a load, to try and kill something for supper; we found a musk-ox, but made rather a clumsy mess of killing it, and the animal was badly heated before we finished it off. The meat was consequently discoloured, and Saltatha declared this to be an unfailing sign of some great misfortune at hand. The women had made us a few pair of moccasins each, but not nearly enough for the tracking-work that we should have to do when we turned up stream; and our stock of provisions, instead of the bales of dried meat that we had expected to enable us to travel without waste of time in hunting, consisted of ten dried deers'-ribs, so full of maggots, from having been imperfectly cured, that we threw them away on the second day out. Our

flour and pemmican had of course been finished
long ago, and we drank the last kettleful of tea
before leaving Musk-ox Lake, but as the Labrador tea grows all over this country in profusion,
this did not much matter; tobacco too was nearly
at an end.

The lake was still full of floating ice, but we
had no trouble in passing the canoe into the river
at the north end, and found the stream considerably increased in volume by a couple of large
tributaries that come in from the opposite sides
of the lake. After dropping down two or three
miles with a sluggish current, we heard the roar
of a rapid, and put ashore on an island in mid-
stream as soon as we sighted broken water. It
was lucky we did so, as there was a heavy over-
fall impossible to run, and we were obliged to
portage the whole length of the island and then
shoot the tail of the rapid. Here we put ashore
to patch the canoe, which was leaking badly, and
pulled out big trout as quickly as we could throw
in the spoon-bait; we found this could be done at
the foot of all the rapids, so one need not take
much thought about provisions in this part of the
stream. After another small rapid, which was
run with a full load, the river, heading straight
to the north, passes through a small lake and
emerges as a broad canal-like waterway with very
slight current, flowing through the roughest part
of the ironstone country that we had yet seen;
the banks were steep too, and we could put the

canoe alongside a natural wharf in any spot for a distance of five or six miles. In passing down these reaches we saw and killed musk-ox, but the caribou seemed to shirk the labour of crossing the confused masses of rocks, and none of these animals were seen till we reached a less rugged district. Again the channel widened out into a lake, two miles in length, with an ugly rapid at the north end; this we negotiated with the precaution of leaving guns and ammunition ashore, and directly afterwards Saltatha caused some excitement by saying he had caught a glimpse of a man walking on a neighbouring ridge; we put ashore, but could find no tracks, and came to the conclusion that it was Saltatha's imagination. A long day's travel was made successfully, and by ten o'clock we were clear of the ironstone and slipping quietly along through a pleasant sandy country. We camped at the foot of a high sand-butte covered with flowers and moss, and found a bunch of willows on the bank of the river. There were indications that some one had camped on the same spot many years ago; small sticks had been chopped with an axe, and bones of caribou were lying in heaps on the ground. The Yellow Knives at once said it was an old Esquimaux camp, and it was evident that they had little inclination to go any farther down stream; more probably the chopping was done by a band of Dog-Ribs, whose hunting-grounds lie to the west, or possibly by the members of Stewart's and Anderson's expeditions. On mounting the butte we saw that the country northward presented a much more fertile appearance than anything we had seen on the south side of the watershed. There was a luxurious growth of grass over the sandy ridges, and during the two months of summer one could imagine oneself back on the prairies of Alberta; the willows here too grew to a better size, and, as far as we descended the river, we had little trouble about fuel; in the winter, of course, the willows would be all drifted over with snow, and it would then be no easy matter to make a fire. This stream heads in the woodless country; consequently there is no drift-timber, and not a single pine-tree is to be seen along its course.

We had a pleasant camp enough that night, but rebellion was rife and burst into flame on the following morning when we ordered the men to take their places in the canoes. This is the hopeless part of having to rely on natives for travelling in the Barren Ground; they have no courage outside their own country. If we had had a good crew of half-breeds from Red River or the upper country of British Columbia we might even now, notwithstanding the lateness of the season, have pushed far out towards the northern sea-coast, and possibly have made the acquaintance of some of the scattered bands of Esquimaux who live there in happy ignorance of any more comfortable form of life. But we were practically in the hands of the Yellow Knives, for although I would myself have taken the risk of steering, none of the men who were willing to go knew how to stitch up a broken canoe, and it would have been madness to push on without this knowledge. Moise, our half-breed interpreter and steersman, who was an engaged servant of the Hudson's Bay Company and bound by his contract to obey Mackinlay's orders in everything, showed the Indian side of his nature by joining the mutineers and refusing to take his position in the stern of the canoe. For two hours we argued the matter on the bank of the river, and at one time I thought we should certainly have come to blows. Marlo and Carquoss were the ringleaders, but Saltatha was inclined to stand by us, although afraid of giving offence to the other Indians. The result of the dispute was that the worst two deserted, taking with them the little canoe, while Noel and Saltatha, tempted by many promises of great reward when we reached the fort, agreed to come with us, and Moise sulkily went back to his duty. After we had thus got rid of the element of discord things went on better; but the loss of the little canoe, besides doing away with our chance of crossing overland to Bathurst Inlet, increased the risk of losing all our possessions by one disaster. A pretty poetical thing is a birch-bark canoe, as it leaps down a sparkling river among its native birch woods, but too frail a craft for a long journey in the rock-bound country beyond the line where timber grows. No chance here to strip the bark from a birch-tree and put a new side in a canoe that has struck a rock in the foaming rapid, or if needs be to build a new canoe altogether; three square feet of birch-bark, a little gum, and a bundle of fibre were our only resources for effecting repairs.

The day's journey began with a rapid, below which was a reach of quiet water gradually broadening out into a lake some eight miles in length; its surface was covered with ice at the north end, but we found an open channel close ashore on the west side and effected a passage through by skirting the bays. Several bands of musk-ox were seen, and there was always too much anxiety among the men to put ashore and shoot, or to do anything except push steadily on; just as we were leaving the lake a magnificent bull appeared on the top of a high ridge, and, standing on a flat rock within one hundred yards of us, leisurely surveyed the first human beings who had encroached upon his sanctuary for so many years.

Below the lake the river makes a sharp bend eastward, and for three miles is nothing but a succession of rapids. Moise when once at work was a splendid steersman, and he certainly handled the canoe with great skill through this difficult piece of navigation; we passed the mouths of two big streams coming in from the west, and at camping-time shot into a quiet sandy lake and put ashore for the night. A musk-ox that I killed from the door of the lodge, and the unlimited number of trout that we could catch in the river, enabled us to spend a peaceful Sunday without hunting. We explored towards the east, and came once more upon the iron country, which seems to run with a sharply defined edge in a north-easterly direction. There were few lakes out of the course of the river, but long stretches of flat grassy muskegs extended as far as the eye could see to the west. Four-footed game was plentiful, especially musk-ox; the caribou that we saw were generally solitary bucks, but it was now nearly time for the does to be coming back from the sea-coast; of the smaller animals we often came across a skulking wolf, a wolverine, an Arctic fox, or a hare, while the holes in the sand-hills were the abode of numerous *siffleurs* and ermines. A ferocious little mouse, brown in summer, but turning white as the winter comes on, is very common all over the Barren Ground; if disturbed from a tuft of grass it will turn on a man and dance with impotent rage at his feet; these mice naturally fall an easy prey to the hawks and owls, which make a good living here during the summer months. Beyond these predatory birds little feathered life was visible in this part of the country; a few gulls, terns, and skuas flitted along the reaches of the river, and occasionally a loon or a long-tailed duck could be seen in the lakes. The Canada goose and grey wavy were breeding in the marshes, but not in great quantities; the main body of geese go right out to the coast to lay their eggs, and do not start for the South till the end of August.

In the early morning we made a short portage over a small cascade immediately below the camp, and found that the river still held its northerly course through a chain of small lakes connected by short stretches of bad water. We made one more portage at mid-day and ran several rather nasty rapids. After dinner we were obliged to portage fully a mile to avoid an impassable reach, and then took more risk than we were justified in doing with our only canoe by running a couple of miles of broken water, full of boulders and with such a heavy sea that we shipped a good deal of water; luckily we did not touch anything, and dropped safely into a long narrow lake, on the east side of which camp was made for the night. This was the most dangerous day that we made; as although we always put ashore to inspect the rapids in case we might discover a waterfall below, we became emboldened by success and ran in safety through some places that we should not have attempted. Back's map of the river would have been a great help to us, but neither this nor an account of the previous journeys that had been made down the stream was procurable at the fort.

The next day a curious blue haze hung over everything, closely resembling the smoke of a

forest fire at a distance from the scene of con-
flagration. The lake that we had camped on
proved to be about six miles in length, with the
usual rapid at its north end connecting it with
another lake, the size of which we could not at
first determine owing to the murky state of the
air; nor could we at once find its outlet, but by
keeping in a north-easterly direction soon felt
the influence of a current, and found the volume
of water much increased by the junction of a
tributary, which we afterwards discovered came
in from the north-west. On the east side of the
stream, just as it left the lake, we noticed a circle
of flat stones standing on end, evidently put up
by human hands, and on landing discovered unmistakable signs of a band of Esquimaux having been encamped there not very long before.
Seven small oval-shaped enclosures, surrounded
by rough turf-heaps six inches in height, had been
the dwelling-places, but we could not determine
whether these low walls were the foundations of
snow-houses or deer-skin lodges; there were several blackened fireplaces outside, but the fires must
have been very small judging from the charred
stumps of tiny green willow twigs, and we saw
no wood within several miles of the encampment.
The stones propped on end had been used probably for drying meat, and for tying up the dogs
to keep them from stealing. Bones and horns
of musk-ox and caribou were lying about in every
direction, and their numbers showed that this

must be a favourite camping-place of the Esquimaux; some of the musk-ox horns had been cut
into rough spoons, and several were found in a
half-finished condition. A flat stone kettle was
picked up with the grease still sticking to it, and
a small piece of copper let into the back, possibly an arrangement for a handle, showed that
these people are able to work this metal; there
were also a few bone arrow-heads scattered about
in the camp. If any further proof were necessary
to determine what tribe of people had camped here,
it was forthcoming in the form of several pieces
of undressed sealskin with the hair on, and these
seemed to be of greater interest to our crew than
any of the other discoveries; arrow-heads, spoons,
and kettle were dropped in the contemplation of
the skin of an animal they had never seen, and
they instantly demanded a description of the seal.
After we had told them all we knew upon the
subject, we asked their opinion as to the length
of time that the Esquimaux had remained here,
and when they had left. Saltatha, reading the
signs that a white man might miss, came to the
conclusion that they had come here in the autumn,
as was proved by the hard horns of male caribou
lying about, that they had stayed here through
the winter, and left late in the spring with dogs
on the last snow, about six weeks before our arrival. He thought too that they made a practice
of coming here regularly, in the same manner that
the Yellow Knives come to the head-waters of

the river, as the bones appeared to him to have belonged to animals killed at widely differing dates. We found hiding-places among the rocks close to the edge of the river, which had evidently been used for concealing men engaged in spearing the swimming caribou. The only weak point in Saltatha's theory seemed to be the absence of any carcasses of freshly killed caribou; but it is possible that the Esquimaux may have left before the females came out so far, and the animals would have been later than usual in arriving here owing to the backward nature of the spring.

When we had thoroughly inspected everything we left again down stream, with a swift current and good water without rapids for eight miles, where we found another lake running more to the eastward than the general course of the river; on the west side of this lake we were obliged to camp, as a strong head-wind raised too much sea to travel against, and rain was falling in torrents. We explored the shore of the lake in hopes of finding further traces of the Esquimaux, but made no discoveries of any kind. No musk-ox were seen this day, but there were enough caribou to provide food for the party.

With better weather we made an early start in the morning, the river on leaving the lake bending a little more to the eastward, with a swift current for several miles, and two rapids which we ran in safety. A short distance below the second rapid the current slackens and the stream gets rapidly broader, till, with a sudden sweep to the south-east, the whole length of Beechey Lake comes open; a long narrow sheet of water, twenty-five miles in length, and nowhere more than two in breadth, lying east and west, and forming a well-defined elbow in the course of the Great Fish River. With a light fair wind, and a blanket set for a sail, we ran down the lake and pitched our lodge on the north shore. Two days were spent in exploration, but again we failed entirely to find any signs of the Esquimaux. Towards the east end of the lake the iron formation shows up once more, and the country is rough to travel through. There was a slight difficulty about provisions at this time as game was scarce, and, though we fully expected to catch fish in the lake and put out our net both nights, not a single fish was taken; just at the critical time, however, a few female caribou with their young turned up on their way back to the South, and we were relieved of all anxiety.

As we had promised our crew that we would not descend the river beyond Beechey Lake, and it was already the end of July, orders were reluctantly given on the third day to start up stream with the intention of doing a little exploration to the northward of the old Esquimaux camp, to see if there was any feasible route from there to Bathurst Inlet, as there were no signs of these people having camped in any other place along the river. It seemed a pity to abandon the voyage just at the interesting time, after we had got over all the difficulties of the upper part of the river and had now only a broad stream to follow, with a great deal of easy lake-travel, to reach the Arctic Ocean, and the scene of the final sufferings of the members of Sir John Franklin's last expedition. On the other hand, we had no object in going down to the sea, and there is little pleasure to be got out of a journey of this kind with an unwilling and untrustworthy crew; our canoe, too, which was already leaking badly, would have been of very little service for sea work.

As far as Beechey Lake the south side of the Great Fish River is free from any large tributary streams, so that, if our canoe had been smashed up in a rapid, and we had been able to save guns and ammunition, it would have been easy enough to follow the river on foot; but on the north side there are several large streams to be forded, and a long detour might be necessary to find a spot shallow enough for this purpose.

There was much more enthusiasm displayed by the Indian portion of the crew on the upstream journey, and no encouragement was needful to get a good day's work done. In the river stretches the tracking line was used, and three men at the shore end of it kept the canoe travelling at a lively pace except in the very strong water; in mounting the second rapid a mistake on the part of Noel, our bowsman, caused a heavy collision with a rock, and several hours were spent in putting in a patch of birch-bark. On the second night we pitched our lodge on the sandy lake within sight of the Esquimaux camp, and found a considerable stream coming in from a north-westerly direction. I cannot find any mention of this stream in the accounts of the two former journeys down the river, nor is it marked on the maps; it was probably unnoticed on both occasions, as it comes in at the west end of the lake, out of the course of a canoe passing up or down the main river.

Mackinlay, Murdo, and myself started on foot the following morning, to explore this stream for a couple of days, taking David with us in case we came across any of his countrymen. The malcontents were left in charge of the camp, with orders to kill caribou if any passed, and partially dry the meat to save the waste of time caused by having to hunt for our living as we travelled; they were also to thoroughly gum the canoe, to stop as much as possible the leaking which was getting serious.

We struck out along the bank of the stream, carrying nothing but a gun and a blanket apiece, and at dinner-time were lucky enough to find a flock of moulting Canada geese, unable to fly; four were shot, and two eaten at once, while the other two were stowed away among the rocks for use later on. We had a long day's walk through a pleasant grassy country, and towards evening crossed an unusually high range of hills through which the river cañons. Finding a few willows here, we left our blankets, and walked on along the bank for an hour or two, finally climbing a solitary sand-butte at sundown for a last survey of the country before turning our faces to the south.

Far away towards the north-west we could trace the windings of the stream to a ridge of blue hills, which formed the horizon under the setting sun. How these blue ridges in the distance tempt one to push on and see what lies on the far side! And the experience that nine times out of ten you would have done better to stay where you were is never sufficient to overcome this feeling; to this day I can seldom resist it, although game may be plentiful at the door of my lodge and everything that one desires in a wild country is close at hand. Below us lay a broad valley, so green and fertile in appearance that we could hardly realise that for nine months in the year it lay frost-bound and snow-covered under the rigour of an Arctic climate. In the middle of this valley, close to the bank of the stream, was a black object that we had long ago learnt to recognise at a glance, an old bull musk-ox feeding in a patch of willow-scrub; he was sacrificed for our night's rations, and, loaded with meat and marrow-bones, we re-turned to the cañon where we had left our blan-kets. There was a distinct twilight, and late in the night David awoke me to draw my attention to the first star that we had seen for many weeks. "See," he said, "a star already; it is past middle summer, and we have not yet seen the sun all night." It was the first summer he had ever spent without seeing the midnight sun, as, since he had been left at the Peel River Fort by a band of Esquimaux who come there annually to trade, he had passed his life within the Arctic circle.

The only signs that we saw of people having travelled along this valley were occasional *cache*-marks made by piling up a heap of small stones in a conspicuous position, to denote the carcass of an animal hidden in the rocks close by; but it seems such an easy route and leads so nearly in the direction of Bathurst Inlet, the nearest point on the sea-coast, that it is probably used regularly by wandering bands of Esquimaux on their way to and from their inland hunting-ground.

This was the end of our voyage of discovery, though I should have liked to have pushed on another day or two; but we wanted a small canoe to be certain of reaching the coast, which must have been within sixty miles of us, as there are sure to be many lakes to cross *en route*, and making long detours on foot would be an endless task. The fine weather also had broken, and heavy showers of rain came driving in front of the north wind, while the rest of our crew that had remained with the canoe were not too trust-worthy, and, with the exception of Saltatha, in

whom both Mackinlay and myself had great confidence, were quite capable of leaving us to find
our way out of the country on foot. We had to
content ourselves with the hope that in a future
summer, with an earlier season and a better crew,
we might find an opportunity of exploring thoroughly this promising valley in the Barren
Ground. But now I must turn my attention to
my long journey of seventeen hundred miles,
mostly upstream, to cross the Rocky Mountains
by the head-waters of the Peace River before the
winter set in; and even if I could manage this
there were still many hundred miles of mountain
and forest to be crossed before I saw the shores
of the Pacific and the abodes of civilization.

When we reached the lodge we found that the
Indians had made a stupid slaughter of caribou,
and, not contented with taking as much meat as
we could carry, had been recklessly killing the
females and young that were now passing in
great numbers. The love of killing seems deeply
rooted in the nature of most men, but the Yellow
Knives have it more fully developed than other
people. This indiscriminate slaughter is especially
culpable in a land where ammunition is scarce,
and not to be replaced when wasted by needless
firing.

The next morning we picked out of our trading-stock a few presents to be left in the Esquimaux camp, as a sign that there were people in
the interior willing to be on friendly terms with

the people of the coast. Knives, axes, beads, and
files, a couple of hand-mirrors, a few strips of
red cloth, and a flannel shirt or two were stuffed
into a copper kettle, which would be itself the
biggest prize of all. On lifting the lid, the first
object to meet the eye of the wondering Esquimaux would be the photograph of the Protestant
missionary at Fort Resolution, which David had
been keeping among his small stock of treasures;
it was a photograph of a Church of England
clergyman, in clerical costume, and should certainly give the Esquimaux a favourable idea of
the style of man who had visited their camping-
place. We also put in a note asking anyone who
might read it to let us know in what manner
it had come to hand, as it is uncertain whether
these scattered bands of Esquimaux ever visit
the Hudson's Bay Company's summer trading-
post on Marble Island, which lies a great distance away at the mouth of Chesterfield Inlet, or
whether they only know of the white men by
hearsay from other tribes that trade annually
with the Company. The kettle was carefully
stowed in one of the pits made for watching the
swimming caribou, and a canoe-pole, bearing a
gaudy cotton handkerchief for a flag, planted
alongside to attract attention. Everybody tried
their handiwork at sketching our story with burnt
sticks on the conspicuous flat rocks close to the
river: there was a picture of a canoe, with seven
upright black lines supposed to represent seven

men; another of a Yellow Knife and an Esquimau (though the artist could not say which
was which) shaking hands with the greatest af-
fection; while David was certainly entitled to the
first prize for a bloodthirsty sketch of a misshapen
musk-ox, with a thin black line, again supposed
to be a man, transfixed on the point of his horn.
When we thought we had represented everything
to perfection, we turned our backs on the land
of the Esquimaux and plodded away up stream,
`tracking and portaging in the river-stretches, and
paddling through the lakes which are always a
great help in mounting a stream.

We now came in for a spell of really bad
weather, which made the uphill work very laborious. A heavy unceasing downpour of rain,
and sometimes sleet, continued day after day,
accompanied by strong winds. The men all
worked well and without much grumbling, although we were never dry and in many places
the tracking had to be done waist-deep in water;
at night we slept in our wet clothes, on the wet
ground, rolled up in our sopping blankets. This
is the killing weather, and one needs perfect
health to resist its effects; the dry cold of a northern winter is child's play in comparison. Saltatha, who had hurt himself by a nasty fall while
carrying a heavy load over a portage, broke down
completely at this time, and was unable to work
during the rest of the trip. We could do nothing for him, as there was no medicine of any

kind in the outfit, and he had to take his chance with the rest. I think he came very near dying while we were running down Lockhart's River; he lost all strength and was spitting blood freely for a fortnight, but ultimately recovered in a miraculous manner. We worked long days tracking up-stream, but were continually delayed by having to patch up the canoe every time she touched a rock; it was just as well we did not go down to the mouth of the river, for she would certainly not have stood another three weeks' work of this kind. Another trouble was the scarcity of moccasins, which were completely worn out by a single day's walk on the sharp rocks along the river's bank.

In eight days we reached Musk-ox Lake, and, finding the wind too strong to paddle against, we put ashore on the east side and took advantage of a little sunshine to thoroughly dry all our belongings. From this camp we saw the last musk-ox, and, crossing the bay with a canoe, went in pursuit as our meat supply was short. Some of the guns were posted, and others tried to drive the animals, but we made a mess of the hunt and the whole band escaped; my last remembrance of the animals that I had started out a year before on purpose to kill, being a stern view of a grand old bull disappearing at a gallop over a ridge, and a puff of dust just behind him, marking the spot where a badly aimed rifle-bullet had struck the ground. A caribou, however, supplied us with meat, but we had some trouble in picking him up, as he was killed in the water and it was no easy matter to tow his carcass ashore against the gale of wind that was raging. Mackinlay and myself for once got ahead of the wolverines on this occasion. We saw three coming our way before they saw us, and, lying behind a rock, bowled them all over; a right and left at wolverines is seldom brought about in a lifetime, but it is very satisfactory when one thinks of the stolen *caches* and consequent hard times that these wily brutes are responsible for.

From the south end of the lake I walked ahead with Mackinlay, starting early in the morning, and at mid-day sighted three lodges on the Aylmer Lake divide. We fired a signal-shot which brought everybody out, and we were soon surrounded by Capot Blanc's brigade, and deluged with questions as to what had happened and why we had come back alone; for surely something evil had taken place in the country that always slopes downhill. With our small command of the Yellow Knife language, and plenty of signs, we made them understand that the canoe was by this time at the first lake, and the water was so low in the river that it would be necessary to portage the whole distance. All the available men and women went to help our crew to carry the loads, and by sundown our lodge was once more planted by the water that finds its way to the Great Slave

Lake and runs a course of a thousand miles before falling into the Arctic Sea.

It took half a day to settle accounts with the Indians who had been working for us on our way up to Musk-ox Lake, while the women were busy gumming the canoe and getting her in order for the run down Lockhart's River. A good proportion of the wages due were paid out of the remainder of our trading-stock that had been intended for the Esquimaux if we had met them. The box that contained this small supply of goods had been an object of strife the whole time. The Indians had the strongest objection to any of the products of the Grand Pays passing through their country being given to strangers, and we had been careful not to let them see the gaudy contents of the box, or we should have been troubled with the constant begging that the Yellow Knives think will eventually gain them the object they desire. Imagination had run high as to the contents of the fairy casket, and there was a great rush when it was announced that any of the men to whom wages were due might take what they fancied. They had seen pressed bales of blankets landed at the fort on the arrival of the yearly outfit from Winnipeg, and had been surprised at the number of blankets that could be squeezed into a small space; there was an idea prevalent that our box had been packed on the same principle, and might contain an abundant supply of all the good things that only the white

men know how to make. Some disappointment
was shown when it turned out that we had only
been speaking the truth in answering their petitions by telling them we had such a small stock
that nothing could be spared. The trade went off
to the satisfaction of both sides; the Indians obtained the trinkets so dear to their vanity, and
we lightened our load for the numerous portages
that lay between us and the Great Slave Lake.
There was some question as to what it was best
to do with Saltatha; whether to leave him here
with his friends, or to let him take his chance of
the canoe journey to the fort, where medicine
could possibly be obtained; at his own request we
decided on the latter course, and during the first
few days his health seemed to improve.

The route that we were now to take was the
same that Back and Anderson had both chosen,
following the Lockhart's River down-stream
through the immense lakes that lie in its course,
gradually bending to the south-west, and avoiding the impassable obstructions in the lower part
of the river by portaging through a chain of lakes,
the last of which is only three miles distant from
the north-east end of the Great Slave Lake. The
boat was to meet us on August 1st, and as it was
already several days past that date we determined to travel our best, although there was a
chance of getting windbound in any of the big
lakes.

CHAPTER XIII

LATE in the afternoon, with a great improvement in the weather, our canoe was afloat on Aylmer Lake (known to the Indians as the Lake of the Big Cliffs), over which she had been dragged on a dog-sleigh five weeks before. The following evening was passed into the short stretch of river that leaves its east end, and camped late on the south shore of Clinton Golden Lake, or, as the Yellow Knives call it, the Lake where the Caribou swim among the Ice. The vast body of water opened out before us into apparently a perfect circle, and now for the first time we were in doubt as to our course, for there was nothing to indicate the point at which the river leaves the far end of the lake; the east shore was invisible from the slight hill behind our camp, although it was a clear bright morning. We had two maps with us, one, the latest issued under the Dominion Government's directions, and the other, an old 1834 map of Arrowsmith's which we had discovered at the fort; they offered very divergent opinions as to the general lay of Lockhart's River, and it says little for later geographical research that the older map should have been by far the more accurate of the two.

216

We put out at three o'clock in the morning to take advantage of calm weather to make the crossing of the lake, and after paddling about eight miles went ashore on an island to cook breakfast and reconnoitre. From here we could see the faint outline of land to the east, and made out that what had appeared a circle consisted in reality of three enormous bays, one heading east, one south-east, and the third south-west. Which was the right one to take? An appeal to Saltatha and Noel, who were supposed to have local knowledge, produced no results; Noel said he thought the east bay was the right one, while Saltatha, pointing south-west, said perhaps that was the correct course to follow. It ended in our taking the middle bay, and, for the benefit of the next party that crosses this lake, I may state that there is a peculiar conical butte lying roughly twenty miles south-east from this island; it is just visible above the horizon, and is a capital leading mark to bring a canoe into a long narrow arm of the lake, which afterwards broadens again into a huge round sheet of water, and here, by keeping close to the east shore for five miles, the entrance to the river will be found. It was in great uncertainty that we headed our frail vessel across the broad traverse with a blanket set in front of a light fair wind; at noon we again put ashore on an island, and, killing a caribou, made a long halt for dinner. We climbed to the highest point of land but could make nothing out of our survey, and continued coasting along the island till we reached its south end, and then found ourselves in the channel I have mentioned. No current was noticeable, and we pushed on through the winding waterway, in fear that it might be a *cul de sac* and we should have to turn back and try our luck in some other direction. On landing, however, we saw a sheet of water ahead of us, so broad that the far shore was below the horizon, and, on passing out of the channel we had been following, pitched camp on the east side of the lake, still uncertain as to where the river lay. Very early in the morning we were under way again, and followed the land to make sure that we did not pass the opening of the river, if indeed we were anywhere near it. About six o'clock there came a shout from the bowsman, that he saw a pole planted among the rocks ashore, and the canoe at once began to feel the influence of a slight current. Rounding a low point, a reach of strong running water lay before us, and we landed to see what was the meaning of the pole. A broken piece of *babiche* hanging from it told the old story of a rifled *cache,* another evidence of the wolverine's handiwork.

Among the Indians who had come to the fort during the winter to trade fur was a hunter generally known by the name of Pierre the Fool, though it seems hard to understand how one of the most intelligent Indians in the country of the Great Slave Lake had earned this *soubriquet.*

Pierre had been much interested in our expedition. Every summer he pitched his lodge where the river leaves the lake in which the caribou swim among the ice, to make dried meat to sell at the fort; his hunt this year had been successful, and, when he broke up his camp, he had faithfully kept his promise to leave us a *cache* of pounded meat and grease, but the wolverines had reaped the benefit. Just below the camp we saw plain evidence of the slaughter he had made among the swimming caribou; what we took at first for a bunch of remarkably big willow sticks proved to be the horns of fifty or sixty bucks, lying in shallow water at the edge of the stream; and enough meat to keep an Indian family for a year, if properly cured, was rotting in the sun.

After a mile of strong running stream the river falls into another lake, and immediately makes a sharp bend to the south-west, and, during the rest of the descent, we travelled in that direction with little variation till we reached the Great Slave Lake. Saltatha now began to recognise the country, and there was no more doubt about the way; but had we been left to our own judgment, we should have certainly gone wrong in this first lake, as there is a promising bay heading in to the south. None of the maps show this bend in the stream at all correctly, nor do they take any notice of the next lake, the Indians' Ptarmigan Lake, a large sheet of water fully twenty miles in length, which Pierre the Fool afterwards told us lies within a short portage of the west bay of Clinton Golden Lake.

We now fell in again with the big herds of caribou. For the last few weeks we had only seen enough to provide us with meat, but here they were in their thousands, and I am sorry to say that our crew did far too much killing, during the short spell of bad weather which forced us to camp on Ptarmigan Lake. The excuse was that the hides were now at their best for coats and robes; but even so, far more were killed than could be used for this purpose.

We made rather a risky passage down the lake in front of a strong wind and heavy sea, and at the west end found an ugly rapid six hundred yards in length: the cargo was portaged and the canoe run light in safety; and, after crossing a short lake, another rapid was negotiated in the same manner. In this second portage stood a solitary pine-tree, round which we all crowded as in welcome of an old friend after our long journey in a woodless country. Just below there was an impassable rapid, the only real impediment to navigation from the head of Mackay Lake to the foot of Artillery Lake, a distance of four hundred miles. Below the portage we ran five or six miles down a steady swift current, occasionally widening out into a small lake, with caribou continually swimming across the river ahead of the canoe, and late at night camped on the edge of a huge lake with a clear horizon to the west. This proved to be Artillery Lake, and at four o'clock next morning we were running down the south shore, in front of a gale of wind with our smallest blanket set for a sail. The day was much colder, with a few flakes of snow flying, and everybody was pleased to put ashore in a clump of pine-trees at dinner-time; the wind moderated towards evening, and, crossing to the north shore, we camped once again in the strong woods. The timber line is much more clearly defined here than on the other routes by which I approached the Barren Ground; the outlying clumps of pines extend to a very short distance, and their growth ceases entirely within seventy miles of the Great Slave Lake. If it should ever again prove necessary to reach the Arctic Sea by way of the Great Fish River, Artillery Lake would, in my opinion, be by far the best place at which to build light boats for the voyage; the timber is quite large enough, and only one portage has to be made to reach the Aylmer Lake divide.

The next morning we reached the end of Artillery Lake, which we reckoned roughly at forty-five miles in length, and passed into a narrow channel with hardly any current. Towards midday a couple of small canoes appeared ahead of us, and the usual formalities of saluting ensued. When they came alongside the occupants were asked for the news, and they informed us that the burnt Indian was drowned, that the caribou had been passing more thickly than ever known before, and that the fort boat had not yet arrived at the appointed meeting-place. The burnt Indian seems to have been badly out of luck. He had rolled into his camp-fire during a fit, and was found with his feet burnt off; after being doctored by the missionary for many months, and cured as far as it was possible to cure such a case, the cripple had left the fort with some of his relations to get back among the caribou, but on the second day out was drowned by capsizing his canoe. We could not account for the non-arrival of the boat, as we ourselves were already a fortnight later than the day agreed upon for meeting.

Round the next bend of the stream were six lodges, and the first greeting we received was from old Syene, the Medicine Man. There was no doubt that the caribou had been passing, as the children and dogs were rolling fat, and an unmistakable air of plethora from much feasting hung over the camp. Only four days before there had been one of those big slaughters, which one would think could not fail in a short time to exterminate the caribou. A large band had been seen to start from the opposite bank, and was soon surrounded by seven hunting-canoes; the spears were kept going as long as there was life to take, with the result that three hundred and twenty-six carcasses were hauled ashore, and fully two hundred of these left to rot in the shallow water. Every lodge was full of meat and grease in various forms, and there would be a cargo for the boat to take back to the fort. Pierre the Fool, who was camped here, was in great form, and at once presented us with a bunch of smoked tongues and a bladder of marrow grease. He gave us a great deal of information about the country eastward of Clinton Golden Lake, and in a much more intelligent manner than the usual Indian method of constant repetition; he told us there were fewer lakes in that direction than in any other part of the Barren Ground that he had visited, but he was always obliged to take a small canoe with him, to cross a big stream running in a southerly direction, three days' easy travel from Clinton Golden Lake. Once, when he had pushed out farther than usual, he had seen smoke in the distance, and came upon a camp that the Esquimaux from Hudson's Bay had just left; they had been cutting wood for their sleighs in a clump of well-grown pines, and Pierre, who shares the dread which every Yellow Knife has of the Coast tribes, had been afraid to follow them. From the fact of his having seen the pine-trees, which are said not to extend far from the salt water of Hudson's Bay, he must have been within a short distance of the coast.

On the day after our arrival in the encampment a general movement was made; the lodges were thrown down, and the women and dogs received heavy loads to carry to the Great Slave

Lake. Lockhart's River on leaving Artillery
Lake becomes a wild torrent, falling several hundred feet in twenty miles, and is quite useless
for navigation, so we had to make use of a chain
of lakes, eight in number, lying to the south of
the stream. This is by far the prettiest part of
the country that I saw in the North, and it was
looking its best under the bright sunshine that
continued till we reached the fort. Scattering
timber, spruce and birch, clothed the sloping
banks down to the sandy shores of the lakes;
berries of many kinds grew in profusion; the
portages were short and down hill; and caribou
were walking the ridges and swimming the lakes
in every direction. A perfect northern fairyland
it was, and it seemed hard to believe that winter
and want could ever penetrate here; but on the
shore of a lovely blue lake Pierre the Fool pointed
out a spot where the last horrors of death and
cannibalism had been enacted within his memory.
Sometimes a column of smoke would be seen
ahead, and we paddled by a lodge where the fat
sleepy children were revelling in the abundance
of grease. Late on the second day a white object on the shore attracted general attention: "It
is a wolf, a white caribou; no, a man, a man in
a white shirt,—it must be one of the boat's crew";
and so it proved to be. The white shirt was a
libel, but the clean canvas jumper quite deserved
the admiration it had received, especially in contrast with our own rags. The boat had arrived

from Fort Resolution in charge of François Mandeville, another brother of Michel the fort interpreter. François had been alarmed at not finding us at the meeting-place, and had immediately dispatched four of the crew in a large canoe, with a supply of tea, tobacco, and flour, to ascend the river in hopes of finding us. But the relief party had come across the fresh tracks of caribou in the first portage; it was long since they had tasted meat, so the canoe was put down in the woods, and the "big masters," who were supposed to be lost in the Barren Ground, were forgotten. The man we met had come on to see some relations who were camped among the lakes, and, as he was discovered to be possessed of tobacco, we made him share up, and sat on the beach enjoying the first smoke for many days, and hearing the accounts of what little events had happened during a short summer on the Great Slave Lake. But it was getting late, and we still had the longest portage to make. At the end of the last lake we abandoned the canoe that had done me such good service on two long journeys, and with loads on our backs followed the well-worn trail that the Indians have used from time immemorial as a route to their hunting-grounds. A natural pass with a steep descent led between the rough broken hills on each side, and a three-mile walk brought us within sight of the waters of the big lake. Below us, close by the edge of the bay, there were already several lodges planted, and over a white tent floated the old red ensign bearing in the corner the letters H. B. C. so well known throughout the whole dominion of Canada. A shot from the last ridge aroused the encampment, and soon a general fusillade took place; a fleet of canoes, running with blankets set to a fair wind far across the bay, took up the firing and headed for the shore, while every Indian within sound of gun-shot hurried to hear the news and join in the trading which was sure to take place on our arrival.

Here we found everything that a man in the wilds longs for, flour, bacon, tea, tobacco, sugar, a packet of letters from England written many months before, and a bottle of brandy, the first "fire-water" that had come our way for a year. Women and dogs heavily loaded with bales of meat and bladders of grease kept dropping in from across the portage; a dance was set on foot and kept up all night round the huge camp fires, while the tall pine-trees looked down on a scene of feasting and revelry such as had probably never been known on the shores of this pleasant bay.

Poor Saltatha, who had been very bad for the last week, crawled into our lodge late at night, and threw himself down on a blanket in a state of utter exhaustion. In spite of the best law in Canada, which forbids a white man to given an Indian any intoxicating drink, under penalty of a $200 fine, I determined to try if brandy could do

him any good. Saltatha had never tasted the
strong water, but had heard much of its wonderful qualities, and made no objection to trying the
cure. I gave him a small dose, but it had a
wonderful effect; his eyes became round and big,
and once again he started the dismal chant that
he had been so fond of during our musk-ox hunt
last winter. He was hopelessly drunk, and, when
he was seized with a violent fit of coughing and
his head fell on the blanket like a dead man's, I
thought I had made a sad mess of my doctoring.
Early in the morning I got up to see if he was
dead, and was relieved to find him much better
and keen for some more brandy, which I refused;
he had had very pleasant dreams he said, and the
pain had gone from his chest to his head. From
that time he improved in health, his strength came
back rapidly, and when I left the fort a week later,
he looked as well as ever.

Two days were spent in trading for the meat
which kept coming in, and during this time we
sent out a hunting-party to kill fresh meat, which
we hoped would keep till we reached the fort if
we made a good passage. At Resolution times
were very hard; few fish were being caught, and
the return of the boat was anxiously expected.
Many caribou were killed, and our ship was well
loaded with fresh meat, besides over three thousand pounds of dried meat, two hundred pounds
of grease, bunches of tongues, coils of *babiche*

and sinew, and a little fur that had been killed during the spring.

The Indians all left on the evening of the second day, and early the following morning we put to sea in a flat calm. Before leaving we went through the ceremony of cutting a lop-stick, as is the fashion of the North, to commemorate our expedition. A conspicuous pine was chosen, a man sent aloft to lop off the lower branches, while Mackinlay and myself cut our names on the trunk; then everybody discharged their guns at the tree, and the performance was ended. Often in the lonely waterways of the Northern country one sees a lop-stick showing far ahead on the bank, and reads a name celebrated in the annals of the Hudson's Bay Company or in the history of Arctic exploration. These lop-sticks are easily distinguished landmarks, well known to the *voyageurs,* and many an appointment has been kept at Campbell's, Macdougal's, or Macfarlane's tree. In giving directions to a stranger it is hopeless to describe the points and bends of a monotonous river highway, but a lop-stick does the duty of a signpost and at once settles the question of locality.

Two hundred miles of the Great Slave Lake lay between us and the fort, but a steady wind came from the north, and the shallow-draught York boat ran in front of it so well that on the fourth night we camped on the Mission Island within a couple of miles of Fort Resolution. A worse boat for the navigation of the lake could hardly be imagined. A huge square sail, set on a mast shipped right amidships, does good work so long as the wind is abaft the beam; but when a head-wind springs up, too strong to row against, it is a case of hauling ashore on the beach, as no anchor is carried. Steep cliffs on a lee shore have to be carefully avoided, for it is impossible to propel such a vessel to windward in a heavy sea. On the present occasion, however, we were in great luck, and I never remember a more pleasant voyage in a sailing-boat. A run up the English Channel in a well-found yacht, with fair wind and sunshine, is enjoyable enough; but there are seldom any blankets to lie about in on deck, and there is always some stray peak or jib-halliard that wants pulling on, besides continual threats of setting or stowing a topsail, which prevents your settling down into a comfortable position. Here we had nothing to worry us; the wind blew fair, and we lay in our blankets, smoking and looking at the land, as the boat glided along the narrow blue lanes, among islands that the foot of white man had never pressed. Four times a day we put ashore to boil the kettle, and at night slept by the side of a huge fire in the thick pine-woods; darkness lasted many hours now, and prevented navigation among the countless islands and outlying rocks. On the fourth day we crossed the Grand Traverse, and, leaving the Ile de Pierre after nightfall, ran for Mission Island with a strong wind blowing in from the open lake. Crossing the mouth of the big river was rather risky work in the dark, as the sandy battures ran far off to sea and the waves were breaking heavily in the shallow water; the sounding-pole gave only four feet in one place, but we ran across without touching, and at midnight camped at the back of Mission Island.

The sun was just rising on Sunday, August the 24th, when we ran the boat on the beach in front of Fort Resolution, and a glance at the faces that gathered round told us that living had been none too good, and that a man is sometimes better off among the caribou than depending upon an uncertain fishery for a livelihood. With all thanks to priest and parson, Indian and half-breed, for the kind welcome they gave us, I noticed many an eye glancing furtively at our rich cargo from the land of plenty; and the rejoicings that day may be attributed equally to joy at our safe arrival and to the influence of a feast of fresh meat after many weeks of short allowance.

I could afford to make only a short stay at Resolution, as the season was far advanced, and I had to start at once to avoid the chance of being caught by the winter during my long journey. Of the three routes that might enable me to do this I should have preferred the ascent of the Liard River, which falls into the Mackenzie at Fort Simpson. From its head-waters at Dease Lake, in the once celebrated mining district of

Cassiar, the Pacific Coast is reached at Fort Wrangel in Southern Alaska without difficulty; but the Liard itself is full of terrors, even for the hardy *voyageurs* of the North, and although Mr. Camsell offered every inducement to men to accompany me he was unable to get together a crew. Formerly the Company had an establishment at Fort Halket on the west branch of the Liard, but the difficulties of conveying supplies, and the frequent occurrence of starvation, made it a hard post to maintain; finally a boat's crew were drowned by a capsize in one of the worst rapids, and the fort was abandoned. The Athabasca I had seen, and not caring to go over old ground I decided on ascending the Peace River to its headwaters in the neighbourhood of Macleod's Lake on the west side of the Rocky Mountains, and, crossing the small divide, to run down the Fraser River to Quesnelle a small town on the southern edge of the Caribou Gold Fields of Northern British Columbia.

The *Wrigley* had made her last up-stream voyage for the year, and was daily expected from Fort Smith. I was thus obliged to depend on canoe travelling to reach Chipeweyan on the Athabasca Lake, some three hundred miles distant; if we had arrived at the fort ten days earlier I could have saved much valuable time by making this part of my journey by steamer.

Taking advantage of frequent experience that it is better to leave a fort overnight, even if camp be made within a couple of miles, than to trust to an early start in the morning, it was after sun-down on the 26th when I said good-bye to Resolution, not without a feeling of regret, and the hope of seeing at some future time the place where I had been so well treated. There are few spots in the world in which one can live for a year without making some friends, and when I left this lonely trading-post there were many faces on the beach that I should like to see again. Saltatha was the last man to shake hands with me as I stepped into the canoe; he tried to extract a promise from me to come back the next summer for another expedition in the Barren Ground, and was much disappointed when I told him that I certainly could not return for two years, and perhaps not even then. No need to feel pity for the people left behind, although I was going to civilization and all the good things that this word comprises. A man who has spent much time under the influence of the charm which the North exercises over everybody wants nothing better than to be allowed to finish his life in the peace and quietness which reign by the shores of the Great Slave Lake. Ask the priest, when you meet him struggling against a head-wind and driving snow on his way to some Indian encampment, whether he ever sighs for his sunny France. "No," he will tell you; "here I have everything I want and nothing to distract my thoughts; I enjoy perfect health, and I feel no

desire to go back to the worries of the great
world." So it is with the fur-trader; the mysterious charm has a firm hold on him, and if he is
in charge of a post where provisions are fairly
plentiful and the Indians not troublesome he has
a happy life indeed. I was sorry to have missed
seeing the Mackenzie River, La Grande Rivière
en Bas, as they call it at Fort Resolution, but to
do this meant spending another winter and another summer in the country, and I could not
afford the time.

The first evening out from the fort we camped
near the mouth of the Slave River, on the same
spot where I had spent a night with King Beaulieu and his family more than a year before. My
crew now consisted of Murdo Mackay and three
half-breeds, while Mackinlay, who had proved
such a trusty companion during our summer
journey, was to accompany me till we met the
steamer. This happened the next morning, and
after an hour of hurried questions and answers,
and farewells to men who seemed more like old
friends than comparative strangers whom I had
met once the year before, the *Wrigley* put her
head down-stream, and we continued our voyage
through the wilderness of pines, cotton-wood, and
willow.

Pierre Beaulieu was captain and guide of the
canoe, and a right good traveller he proved to be;
no lying snug in your blankets in the early morning, but breakfast in black darkness, and the pad-

Starting Up the Peace River

dles or tracking-line in full swing at the first sign of the coming day. Sometimes he would put ashore and start us off through the woods, with canoe and cargo on our backs, to drop on the river again at the end of the portage, and find that we had saved many miles of laborious up-stream work by cutting across a bend of the river. The tracking till we reached Fort Smith was bad, as the banks were usually soft muddy sand, while the land-slips had sent so many trees into the river that it was often easier to paddle against the stream than to pass the line round the obstruction. Ducks and geese were plentiful enough, but Mackinlay had been liberal in the matter of provisions for our voyage, so we only took the most tempting shots, but if it had been necessary we could have made our own living without difficulty. Early on the sixth day we came in sight of Fort Smith, and found Mr. Flett in charge, with the house much improved and made fairly comfortable in readiness for the winter; but there was no time to be spared, and the next day saw us driving across the portage in a waggon to take a fresh crew to Chipeweyan. No canoe was available, but José Beaulieu, another of King's numerous brothers, lent us a skiff, which answered the purpose well enough. Mr. Flett took the opportunity of going up to headquarters, and enlivened the journey with many stories of over forty years' experience in the North. Among the new crew was a deaf and dumb half-breed, a capital worker and always good-tempered, in spite of the cold drenching rain that continued till we reached Chipeweyan; some of his conversations by signs were very amusing, and one could almost wish that all these boatmen were deaf and dumb to avoid the constant chatter which they keep up round the camp-fire when they know that you understand them. One day we made a splendid run in front of a gale of north wind, but nearly came to grief through our steersman's recklessness in trying to force the boat over a rapid under canvas; she took a sheer in the swirl of an eddy, and the sail jibbed with such violence that we were within an inch of a capsize. Provisions ran short on the last day, but just as we were talking of camping early and going after duck for supper a little black bear turned up on the bank; I was lucky enough to kill it, and we enjoyed a royal feast of fat bear's meat instead of a night's starvation. On the fourth day we entered the Athabasca Lake, and forced our way to the fort against a strong head-wind; it was another Sunday arrival, and we did not show to advantage in comparison with the bright dresses and gaudy belts and moccasins of the dwellers at the chief post of the Athabasca district. A little snow was whitening the ground, the goose-hunt was at its height, and the array of nets showed plainly enough that it was time to make preparation for the Fall fishing. Dr. Mackay was away inspecting Fort Vermillion on the Lower

Peace River, and would not be back for several days.   An unexpected difficulty now turned up; there was no crew forthcoming for the next part of my journey, and everybody advised me to take the ordinary route by the Athabasca River. However, two of my Fort Smith crew, José and Dummy, finally agreed to go to Vermillion, although neither of them had been there before, and Murdo, who was very anxious to accompany me across the mountains, obtained leave to come with me till we should meet Dr. Mackay on Peace River; if he could get extended leave from the head officer of the District he was to come right through.

CHAPTER XIV

By this time it was well on in September, and eight hundred miles had to be travelled to reach the Rocky Mountains and when these were sighted there were still two hundred miles to MacLeod's Lake, the farthest point I could reasonably hope to reach by open water. The first night we camped in the Quatre Fourches, the channel connecting the lake with the main stream of Peace River. The banks were thickly peopled with Indians and half-breeds, drying whitefish which were being taken in marvellous numbers; white and grey wavies and ducks of many kinds were flying overhead in large flocks, and rising in front of the canoe at every bend of the stream; plovers and other wading birds were screaming over the marshes, and I noticed a good many snipe; but who would fire a charge of ammunition at such a wretched little mouthful when geese were plentiful? Without going out of our way to hunt, we could have loaded the canoe with wild-fowl, but of course only killed as many as we required for food.

At the end of the Quatre Fourches we passed into the main stream of Peace River, and, with a sharp westward turn, commenced our ascent of the easiest of all the Northern waterways. From its junction with the Slave River to the first range of the Rocky Mountains, with only the obstruction of the shute some forty miles below Fort Vermillion, its course is navigable throughout for a light-draught steamer, and, but for this shute, would be an invaluable route for supplying the Hudson's Bay Company's upper river-posts.

The lower reaches of the river present exactly the same appearance as the country we had passed through in ascending the Slave River; a broad stream with low sandy banks, densely timbered, with often a huge sand-bar, the resting-place of many geese, stretching far out into the stream. We were rather handicapped by not knowing the river and missing the best tracking; an old hand would have known all the correct crossings to take advantage of an easy bank to track from, or an eddy to paddle in. Nor could we well risk the short cuts, as a promising channel would often end in dry sand and instead of running through into the river, or turn out to be the mouth of a tributary stream. After our usual halt for dinner on the third day we saw a canoe coming down stream, and, crossing over, found that it was Dr. Mackay on his way from Vermillion; both canoes put ashore and we had the usual cup of tea and an hour's yarn together. The Doctor was anxious to get back to Chipeweyan, to begin his Fall fishing and make every possible preparation for keeping up the food-supply for the winter; I had no time to spare either, and darkness must have found us camping many miles apart. These stray meetings in the wilderness are always a pleasant recollection, and on first returning to civilization one is surprised at the manner in which people pass each other with a nod, till one realises the fact that there are too many people about for a more lengthy salute. Murdo obtained leave to come with me across the mountains, subject to the condition that he was to return in the spring if he received orders to that effect from headquarters at Winnipeg.

The same evening we hauled up an insignificant rapid, caused by a contraction in the channel; a limestone formation, with many fossils, shows up here for a few miles of the river's course, and is noticeable again at the shutes and in several spots along the river. We broke the canoe rather badly in mounting this rapid, and during the rest of our journey to Vermillion had to bale out frequently. Day after day we followed the winding course of the river, which bends and doubles on itself through the flat country, and at last made out a landmark in the Caribou Mountains, lying to the north and stretching in that direction as far as we could see: an inviting range of hills, clear of timber on the slope, and their round summits sparsely dotted with pines; a favourite hunting-ground for the Indians of Vermillion, but none of the white men of whom I made inquiry seemed to have any knowledge of the extent or nature of this solitary range, rising so conspicuously from the dead level of muskeg and pine forest.

Just as we were starting on the tenth morning a light puff of west wind brought us the first sound of a distant roar that we knew must be caused by the shute, and a couple of hours' tracking brought us to a small Company's trading-post, known as Little Red River, from a stream bearing that name which here joins the Peace River from the south. The establishment was deserted, although it was to be kept open during the winter; so we passed on and soon came in sight of a low white wall of water extending across the whole width of the river. Dr. Mackay had told me to make the portage close under the fall on the south side, or we should have been at a loss to find the only place where it is possible to take the canoe out of the water. In a strong running current, with the spray falling over her bow, we put alongside a ledge of rock six feet above us, and two men, standing on a submerged ledge, not without difficulty passed everything up to the others above; the distance to carry was very short, and we were soon afloat again above the fall. The shute is not more than eight feet in height, but is of course a complete barrier to navigation. I think the scene from the south bank is one of the most beautiful in the whole course of the loveliest of rivers. It was a bright afternoon when we made the portage, and the white broken water of the cascade showed in strong contrast to the broad blue stretches above and below; several rocky, pine-covered islands stand on the brink of the over-fall, as if to give a chance to any unlucky traveller who may approach too near the danger; fully three-quarters of a mile away on the far side stands the gloomy forest of black pines, relieved by a glimpse of the open side-hills of the Caribou Mountains. Another small portage was necessary a mile or two above; but from the spot where we camped that night we never had to lift canoe or skiff out of the water till we reached the foot-hills of the Rocky Mountains.

The next day we passed a couple of Cree lodges, and finding moose-meat plentiful made the most of our opportunity, as a gale of wind sprang up right ahead and prevented travel.

It was not till sundown on the eleventh day from Chipeweyan that we completed our journey of two hundred and eighty miles, and put ashore at the Company's trading-post at Fort Vermillion. Here the appearance of the country suddenly changes; stretches of open prairie dotted with small poplars take the place of the pine-woods, and the sand-bars in the river begin to give way to gravel, and the banks rise higher and higher as one journeys up-stream. We reached Vermillion late in September, in the full glory of the autumn; the sharp morning frosts had coloured the poplar leaves with the brightest golden tints, and the blue haze of an Indian summer hung over prairie and wood. Away on the Great Slave Lake a half-breed had told me of the beauties of Vermillion as a farming country, and had explained that all the good things of the world grew there freely, so that I was prepared for the sight of wheat and barley fields, which had this year produced a more abundant harvest than usual; potatoes and other vegetables were growing luxuriously, cattle and horses were fattening on the rich prairie grass, and it seemed that there was little to be gained by leaving such a fertile spot in the face of the winter that would soon be upon us.

Vermillion is also an important fur-post, and probably to-day the best in the North for beaver and marten; but there are several free-traders on the Peace River, and the Company have to carry on their business with the extra difficulty of competition, which always raises the price of fur. It is all very well to say that no Company should have the monopoly of trading over so vast a territory, but after all the Indians are little benefited by the appearance of the free-traders. The Hudson's Bay Company have always treated the Indians fairly and leniently, taking the greatest care only to import articles absolutely necessary to the welfare of the natives. Guns, ammunition, blankets, capotes, dress-stuff for the women, and tea and tobacco, have always been the principal contents of the store; and these are sold at absurdly low prices, when the cost of the long and risky transport is considered. The Indians' love of gaudy colours was always indulged, but the goods were of the best material. Then came the free-trader with a stock of bright cheap clothing, a variety of dazzling tinsel, or perhaps a keg of molasses, which attracted the eye and palate of the wily hunter, so that he would give up his rich furs for the worthless trash, only to find himself short of all the necessaries for maintaining life in the woods when the snow began to fall again. No amount of experience enables him to resist the temptation; but the long enduring Hudson's Bay Company always listens to his tale of woe and helps him out of his difficulties, accepting his promise, ever readily given and as readily broken, to hand in his fur in the following spring to the officer in charge of the post. Whenever the often-told story of a band of Indians caught by the horrors of starvation reaches the fort, the Company sends to the rescue, and every winter saves many a man from death, while the free-trader, having taken as much fur as he can out of the country during a short summer's trip, is living at ease on the confines of civilization. The days are long gone by when a prime silver fox could be bought for a cotton pocket-handkerchief, but still the rumours brought from this little known

Northern country attract the venturesome trader, usually to his own loss, and always to the up-setting of the Company's wise system of dealing with the Indians.

Vermillion has a comparatively large population, outside the numerous *employés* of the country. Both the Protestant and Roman Catholic churches have missions here, and several half-breeds have taken up an irregular method of stock-raising and small farming to help out the uncertain living afforded by fur-trapping. Mr. Lawrence, a practical hard-working farmer from Eastern Canada, has been successful with a farm three miles above the fort; but for many years to come there is not the slightest reason for that emigration of farmers to Peace River which wild enthusiasts clamour for. So much talk about this scheme has lately appeared in the Canadian newspapers, mostly, no doubt, as one of the political cries which find such favour with the statesmen of Ottawa, that I cannot allow this opportunity to pass without a word of warning to any intending settler. I made careful inquiries and observations along the whole length of Peace River, and I do not for a moment deny that in some parts of its course crops of wheat and barley may be raised in favourable seasons, as the well-managed farms of Mr. Lawrence, at Vermillion, and Mr. Brick, hgher up at Smoky River, fully attest; but these farms, and all the spots in which grain ripens, are in close proximity to the bed of the river, and here the amount of arable land is limited. Climb the steep banks and take a glance over the millions of fertile acres which the philanthropic politician wishes to see cultivated; notice the frost on a summer's morning, and make the attempt, as has often been made already, to raise a crop on this elevated plateau. In ten years' time this may be a cattle-country, although the hay-swamps are insufficient to ensure enough feed for the long winter; but let us have an end of this talk of sending poor settlers to starve in a land unable to supply food to the Indian, who is accustomed to a life of continual struggle with a relentless nature.

Mr. Wilson entertained me royally at the fort, but here again was the same trouble that I had found at Chipeweyan; no crew was procurable, and there was a journey of three hundred and fifty miles to Dunvegan before I had any chance of getting men. José and Dummy, who had both worked right well up to now, considered they were far enough away from their beloved Fort Smith; and José had an extra attraction in Dummy's sister, who was waiting his return to make him happy for ever, but was not very reliable in case of a more prepossessing admirer coming to the fore. José made a touching speech at parting: "God made the mountains, the lakes, and the big rivers," he said. "What is better than drifting down Peace River singing hymns? You are going up-stream to cross the big mountains back to your own country; I am going down-stream to marry Dummy's sister; I shall think of you many times." Dummy smiled and nodded affectionately, and the pair shot out into the river with my canoe, leaving me on the bank with only Murdo for my crew and no means of conveyance.

Now if I could have got a small dug-out wooden canoe, and pottered away up-stream with Murdo, tracking in turns, we should have got on very well; but unfortunately there was nothing but a large and somewhat clumsy skiff available, and this we finally had to take. The evening before we were to start I received a visit from a man whom I shall allude to as John. Long before in merry England he had seen better times, and was evidently intended by nature for a sedentary life, or any other kind of life than the physical activity necessary to accomplish quickly and successfully a boating-trip up a swift-running river; in reality he was powerful enough, and but for his extraordinary laziness might have earned a good living anywhere. John told me he wished to leave Peace River and cross the mountains to Quesnelle, and would be glad to render me every assistance in his power if I would let him take advantage of this chance to get out of the country. In spite of the warnings of Mr. Wilson and everybody else who knew John's character, I went on the theory that when one is shorthanded any kind of a man is better

than no man, but was speedily disabused of this
idea after leaving the fort. He turned sulky
when he found that I would stand no shirking,
and was painfully slow on the tracking-line, awkward in letting go or tying a knot, and, although
he had been five years at boating, absolutely without knowledge of the duties of bowsman or
steersman. In addition to this he was just as
useless in camp, and conceived a violent hatred
to Murdo, who fully reciprocated the feeling.
Once, on being heartily cursed while he was
tracking, John threatened to desert and go back
to Vermillion, but when we ran the skiff ashore
and offered to help him build a raft and to give
him a week's rations, he hastily withdrew his
proposition. I hoped to be able to leave him at
some fort *en route,* but I found John was too
well known, and no one would accept the horrible
responsibility of keeping him for a winter on any
terms. A man like this takes all the pleasure
out of a journey when good temper is the almost invariable rule, and everybody takes his
share of the tracking and wading, the paddling
and poling, as part of the ordinary day's work.

At this time of year, when the water is at its
lowest, tracking is a comparatively easy matter,
and taking half-hour spells at a sharp walk we
made good day's journeys, although we should
have done much better with a canoe. It was a
hard time for moccasins, but we could get them
at every fort we passed; sometimes we found an

Indian encampment on the bank, and a small present of tea and tobacco to the women ensured neat patches over the gaping holes in the moose-skin soles.

The fourth day out from Vermillion we reached the mouth of Battle River coming in from the north, and found a small trading-post with a French half-breed in charge. He told us that the Indians had been killing a great many moose, and that he had already bought the dried meat of sixteen as a start towards his winter stock of provisions; black bear too were numerous on Battle River, and there were reports of grizzly having been seen. This would probably be one of the best points from which to enter the unknown country between Peace River and the Great Slave Lake.

I never remember to have seen in any part of Canada such a fine autumn as we enjoyed between Vermillion and the Rockies; there was hardly a day's rain the whole time, and, although a sharp white frost usually made a cold camp, the days were bright and at times almost too hot for tracking. Often we saw the fresh tracks of moose and bear, but never happened to see an animal of any kind, and as we could afford no time for hunting did not fire a single shot at big game; geese and ducks we could have killed every day if there had been any necessity for doing so.

Fifteen days of continuous travel from Vermillion took us to the junction of Smoky River, the principal tributary of the Peace, flowing towards the south-west not far from some of the head-waters of the Athabasca. This junction is rather an important point, as it is close to the end of the waggon-road to the Lesser Slave Lake, lying seventy-five miles to the south. Here the trading-goods brought overland are loaded on to scows and boats, to be sent down-stream to Vermillion and up-stream to Dunvegan, St. John's, and Hudson's Hope. A little above are Mr. Brick's mission and the farm that I have already spoken of, besides a settlement of half-breeds, more hunters than farmers, well known as the laziest and most worthless gang on the whole length of Peace River. Many efforts have been made to get these people to pay more attention to their potato-patches as the game is getting killed out, but all in vain; sometimes they will fence in a piece of ground and plant seed, but will take no further trouble with the crop, and generally use their fence-rails for firewood during the next winter. Lukily whitefish are very plentiful in the Lesser Slave Lake within two days' journey, or starvation would certainly play havoc at Smoky River.

I enjoyed a long talk with Mr. Brick in his pleasant home in the wilds, where we spent a night; he kindly furnished me with supplies that I was short of, and three days afterwards we arrived at Dunvegan, another celebrated fur-

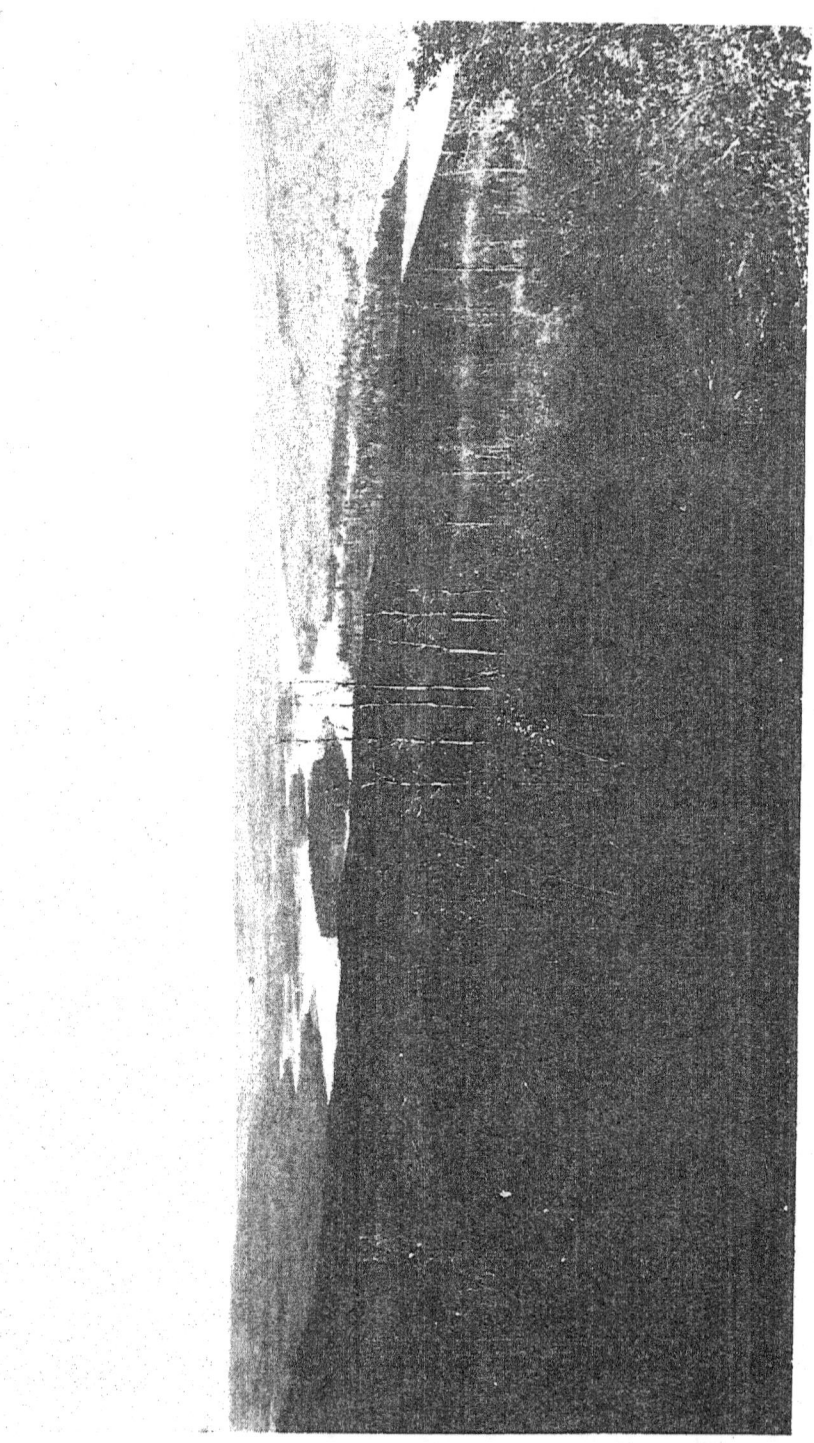

Junction of the Peace and Smoky Rivers

post, situated on the north bank of the river at the foot of a high bluff known as the Cap. Here again was abundant evidence of the fertility of the soil in the crops harvested by the Company and the missionaries. Across the river, twenty miles away, is the Company's cattle-*ranche,* where the oxen used on the waggon-road are raised and a fair amount of beef is annually killed. Some thoroughbred stock has been imported and should prove successful, but of course there is no paying market for a large amount of cattle, although there are plenty of hungry people who would be glad of a chance to eat beef.

At Dunvegan, besides Mr. Round who was in charge of the fort, I met Mr. Ewen Macdonald, the chief of Peace River District, with headquarters at Lesser Slave Lake. He had just finished his inspection of the upper river-posts, and had left Hudson's Hope, the last establishment east of the mountains, a few days previously; he reported that the snow was already low down on the foot-hills, and advised me strongly to give up my attempt to cross the Rockies so late in the autumn. He told me, however, that a free-trader was expected in from the west side of the mountains, and if I was lucky enough to meet him I should probably be able to secure the service of some of his crew who would be returning to Quesnelle.

Above Dunvegan the valley of the river contracts, the banks rise for several hundred feet in height, and the strength of the current increases. The hundred and twenty miles to St. John's took us seven days and a half to travel, and in many places we had to keep two men on the line to stem the strong water; the tracking too was bad, as the banks had fallen in several spots, and John, who had been up and down the river three times before, proved a very poor pilot. The weather was colder, and a sheet of ice formed over the back waters and close to the bank out of the current.

At St. John's we found Mr. Gunn busy with a band of Indians who were taking their winter supplies, and I had a chance of hearing their accounts of the wilderness to the north in the direction of the Liard River; they described it as a muskeg country abounding in game and fur, but a hard district to reach, as the streams are too rapid for canoes and the swamps too soft for horses to cross. They occasionally fall in with a small band of buffalo, but have never seen them in large numbers. Sometimes by ascending Half-way River, a stream adjoining Peace River twenty-five miles above St. John's, they meet the Indians from Fort Nelson on the south branch of the Liard.

We had now passed out of the Cree-speaking belt and the language became that of the Beaver Indians, a far inferior language to Cree, resembling in sound and in many of the words some of the dialects of the Chipeweyan tongue.

Mr. Gunn had learned to speak Beaver fluently, and was now going up to Hudson's Hope to interpret; he was a great help to us both as pilot and on the line, and with two men always tracking we took little notice of the strong stream which we found throughout the fifty miles to the next fort.

Snow was falling heavily when we left St. John's, and it looked as if the winter had set in, but next day the ground was bare again, and a west wind from across the mountains blew warm as a summer's breeze. We camped for a night at the mouth of Half-way River, heading towards the north through a wide open bay which seems to invite exploration. A considerable quantity of gold dust has been taken out of some of the gravel-bars along this part of Peace River, and Half-way River is supposed to be a paradise for the miner and hunter, but I could not hear of any white man having ever penetrated far up this valley. On the afternoon of Sunday, October 26th, on rounding a bend in the river, we caught our first glimpse of the snowy peaks of the Rocky Mountains that I had travelled so far to reach; but the sublime is often mixed with the ludicrous, and when John in his admiration of the scenery slipped off a narrow ledge of shale along which he was tracking and fell with an oath into the river, the snowy peaks were forgotten in the joy that always greets other people's misfortunes in this sort of travelling.

A short distance below Hudson's Hope we passed a remarkable group of high basaltic islands, differing entirely from anything in the neighbourhood, and affording a strong contrast to the low gravelly islands so numerous in the course of this river. In the afternoon of the 27th we unloaded the skiff and hauled her up on the beach in front of the fort, to lie there till anybody might want to run her down-stream the following spring.

Hudson's Hope is a small unpretentious establishment, standing on the south side of Peace River, a mile below the wild cañon by which this great stream forces its way through the most easterly range of the Rocky Mountains. The Indians were all encamped in their moose-skin lodges on the flat close to the fort waiting for the trade to begin, and I was surprised to hear how few representatives of the once numerous tribe of Beavers are left. It is the same at St. John's and Dunvegan, and the total Indian population of the upper Peace River cannot exceed three hundred, an immense falling off since Sir Alexander Mackenzie first crossed the mountains by this route. The biggest lodge was occupied by Baptiste Testerwich, a half-breed Iroquois, descended from the Iroquois crew left here many years ago by Sir George Simpson, formerly Governor of the Hudson's Bay Company. Baptiste had a house at Moberley's Lake twelve miles to the south, and is well known as the most successful and most enduring of moose-hunters. A remarkable point about the man is his hardiness and indifference to cold; in the dead of winter he wears no socks in his moccasins, which to any other man would mean a certainty of frozen feet, and the Indians say that his feet are so hot that the snow melts in his tracks in the coldest weather.

Once again arose the trouble about guides to take us to Macleod's Lake. John had been there before, but I had already seen too much of his piloting to trust myself in his hands, and was quite sure that he would lose his way if there was the least possibility of doing so. The free-trader from across the mountains had not yet arrived, and as it was getting late in the year there was a chance of his being frozen in before he reached Hudson's Hope. Besides the Peace River route there is the Pine River Pass, farther to the southward, heading almost directly to Macleod's Lake. A party of surveyors once came through this pass several years ago, and the Indians use it habitually in the summer; but none of the Beavers would volunteer to guide us through at this time of the year, as a heavy snowfall might be expected immediately.

I decided to wait a few days for the trader, and we had a very festive time at Hudson's Hope; a ball was given every night, and the moose-dance, rabbit-dance, and duck-dance were kept up till the small hours. A ball is not an expensive entertainment at an out-of-the-way trading-post; no invitations are necessary, but a scrape of the fiddle at the door of the master's house fills the ball-room in a few minutes. If the master is in a liberal state of mind, a cup of tea is provided for his guests, but in any case the river is close, and if anyone is thirsty there is plenty of water. On the third night the ceremonies were interrupted by the sound of a gunshot on the opposite bank, and an Indian came across with the news that the trader had arrived at the west end of the cañon with two small scows, and that some of his crew were going back to Quesnelle.

Baptiste lent me a horse on the following day, and I rode over to interview the new arrivals. A fair trail, twelve miles in length on the north side of the river, leads to the navigable water above the cañon, while the stream runs a circuitous course of probably thirty miles. I could get little information as to the nature of this cañon; even the Indians seem to avoid it, and, though accounts of it have been written, nobody appears to have thoroughly explored this exceptionally rough piece of country. I went down a few miles from the west end, but found the bluffs so steep that I could seldom get a view of the water, and could form no idea of the character of the rapids and waterfalls. There is some quiet place in the middle of the cañon where the Indians cross on the ice, but beyond this they could tell me little about it.

Right in the centre of the gap by which the trail crosses stands the Bull's Head, a solitary mountain well known to travellers coming from the west, as it can be seen many miles away, and in full view to the south is a huge flat-topped mountain, covered with perpetual snow and fit to rank with any of the giants of the main range. The trail reaches a considerable elevation above the river level, and from the summit the upper waters of the Peace are seen winding away to the west, through a broad valley flanked by hills of ever increasing height, as far as the eye can reach. Close to the river the slopes are open or thinly timbered with pine and poplar, but the big mountains are clothed nearly to their summits with the dense, almost impassable, forest growth which is such a common feature in the scenery as the Pacific Coast is approached.

At the far end of the portage, on the bank of the river, stand a rough shanty and trading-store. Here I made the acquaintance of Twelve-foot Davis, who acquired this name, not from any peculiarity of stature, but from a small though valuable mining claim of which he had been the lucky possessor in the early days of British Columbia. A typical man of his class is Davis, and his story is that of many a man who has spent his life just in advance of civilization. Born in the Eastern States of America, a 'Forty-niner in California, and a pioneer of the Caribou Diggings discovered far up the Fraser River in

'Sixty-one, he had eventually taken to fur-trading, which has ever such an attraction for the wandering spirit of the miner. Here among the mountains and rivers where formerly he sought the yellow dust he carries on his roaming life. There is a strong kinship between the two enterprises; the same uncertainty exists, and in each case the mythical stake is always just ahead. No failure ever damps the ardour of miner or fur-trader, or puts a stop to his pleasant dreams of monster nuggets and silver foxes.

Davis was making all possible haste in packing his cargo across the portage with horses; an Indian and a half-breed were going back to Quesnelle, and would gladly enter my service as guides. A small stock of goods was to be left at the west end of the portage, and Thomas Barrow, the only white man who had come down with Davis, was to remain in charge of the trading-post during the winter.

CHAPTER XV

ON November 5th I camped at the head of the cañon with my crew, Murdo, John, Charlie, a half-breed from Quesnelle, and Pat, a full-blooded Siccanee from Fraser Lake ready to make a start up-stream the following morning with a long narrow canoe dug out of a cotton-wood log. But in the night the weather changed; snow fell heavily, a severe frost set in, and ice was forming rapidly along the banks. Baptiste, the Iroquois, who had come across the portage to see us off, had brought me a dozen pair of the best moose-skin moccasins from his daughters, who were beyond compare the *belles* of Hudson's Hope. Baptiste had spent many years of his life in this part of the country, and I was quite ready to listen to his opinion on the chances of getting through to Macleod's Lake. He would not hear of our starting with a canoe under the changed conditions of weather: it was the winter; the ice would catch us in less than three days, and we should be lucky if we could get back on foot through the deep snow. His advice was to wait a fortnight till the river set fast, and occupy our-selves in making hand-sleighs, while he would make us five pairs of snow-shoes, and then we might walk the two hundred miles to Macleod's Lake in comfort. Accordingly I gave orders for the lodge, which we still had with us, to be pitched in a clump of poplars a short distance above Barrow's house, and we busied ourselves with cutting birch and bending sleighs in readiness for our trip.

The cold snap continued for several days, but very little ice was running, although the eddies and backwaters were frozen up; then the weather grew milder again, and I could see that we had missed our chance. It was past the middle of November, and the river, by all accounts, is usually frozen solid at this time of year; it seemed too risky to start out so late to try and make a passage with open water. Meantime we were taking things easily when, as it turned out, we should have been travelling; there was not much to shoot beyond wood-grouse and rabbits, but with these we could keep the pot going, and time went pleasantly enough in short expeditions into the surrounding hills.

And now a warm Chinook wind came sweeping across from the Pacific, and licked up the snow from the ground, while the ice broke away from the banks and drifted down in little floes to be ground to pieces in the cañon. I could bear the inactivity no longer, and, with a recklessness that I had plenty of opportunity to repent later on, gave orders on November 25th for the canoe to be got ready on the morrow to start up-stream and take the chances of being caught by the ice in the main range of the Rocky Mountains. I consulted Charlie and Pat about the route, and they both said they could make no mistake in finding the way to the Hudson's Bay Fort on Macleod's Lake, as they had just come down the river, and Charlie had made the journey the year before; if we could succeed in getting to the junction of the Findlay and Parsnip, just beyond the big mountains, before the ice caught us, there could be no difficulty in reaching the fort on foot in about four days' travel.

At the risk of being verbose and boring any reader who has struggled thus far through the record of my wanderings in the North, I must now enter somewhat fully into the details of travel, and describe minutely the events that happened during the next month, in order to answer once for all the numerous questions that I have been asked as to what took place on that terrible winter journey in the Rocky Mountains. When I reached civilization again, and found that part of the story had leaked out, I received plenty of gratuitous advice as to what I should have done and where I should have gone, from people who had never themselves been in a like predicament, and had no further knowledge of hardship than perhaps having had to pay a long price for a second-rate dinner. I discovered that the easiest method of satisfying them was to let them tell the tale of my adventures in their own way, and assent readily to their convincing proofs that if they had been there all would have gone well. I admit freely that it was a stupid act to leave a supply-post so late in the year, unprovided as we were with the necessary outfit for winter travelling; but think I was justified in trusting to the local knowledge of my native guides to bring our party in safety to Macleod's Lake after we were forced to abandon the canoe.

Walter Macdonald, a son of Mr. Ewen Macdonald of Lesser Slave Lake, and Tom Barrow both gave me every assistance in their power to provision my crew for what is usually an eight or nine days' journey. Meat was not to be had, and there was little chance of finding big game along the course of the river, but a hundred pounds of flour, a few pounds of beans and rice, and a small sack of potatoes, besides plenty of tea and tobacco, would surely last us this short journey, and, even if we found it impossible to travel quickly, a few days of short rations could easily be endured.

It was late in the afternoon of Wednesday, November 26th, when I started the canoe off, and the sun was down before I had settled up accounts and said good-bye to the friends whom I did not expect to meet again for many a long day. The moon was full, and I had no difficulty in finding my way six miles through the woods to an old miner's cabin at which we had arranged to camp for the night. At the first streak of

dawn we were off again, travelling our best with
two and sometimes three men on the line; the
current was strong, but the tracking on the gravel-
bars perfect. That night there was a heavy snowstorm, while the ground froze hard and caused
many a nasty fall on the slippery stones during
the next two days. On Saturday morning cakes
of soft ice began to run, but we found that most
of them were brought down by a large tributary
coming from the north, and above its mouth the
river was comparatively clear of ice. The same
afternoon we reached the entrance to the main
range of mountains, and under the first peak of
the chain tracked up a strong rush of water
with a heavy sea at its foot, commonly known as
the Polpar Rapid, a curious corruption of *la
Rapide qui ne parle pas,* so named by the old
voyageurs from the absence of the roar of
waters which usually gives ample warning of the
proximity of a rapid. Part of the cargo we
portaged to keep it dry, and above the strong
water lay a quiet stretch of river, winding away
in the gloomy black chasm between the huge
mountains, which in many places takes the form
of a sheer bluff hanging over the stream.

We camped just above the Polpar, and another
night's snow made the tracking worse than ever;
often it was necessary to put the line aboard and
take to the paddles, to struggle round some steep
point upon which a coating of frozen snow made
it impossible to stand. Ice was running in large

pans and steering was difficult, but we got on fairly well, and were far in the heart of the mountains when we camped on Sunday night under one of the steepest and most forbidding peaks that I ever remember to have seen in any part of the Rockies.

Monday was really cold, and our difficulties increased; the tow-line was sheeted with ice and three times its ordinary weight, while the channel was in many places almost blocked; poles and paddles had to be handled with numbed fingers, and our moccasins from constant wading turned into heavy lumps of ice; but we pushed on, and at nightfall had passed the mountains and emerged into a more inviting country. It was evident, however, that canoe-work was nearly over for the year, but we determined to make one more attempt, as the junction of the Findlay and Parsnip was not far ahead, and there was just a chance that the ice was coming from the Findlay and we might find the Parsnip, up which our course lay, clear enough for navigation. On Tuesday we made the most dangerous day's travel that I ever experienced in a canoe; the river was far too full of ice to handle even a "dug-out" with safety, and we had to make many crossings in the swift current among the running floes. I made it a point that everybody should keep on the same side of the river to assure our all being together in case of accident, and we had several narrow escapes from being nipped. At dinner-time we came in sight of the broken water of the Findlay Rapid, and found the big eddy on the south side of the river completely blocked with ice. We went through the risky manœuvre of skirting the edge of the eddy with the floes whirling round us in the strong running water, and, finding a solid spot, hauled the canoe over the ice to the shore, making a half-mile portage to the foot of the rapid. A very close shave of capsizing filled the canoe with water; but the second attempt at tracking through the swift current and blocks of ice was more successful, and, as the short day was drawing to its close, we were paddling under a high bluff which prevented our using the tracking-line. Here darkness caught us, and our position was perilous in the extreme; the current was so strong that our best pace was required to stem it at all, and many times we had to drift back to avoid collision with the ice that was grinding past us. A couple of hours' hard work brought us to the first spot at which we could effect a landing, but it was no easy matter to carry the cargo up the frozen bank; we secured the canoe as well as we could, and found ourselves on a small flat covered with willows and abundance of firewood. Towards midnight the grinding of the ice became less noticeable and before daylight ceased entirely; the river above us had set fast and further water-travel was impossible. When morning broke we saw the Findlay branch com-

pletely jambed with ice stretching away to the
north-west, and the Parsnip bending sharply to
the south presented a similar appearance.

A glance at our position is not out of place,
and a good map might have saved us from the
serious trouble we afterwards experienced.

Far away in the mountains of British Columbia, in a country little known to the white man
and at no great distance from the Pacific Ocean,
the Findlay River has its source, while the Parsnip rises close under the Rocky Mountains on
their west side, and, skirting the foot-hills, joins
the Findlay at the spot where we now encamped.
Below the junction the stream, already of considerable size and known as the Peace River,
pours through the black rent in the backbone of
the North American continent many thousands
of feet below the summits of the mountains, and
takes its course towards the Arctic Ocean at the
mouth of the great Mackenzie. The most extraordinary feature in this reversion of the laws of
Nature is the extreme tranquillity of the stream
in passing through the main range, for with the
exception of the Findlay and Polpar Rapid, one
at either end of the pass, there is no difficulty in
navigating a canoe. In passing the eastern range
above Hudson's Hope the cañon is rough to the
last degree, and one would expect to find the
same thing among the higher mountains. A third
branch, the Omineca, once a celebrated mining-
camp, joins the Findlay, but is a much smaller

stream. To reach Fort Macleod we had to follow the Parsnip and turn up a tributary branch
known as Macleod's River, draining Macleod's
Lake into the Parsnip.

I had another long conversation with Charlie
and Pat as to the best plan of action, and pointed
out to them that if there was the least doubt
about finding the lake we might still get back to
Hudson's Hope, as by the aid of a few portages
over ice-jambs one can travel down-stream in
company with the floes long after it has become
impossible to force a passage against them, and
when we reached the east end of the pass it would
be easy to walk through the level country. But
both the guides laughed at the idea of their getting lost, and again reminded me of the fact that
only a few weeks before they had come from
Macleod. If we could cross the Parsnip, they
said, we had only to follow the west bank till we
came to the Little River, and then half a day
would take us to the fort; in four days from now,
or five at the latest, we should reach the end of
our journey. The morning of December 4th
was spent in making a scaffold on which to store
my rather bulky cargo, which of course had to
be left with the intention of returning from Fort
Macleod with a dog-sleigh. After dinner we
started on foot, every man carrying his blanket
and a small load of provisions, kettles, and necessaries of various kinds. I decided to take no
gun, as I only had a dozen shot-cartridges left,

and a gun is always an impediment in walking through the woods, although there is a good old saying in the North that men should not part with their guns till the women throw away their babies.

One thing that I thought might cause some trouble was the fact of our having no snow-shoes, and the snow would soon be deep enough to require them. We took all our beans and rice, but left about thirty pounds of flour in a sack on the scaffold, thinking it needlessly heavy to carry, and that it was better to run short for a day or two than overload ourselves and prevent rapid travelling.

The ice was piled up high on the banks, and we began badly by climbing over a steep hill covered with such heavy timber that the pace was slow, and it was night when we came out on the bank of the Parsnip not more than four miles from our last camp. The next day we did rather better, but, getting among burnt timber and deep snow, had many heavy falls. In the evening we found a jamb in the river, and, making rather a risky crossing with the chance of our ice-bridge breaking up at any moment, camped on the Macleod side, thinking that we were now surely safe enough, and the worst thing that could happen might be a little starvation before we reached the fort. Then came two days of fair travelling, sometimes on the ice and sometimes in the woods, but the latter were so thick that it was hard to get through them at all.

I have never seen a river freeze in the remarkable manner that the Parsnip set fast this summer. The first jamb had probably taken place at the junction of the Findlay; the water had backed up till it stood at a higher level than the summer floods, and the gravel beach was deeply submerged.   There was no appearance of shore-ice, as the constant rise and fall in the water prevented a gradual freezing; jambs would form and break up again, and huge blocks of ice were forced on each other in every conceivable position. Often too the ice was flooded, and it was already cold enough to freeze wet feet; the backwaters were full, and the ice on them usually under water or hanging from the banks without support; the shores were fringed with a tangled mass of willows, heavily laden with snow and their roots often standing in water, while behind, rising to the summit of rough broken hills, was the dense pine-growth of the great sub-Arctic forest.

John caused a good deal of delay by not keeping up, and I did not like to leave him far behind, as he was clumsy on the ice, and there were many treacherous spots where black running water showed in strong contrast to the snow, and the gurgle of a swift current suggested an unpleasant ending to the unlucky man who should break through. Everybody carried an axe or a stick to sound the ice, and, excepting near the banks where the water had fallen away from the ice, there were no mishaps. Further delay was caused by our frequently having to light a fire to dry moccasins and keep our feet from freezing.

On the fourth night after abandoning the canoe we camped close to a coffin hung between two trees, as is the fashion of the Siccanees in dealing with their dead; the guide recognised this coffin, and told me we should certainly be at the fort in two days. Beans and rice were finished, but we had flour enough left for another day, and this we baked into bread to save trouble in cooking later on, and on the following day made a fair journey considering the bad state of the ice.

The next morning, after eating our last bite of bread, we were going to try for the fort, and to lighten our load left behind the kettles, for which we had no more use, while some of us were rash enough to leave our blankets; we expcted to be back with the dog-sleigh in a few days, and could then pick up everything.

The water had risen again in the night and the ice was useless for travelling on, so on the guide's advice we left the river on the west bank, and climbing the rough hills walked along the ridge in a south-westerly direction, expecting every hour to fall upon the little river running out of Macleod's Lake. When night caught us we were still in the woods, and, although there was no supper and snow was falling softly, a bright fire and the prospect of reaching the fort in the morning kept us in good spirits enough. I was one of the unfortunates without a blanket, and was glad to see daylight come again and with it a cessation of the snowstorm. During the last few days rabbit-tracks had been frequently seen in the snow and grouse were plentiful, but we had no means of securing game of any kind.

To make as sure as possible of getting food the next day, I sent Murdo and Charlie ahead without loads to make the best of their way to the fort, while Pat and myself would stay by John, who was already in difficulties, and carry the packs.

Starting without breakfast is the worst part of these starving times. The walking for the first two hours was very hard, through a thick growth of young pines rising among the blackened stumps and fallen logs of a burnt forest, up and down steep gullies, with the snow from the branches pouring down our necks, and our loads often bringing us up with a sudden jerk as they stuck between two little trees. John soon gave up his pack, and left it hanging on a bough, where it remains probably till the present day. About mid-day we came to the end of the ridge and looked up the wide valley of the Parsnip. Far below us we could trace its windings, and branching away to the mountains in the west was a stream that Pat instantly declared to be Macleod's River. Towards sundown we lit a fire on a high bank above the stream, and John in a fatuous manner remarked that he recognised the place where he had camped with a boat's crew some years before. We followed the fresh tracks of our advanced party, and turning our backs on the Parsnip walked on good shore-ice till darkness compelled us to camp. I was rather surprised to find that the river was not frozen up and had much more current than I had expected, but, as both John and Pat were quite certain that all was right, I had not the least doubt that we had at last reached Macleod's River and should arrive at the fort in good time the next day.

Another sleepless night gave me plenty of time for reflection while John was comfortably rolled up in a blanket that I had been carrying all day. Four months had passed, and many a hundred miles of lake and river travelled, since David had seen the first star on that summer's night far away in the Barren Ground; now I thought my journey was nearly over, for two hundred miles on snow-shoes from Fort Macleod to Quesnelle, and three hundred miles of waggon-road from Quesnelle to the Canadian Pacific Railway, counted as nothing. It was true that we had not tasted food for two days, and rations had been short for some time past; but it was by no means my first experience of starvation, and to-morrow evening at the latest we should be in the midst of luxury once more. It was satisfactory to think that we had succeeded in forcing our way through the Rocky Mountains in the face of the winter, and were every day approaching a country made temperate by the breezes of the Pacific; already the cedars, to be found only on the west side of the main range, were showing among the pines.

With the first grey light in the east I roused my companions, and we started on shore-ice at a good pace with the prospect of breakfast ahead. Pat broke through shortly after leaving camp, and, as he was afraid of freezing his feet, we lit a fire to dry his moccasins, and the sun was up when we set out again. A couple of hours later we saw a thin blue column of smoke rising straight up into the sky, and a nearer approach showed that it came from the chimney of a cabin hidden in the woods; a cheering sight at first, but directly we reached the trail leading up from the river I knew that something was wrong, and something wrong at such a time meant something very wrong indeed.

I had spent too much of my life among the woods and mountains to be unable to read the easy writing in the snow; two tracks leading up the river late overnight, and the same two tracks quite fresh coming down-stream and turning up the trail. Murdo and Charlie must be in the cabin, and could not have reached the fort; if they had been coming back with supplies they would never have put ashore with starving men so close up. Pushing open the rough door we found them sitting one on each side of a small fire of cedar-chips that were just crackling into a blaze. "Have you been to the fort, Murdo?" I asked, needlessly enough. "No." "Why not? What is the matter?" "Charlie says it is the wrong river; we are lost, like d——d fools."

Murdo had described the situation concisely enough, and I fully realised the awful position we were in; lost and starving in the mountains with no guns to procure food, no snow-shoes with which to travel over the increasing depth of snow, and no clothes to withstand the cold of mid-winter which was already upon us.

There was still a hope, for Charlie was not quite ready to admit that he was mistaken. Our advance party had turned back on seeing a rapid, and even now could not give me any accurate description of this obstacle to navigation; if it was so bad that a scow could not run down, it was obvious that this could not be Macleod's River, for I knew that no portage was necessary to reach the lake. Pat was still sure that he had recognised many places this morning, but could not say anything about the log-cabin; it stood back from the river, and there was a chance that people, passing quickly down-stream, might have missed seeing it when the foliage was thick on the willows. The best plan seemed to first make sure about the rapid, so we started up-stream to inspect it. I was very doubtful of any good result coming from this move, when I saw that the strength of the current increased, and the mountains on each side of the stream grew higher and steeper. Soon we passed a newly-built beaver-house, which certainly was a strange object on the side of a travelled river, and in a couple of hours reached the rapid. Surely this was enough to make anyone turn back; a heavy shute of broken water down which no scow could ever run without being smashed to pieces; even Pat now acknowledged that he was hopelessly lost. A valuable day had been wasted, and the sun was down before we came again to the cabin, where we decided on spending the night. Three days we had been starving, and it was fully time to take the first steps by which men in our desperate position seek to maintain life as long as possible. A thorough search in the shanty produced nothing of value but an old lard-tin which would serve as a kettle; there were many empty boxes, labelled with enticing names and pictures of canned fruit and of fat cattle that had been converted into "Armour's Preserved Beef" at Kansas City, Missouri; a large number of rotten sacks, marked "Oregon Flour Patent Roller Process," showed that someone had spent a winter here, and an iron bottle containing a little quicksilver proved that he had been a miner by occupation. A board, with a notice in pencil that two men, whose names I forget, had arrived here from Sandy Bar in a day and a half, conveyed no meaning to us.

Among the necessary articles that we had been carrying was a large piece of dressed moose-skin for mending moccasins, and this seemed the most edible thing we could find; five small strips, three inches in length and an inch broad, were cut off and put into the lard-tin to boil for supper. We discovered Labrador tea growing in the woods, and made a brew with the leaves as soon as we thought the moose-skin was soft enough to eat. Rabbit-snares were made by unravelling a piece of string and set in the runs, but after trying this plan on several nights not a rabbit was caught, though we sometimes had the mortification of finding a broken snare. After supper of moose-skin and Labrador tea we felt in better spirits, and with a good fire and a pipe of tobacco discussed our position seriously enough.

Euclid, when he found himself incapable of proving that any particular angle or line was the exact size that he desired, had a habit of supposing it to be of some other magnitude, and by enlarging upon the absurdity of this supposition so completely puzzled the aspiring student that he was glad to admit any statement that the inventor of the proposition suggested. This does well enough on paper, but starving men have no time to put this plan to the test of practice, and when they find that a river is not the one they supposed it to be are at a loss to tell what stream it really is.

Charlie, Pat, and John, who had all been to Macleod's Lake before, told me frequently that they had never heard of any river coming into the Parsnip on the west side between the Findlay and Macleod's River. Now, in a boating journey the talk is always of points and rivers, and the mouth of any tributary is always commented upon, so it seemed unlikely that they should have passed by this large stream without noticing it; nor had they heard of any miner's cabin, which must certainly have been spoken of in a country where houses are scarce. There was a possibility that we had come too far and missed the mouth of Macleod's River, for we had sometimes travelled on the east side of the Parsnip to take advantage of better ice or a thinner growth of timber, and I had heard David say that the Little River was not easy for a stranger to find. In any case it was better to retrace our steps to the mouth of the stream that we had been following, to see if our guides could recognise any landmark, for the hills were conspicuous and sometimes of remarkable shape.

At daylight on December 10th we left the cabin and made tracks down-stream, taking with us the lard-tin in which we had boiled more moose-skin for breakfast. So far we had lost no strength and, with the exception of John, who was always behind, were going strong and well.

It was late in the afternoon when we reached the river and once again stood on the bank of the Parsnip. Across on the east side rose a high-cut bank of yellow clay, a mark that any one should recognise who had ever seen it before; but Charlie and Pat both put on a hopeless blank expression when I asked them if they knew the place. No, they said, they had never seen it before in their lives. Six weeks before they had passed right under that cut bank in a scow, and less than forty miles up-stream would have taken us to the fort if we had only known it. These men were a half-breed and an Indian, supposed to be gifted with that extraordinary instinct of finding their way in all circumstances which is denied to the white man. John was just as much to blame, although it was some years ago that he travelled down the Parsnip; long afterwards, when all the trouble was over, he confided to me, as an excuse for his ignorance, that he had been very drunk when he left Macleod and was unable to make any accurate observations as to courses and distances.

There was nothing to be done but turn down the Parsnip again and keep a bright look-out for the mouth of the little river, in case we had passed it. The ice was too much flooded to walk on, and we camped high up on the mountain-side in heavy falling snow. Another misfortune befell us here; the bottom of the lard-tin was burnt out during the process of melting snow, and we had to give up the small comfort of moose-skin and wild tea. Murdo and myself spent a wretched night cowering over the fire with the snow falling down our backs, for we were still without blankets; daylight saw us struggling through the thick growth of young pines and an increased depth of snow, till at noon, when everybody was thoroughly exhausted and John had nearly given up all hope, we found ourselves stopped on the side-hill by a series of bluffs which no one felt equal to scaling. Fifteen hundred feet below us lay the river, and as a desperate alternative we descended the mountain, with many bruises from stumbling over logs hidden by the snow, to find that the water had fallen in the night, and the ice, though rough in the extreme, was dry enough to travel on. After the night had closed down over the forest we reached the place where the kettles and blankets had been left, and things looked a little brighter with the prospect of tea and a night's sleep; but we knew now that Fort Macleod must lie behind us, although there was little inducement to make another attempt to reach it with such untrustworthy guides. Our only chance of life was to reach the entrance of the Peace River Pass, where thirty pounds of flour lay on a rough scaffold exposed to the mercy of the wolverines!

CHAPTER XVI

Snow fell again in the night and increased our difficulties. For a day and a half we forced our way, sometimes on rough ice and sometimes through the thick willow bushes, with frequent rests as exhaustion overtook us, till we again saw the Siccanee coffin hung in the trees. Here we found the flour-sack that had been thrown away on our up-stream journey, and scraped off perhaps half a pound of flour which had stuck to the sack when wet. At the same time a mouse was caught in the snow, and, with no further preparation than singeing off the hair, was cut into strips and boiled with the flour into a thin soup. Every man carried a tin cup in his belt, so a careful distribution of the precious soup was made, and the last pipe of tobacco smoked; we certainly derived a little strength from this unexpected supply, and our spirits improved greatly for a short time.

The weather now turned colder and its increased severity told on us heavily, for our clothes were torn to rags by pushing through the woods, and a starving man through loss of flesh always feels the cold more severely than a man in good condition. We often had to light a fire to prevent our feet from freezing when wet from walking on flooded ice or breaking through near the shore. The river was still open in places and continually altering its level. John was always far behind, and I expected to see him drop at any time; but he had the advantage of starting fatter than the rest of us, and took good care of himself, always hanging in the rear and coming into camp when the labour of throwing out the snow and getting wood was accomplished. Never once during the whole of this march did he go ahead to break a trail through the snow, which is of course the most fatiguing work of all.

A little before sundown on December 17th, the tenth day without eating anything but small scraps of moose-skin and the soup at the coffin-camp, we staggered among huge blocks of ice, passed the junction of the Findlay, and soon afterwards arrived at the *cache*. It was an anxious moment as I crawled up the frozen bank and waded through the snow to the scaffold; no wolverine tracks were to be seen, and the flour was lying untouched. Camp was made, a kettle of thick paste boiled, and a cupful eaten every half-hour to prevent any ill effects from straining the weakened organs of the digestion.

But we were by no means out of our difficulties yet. Thirty pounds of flour, without meat, is the ordinary amount that would be given to five men for two days, without taking into account the fact that we had been starving for a long time and were now reduced to skeletons. Before us was the main range of the Rocky Mountains; the snow would be drifted deep in the narrow pass, and travel would be slow, if indeed we got through at all. Another serious trouble was the state of our moccasins; as they wore out we had eaten them, and were now wearing rough apologies for shoes which we had made out of the moose-skin that was quickly getting very small under the constant demands made upon it for various purposes.

In the morning I measured the flour very carefully with a cup into different loads, so that I might be able to keep account of the quantity that was used, and, taking a gun and what few cartridges were left, we started for Tom Barrow's cabin, which we hoped to be able to reach in three or four days if the ice should prove good. In this we were terribly disappointed, for at the end of the second day, after wading through deep snow, and frequently putting ashore to light a fire on account of the intense cold, we camped but a short distance below the Findlay Rapid. John's feet were frozen already, and all of us were touched in the face; there was always great difficulty in lighting a match with numbed fingers, but birch-bark was plentiful, and being readily inflammable was nearly sure to blaze up at once. Our only remaining axe was almost useless from having been carelessly left for a night in the fire. Much of the snow had drifted off the ice and was lying three and four feet deep on the banks, increasing the labour of making camp and picking up firewood, for we were too weak to do any effectual chopping even if our axe had been in good condition. Without snow-shoes it was impossible to walk through the forest in the hope of finding grouse; and, after one or two efforts, the exertion of wading waist-deep through snow that reached to the belt was found too great, and the attempt was abandoned.

On the third day a blizzard swept through the pass, completely obscuring the opposite bank of the river, which was here quite narrow. We attempted to travel against it, but found our faces were frozen before going a quarter of a mile. Murdo and myself had always to light the matches, as the other men suffered more from the cold than we did; I knew that my hands were already useless, and that if we continued to force our way against the storm there would be little chance of starting a fire further on. I gave orders to turn back for the camp, and we spent the short day in keeping up the fire that was still burning. Besides the drift, a gust of wind would often send down the masses of snow that had gathered on the branches, putting out our little blaze and filling up the hole that we had dug in the snow, while the boughs themselves often fell dangerously close to the camp. The allowance of flour was cut down to two cupfuls among five men, and this was eaten in the form of paste, which we found more satisfying than bread. The Labrador tea was buried deep under the snow, and from this time no more was obtained.

The shortening of rations produced grumbling in the camp, especially from John, who declared that it was better to eat well while the little flour lasted, to gain strength to take us to the trading-post. Murdo was more sensible in this respect, but was beginning to lose the full use of his head, and, besides the strong aversion he had always shown to John, now developed a passionate hatred to Charlie and Pat, whom rightly enough he held responsible for our position. This ill-feeling among the various members of our party was increased tenfold by an episode which took place on the following day. The morning was very cold but with less wind, and, although our faces froze again, we pushed on for an hour or two and then made a fire on the bank. Here we left the Indian and half-breed drying their moccasins, and continued travelling down stream to make a camp for the mid-day halt, knowing that the others could catch us up easily with the advantage of our road through the snow; this they did just as our fire was blazing up. I asked Charlie for his flour, as so far we had not used any from his load, but when he produced it there was not more than a cupful left in the bag. I had given him five pounds of flour to carry, and at once knew that our guides, who had caused all the trouble, had now been guilty of stealing food, when our lives depended on the scanty store that we had picked up at the *cache*. For this offence, at such a time, there is but one punishment: a man on the point of starving to death cares little whether you cut off the dollar a day that he is earning or not; a blow struck would have fired the train of discontent that was ready to explode; —the only course open to me, if the offenders were to be punished at all, was to put an end to them both with the shot-gun that I carried. For a long time I debated this question while a few spoonfuls of flour were boiled for dinner, and finally decided to let matters take their course; there were still seven or eight pounds of flour left, and by further reduction of rations we might keep ourselves alive for a few more days; the weather might be warmer, the ice less rough, and the snowfall lighter if we could reach the far end of the pass, but at present things looked very black indeed. Flesh and strength were failing rapidly; this loss of provisions would tell heavily, and travelling through the gloomy pass under the high mountains was more laborious than words can describe. It was no good refusing to give the thieves their share of rations, as this might induce them to strike a blow in the night, and deal us the death that they themselves deserved; but the question might still have to be decided, in case of a man dropping, whether his life should be sacrificed and the offenders allowed to go free. If affairs came to the point which everything seemed to indicate, there could now be no fair drawing of lots to see who should die that the survivors might support themselves by the last resource of all.

The weather continued cold, and frozen feet caused many delays; there was no chance here to treat a frost-bite by the tender methods of thawing with snow and rubbing with oil that are practised in civilization, but feet were thrust into a blazing fire and allowed to blister as they would. John and Charlie suffered greatly from this cause, and their pain in walking was much increased. These delays were serious, for although the Peace River Pass lies as far to the south as the 56th parallel of latitude the days were at their shortest.

For three more days we continued wading through the snowdrifts, and crawling over rough ice, continually changing our leader, till on December 24th we were stopped by another blizzard, and forced to lie in camp all day. Rations were by this time cut down to a spoonful of flour in the morning and a strip of moose-skin at night for each man. Not more than a pound of flour was left, and the storm, far too fierce for such wretched skeletons to face, might continue for several days. Our situation seemed utterly hopeless as we crouched over the fire that was with difficulty maintained, and apparently the end had come. There was none of the kindly sympathy for companions in misfortune which men who share a common danger should have: a mutual distrust was prevalent; hatred and the wolfish madness of hunger ruled the camp; and to this day I cannot understand how it was that the fatal spark was never struck, and no tragedy of murder and cannibalism enacted on the banks of that ice-bound river without witnesses save the great silent mountains and the God who made them.

Christmas Day brought rather better weather, although snow was still falling quietly, and, finding open water in the river with shore-ice on which the snow was not so deep as usual, there was a great improvement in our case. An accident, however, occurred which nearly put an end to two of the party. Charlie and Pat, who were leading at the time, ventured too near the edge of the open water and broke through, not only to the knees or waist, as had so often happened, but over their heads in deep water with a strong current, and we had some trouble in pulling them out. It was very important that we should make a fire at once, as the temperature was many degrees below zero, and the men drenched to the skin began to freeze directly. The accident had taken place under a long steep bluff, and from where we stood no firewood was to be seen on our side of the river within a couple of miles. By the greatest good fortune, on turning a point we found a huge tree that had fallen over the

cliff and lay on the beach smashed up into firewood, as if it had been prepared specially for our
use. A blaze was soon started, and the two half-
drowned men left to dry themselves. The most
unfortunate part of the affair was the wetting
of the matches which they carried. I had divided these precious articles among the men in
case of accidents of this kind, for without fire
we should have had no chance of saving our
lives; as it turned out we never ran short of
matches and never once missed making fire, although there was often trouble in procuring
wood; we were far too weak to handle a big log,
but usually found a dead cotton-wood tree, from
which the bark is easily pulled and makes the
best of fires.

In the afternoon we passed the Polpar Rapid,
which was completely frozen up, and emerging
from the pass caught the first sight of the sun,
that had been hidden from us for many days by
the high mountains. The ice below the rapid continued fairly good till nightfall, when we were
forced to camp, although the moon was full and
we tried to travel by her light. But although
it was easy enough to see close ahead, it was impossible to pick out the line of the best ice, and
the labour of travelling was increased by having
to force our way through drifts and piled-up ice
that we might have avoided in daylight.

Soon after leaving camp on the following
morning a grouse was killed, and I think even

this little nourishment helped us a great deal to accomplish our task of reaching the trading-post; this was the only grouse we had seen since we left the *cache,* although on the up-stream journey birds had been plentiful enough. The ice was still rough at times, but in some places the river was open and good shore-ice made the walking easy; the weather was much warmer, with bright sunshine, and there was no danger of freezing our feet. At dark camp was made within a day's travel of Barrow's house, if only we had strength enough to reach it.

The long night passed away, and just before daylight we were staggering among the blocks of ice in a scattered line. There was always difficulty in starting from the camp, for there was a certain amount of comfort in lying in our blankets, and nobody was anxious to try whether he could still stand upright or not. Our inclination during the worst time was to lie down and make no further effort, but after walking half an hour we usually found ourselves in better spirits. Soon after coming out on the ice, I looked back to see how John was travelling, and noticed that he was down. Charlie, who had been behind with him, came up and said that John could travel no longer and intended to stay where he was. I stopped all the men, but Charlie tried to push by me and said that he would not wait for anyone. For the first time I had to use threats to ensure my orders being carried

out, and taking the gun from my shoulder let
Charlie plainly see that I meant to shoot him if
he did not obey. This quickly brought him to
his senses, and John came up very slowly. He
wanted someone to stay with him and trust to
the others sending back provisions, but I would
not listen to this proposal. I told him that it
was only want of courage that prevented him
making any further effort; he was as strong as
the rest of us, and, if he would try, could keep up
quite easily; if he would come on till we reached
the place where we had had dinner on the second
day out with the canoe, we would make him a
camp and leave all our blankets, so that he might
have a chance of keeping himself alive till relief came. On rounding a point we saw open
water ahead, and John, although far behind,
went far better on the smooth ice, and eventually came in not more than an hour after us.
At noon the Bull's Head was in sight, and we
could see the line of hills at the foot of which
Barrow's house lay. The pace was fast for men
in our condition, but we kept up a steady walk,
leaving our blankets when there seemed a certainty of reaching the house that night. The
sun was down when we passed the old shanty in
which we had camped for a night on the way up,
and by moonlight we travelled on, following
close to the edge of the open water and taking
little precaution to test the strength of the ice.
Soon the roar of the cañon was heard, and at

seven o'clock we crawled up the steep bank and stood in front of the cabin. I pushed open the door, and shall never forget the expression of horror that came over the faces of the occupants when they recognised us. We had become used to the hungry eyes and wasted forms, as our misery had come on us gradually, but to a man who had seen us starting out thirty-two days before in full health the change in our appearance must have been terrible. There was no doubt that we were very near the point of death. For my own part I felt a dull aching in the left side of my head; I was blind in the left eye and deaf in the left ear; there was a sharp pain on each side just below the ribs; but my legs, though not well under control, were still strong. We had all completely lost the use of our voices, and suffered greatly from the cracking of the skin on hands and feet, which always results from starving in cold weather; to say that we were thin conveys no idea of our miserable condition. It is needless to go into the details of our recovery; but under Barrow's careful nursing, and restrictions as to the quantity of food allowed, we all came back to health, although for some days our lives were hanging in the balance.

I can never sufficiently thank Tom Barrow for his kind behaviour on this occasion. Of course, everybody is sorry for starving people; but it is rather a strain on this sympathy to have to look after five men so near to death in a small cabin among the Rocky Mountains, with such slender supplies as had been left for a winter's rations for two people. Without a murmur he shared his blankets and his provisions, although he knew that there was a good chance of starving himself in the spring.

Barrow told us directly where we had made our mistake. The river we had turned up was Nation River, and the log-cabin had been occupied some years before by a party of miners, but very little gold had been taken out. Some distance up Nation River was the old trail to the Omineca mining-camp; but of course we should not have known what trail it was if we had found it. The mouth of the Nation River and the yellow cut bank Barrow remembered perfectly, and said there had been much talk about these landmarks on the way down; it seems inexplicable that three men, who had been over the route before, should have made the mistake that so nearly cost us our lives. If we had followed up the Parsnip beyond the mouth of Nation River we should have reached Macleod's Lake on December 12th at latest with only a few days' starvation, and avoided all the misery that continued till the 27th of that month.

In a week communication was opened with Hudson's Hope, and Walter Macdonald did everything he could to help us; but the same thing had happened to him. A band of Beaver

Indians had been caught by starvation at the mouth of the Pine River Pass, and had suffered the same experiences as ourselves. Many had been left by the way, but I think there were no deaths, as provisions were sent out so soon as the news reached Baptiste at Moberley's Lake.

At the end of a fortnight everybody was well enough to travel; and to ease the strain on provisions I sent Murdo, John, and Charlie to Lesser Slave Lake, where they could get fish to support them, and spare the resources of the upper river posts. But even now these men could not travel together, although they had full rations and nothing to quarrel about. Murdo reached the Lesser Slave Lake alone, John arriving several days later, and I found Charlie at Dunvegan, where he had already distinguished himself by robbing from the priest's trading-store. A thorough blackguard was Charlie, and it would have been little loss to the world in general if he had left his bones under the snow in the Peace River Pass; he had begun his voyage badly by stealing fifty dollars from his mother at Quesnelle, and there were several other offences for which the police had hunted him away from the borders of civilization. Pat was to stay for the winter with Barrow, and as soon as Baptiste had made us snow-shoes we pottered about in the woods together, hunting grouse and rabbits, and had soon entirely recovered our strength.

I have never heard any satisfactory explanation of the gradual increase and sudden dying out of the rabbits and lynx, which takes place every seven years throughout the North. Starting from the few survivors of the last epidemic, the numbers increase slowly every season, till in the sixth year the whole country is so overrun with them that a man can travel anywhere with no further provision than shot-gun and snares. Then the disease breaks out, dead bodies are found all through the woods, and scarcely a living rabbit or lynx is to be seen. The autumn of 1885 I spent on the head-waters of the Athabasca, at the east end of the Tête Jaune Pass; the rabbits were then at their height and as plentiful as I ever saw them in England. 1892 will be the next big rabbit-year; but after that famine is sure to be rife on Peace River, as it is harder every year to kill moose, and for the last two or three years the rabbit-snares have kept many an Indian from starvation. This rabbit-question is an important one to consider before starting on an exploration trip in the Peace River country, as in the good seasons there is no danger of running short of provisions.

One day, as we were setting snares together, Pat told me the story of the stolen flour. They had stayed behind to dry their moccasins, and Charlie had explained to Pat that I was keeping the flour for the use of the white men, and that their only chance of getting any was to help themselves; Pat had objected at first, but afterwards gave way when he saw Charlie cooking the flour, and they had eaten about four pounds between them. Judging from Charlie's character I am inclined to believe the story, as Pat in all other respects had behaved well under the pressure of hardship, and had always done more than his share of work in making camp and breaking the trail.

While staying at Hudson's Hope, Macdonald and I walked over to Moberley's Lake, twelve miles to the south, to pay old Baptiste a visit. The house stands within view of the big peaks of the Rockies close to the edge of the lake, but the appearance of the country is rather spoilt by the abundant traces of forest fires that have taken place of late years. The lake is a beautiful sheet of water, ten miles in length, drained by the Pine River, which falls into the Peace a short distance above Fort St. John. Baptiste has a fruitful potato-patch, and his women were catching plenty of rabbits; there was moose-pemmican, too, and dried meat, for the Fall hunt had been successful. The Iroquois gave me a pair of snow-shoes ornamented with tassels of coloured wool, as well as a pair of beaded moccasins which he made me promise not to eat, and came with us to the fort to see us off.

CHAPTER XVII

It was towards the end of January, 1891, that I left Hudson's Hope for Edmonton, a distance of six hundred miles, giving up all further attempt to reach Macleod's Lake. A son of Mr. Brick, of Smoky River, turned up just before I started, and promised to go with Pat to my *cache* at the junction of the Findlay and Parsnip when the days grew long in spring. The rough ice would then be covered with deep snow, and with snow-shoes and hand-sleighs it would be easy to bring away the guns, journals, and many other articles that I had been obliged to abandon.

Two days and a half took me to St. John's, and after a week's stay there a dog-train, carrying the winter packet, arrived, and I took this chance of getting to Dunvegan. Alick Kennedy, one of the very best half-breed *voyageurs* in Canada, was in charge of the packet. The distances this man has been known to run in a day would hardly be credited in a land where people travel by railways and steamboats: moreover, he is a pleasant companion to travel with; his conversation is interesting, and entirely free from the boasting which most of the half-breeds indulge in. Alick was captain of a boat-brigade on the

Arrival of the Dog Train

Nile; and if all the Canadian contingent had been of his stamp instead of the Winnipeg loafers, who were too worthless to get employment in their own country, a different story might have been told of the behaviour of the *voyageurs* on the march to Khartoum.

Five days took us to Dunvegan, where I again met Mr. Macdonald, and travelled with him to the Lesser Slave Lake. From Dunvegan we made the portage straight to Smoky River, crossing a pretty prairie country and camping a night at Old Wives' Lake, where Mr. Brick winters some of his cattle. With a splendid track along the waggon-road, we made the ninety miles to the Lesser Slave Lake in two days, and, judging from the number of people and houses, we seemed to have reached civilization already. Besides the Hudson's Bay establishment, the missions and the buildings of the free-traders, many half-breeds have houses scattered along the lake, and devote part of their attention to raising horses and cattle, though of course whitefish are the main support of life. A favourite haunt for wildfowl is this lake in spring and autumn, but big game and fur have been nearly killed out by the large population, and most of the Indian trade is done at the out-posts nearer to the hunting-grounds.

I spent several days at the fort, being well treated as usual, and February was nearly finished when I started with Mr. Frank Hardistay on my last journey with dogs. The Lesser Slave Lake is about seventy miles in length, and covering this distance easily in two days we travelled down the Little Slave River which leaves the east end of the lake. A good deal of labour has been expended in blasting rocks out of the channel of this river, to enable the steamer from the Athabasca landing to reach the lake, and so avoid the expense of building boats and engaging crews to transport the Peace River cargo, but so far these efforts have proved unsuccessful.

I think we followed the course of this stream about twenty miles, then dived into the thick pine-forest on the east bank, and making a twelve-mile portage came out on the Athabasca River, seventy miles above the landing at the end of the waggon-road from Edmonton. The Athabasca has here the same monotonous look that one becomes so tired of in its lower reaches. When a point was rounded another point exactly similar showed three or four miles ahead, and this continued till we reached the landing, in clear cold weather, on March 3rd; three days later our dogs, bearing the smartest of dog-cloths and with sleigh-bells ringing merrily, rattled into Edmonton, and the wild free life of the last twenty months was over.

The excitement that the arrival of a stranger never fails to create at a lonely Northern fort is rather apt to give that stranger an exaggerated

idea of his own importance; but when I reached
Edmonton I at once realised that there are many
people in the world who have ideas beyond musk-
ox and caribou, dog-sleighs and snow-shoes. An
election was at its height to decide who should
have the honour of representing the territory of
Alberta at Ottawa. Edmonton had been drink-
ing, although it is supposed to keep strictly to
the rules of the Prohibition Act, and before I
had been an hour in the town I found myself
in the midst of a free fight. I was unfortunate
in not knowing the names of the candidates, or
what policy they represented, and as I could give
no clear account as to what I had done with my
vote, I was roughly used by both sides and was
glad to escape to the less boisterous hospitality
of the Hudson's Bay Fort.

There were still two hundred miles of snow-
covered prairie to be crossed to reach Calgary,
but with horses to drag our sleigh, and a house
to sleep in every night, there could be little hardship in the journey. At the crossing of the Red
Deer we saw the iron rails that had already
pushed far out towards Edmonton, but work had
ceased for the winter and no trains were running. As we travelled south the snow became
less every day, till we were forced to change our
runners for wheels when still sixty miles from
Calgary. Late in the evening of March 15th
the whistle of a locomotive told me, more plainly
than anything I had yet heard, that it was time

to pull myself together and take up the common-
place life of civilization; a few more miles of
level country, down a steep pitch or two, across
the frozen stream of the Elbow, and close ahead
the lights of Calgary were blinking over the
prairie.

I am writing these concluding lines in a fashionable garret off St. James's Street. Close at
hand are all the luxuries that only ultra-civiliza-
tion can give, and these luxuries are to be obtained by the simple method of handing over
an adequate number of coins of the realm; there
is no necessity to shoulder your gun and tramp
many weary miles on snow-shoes before you get
even a sight of your dinner in its raw state. But
surely we carry this civilization too far, and are
in danger of warping our natural instincts by
too close observance of the rules that some mysterious force obliges us to follow when we herd
together in big cities. Very emblematical of this
warping process are the shiny black boots into
which we squeeze our feet when we throw away
the moccasin of freedom; as they gall and pinch
the unaccustomed foot, so does the dread of our
friends' opinion gall and pinch our minds till
they become narrow, out of shape, and unable
to discriminate between reality and semblance.
A dweller in cities is too wrapped up in the
works of man to have much respect left for the
works of God, and to him the loneliness of forest

Edmonton

and mountain, lake and river, must ever appear but a weary desolation. But there are many sportsmen who love to be alone with Nature and the animals far from their fellow-men, and as this book is intended solely for the sportsman, a few words of advice to anyone who is anxious to hunt the musk-ox may not be out of place.

I am not quite sure that Fort Resolution is the best point to start from. Fort Rae, on the north arm of the Great Slave Lake, lies nearer the Barren Ground, and the Dog-Ribs are said to be more amenable to reason than the Yellow Knives, while the distance to travel through a woodless country is shorter. Fort Good Hope, on the Lower Mackenzie, would be another good spot to make headquarters; but there is less certainty of finding the caribou in that neighbourhood, and without the caribou there is little chance of reaching the musk-ox. It is not the slightest use starting from a post with the theory that musk-ox can be killed in so many days, and that, by taking a load of provisions sufficient to last for the same length of time, a successful hunt will be made. The only plan is to work your way up slowly, to stay among the caribou in the autumn, and kill and *cache* meat whenever an opportunity offers, ready for a rush on the first snow. Remember, too, when provisions get scarce, as they certainly will at some time or other, the country ahead is as big as the country behind, and the best chance lies in pushing on. To turn back may prove fatal, when another day's travel may put you in a land of plenty. It is possible to reach the hunting-ground and return to Fort Resolution with a canoe in the summer, but the robes are then worthless, and the whole sport savours too much of covert-shooting in July. Make quite sure before you start that you are determined to push on through everything, as even the Great Slave Lake is far to go on an unsuccessful errand. Here, in London, in front of a good fire at the club and under the influence of a good din-ner, it is easy enough to kill musk-ox and make long night-marches on snow-shoes by the flashes of the Northern Lights; but the test of practice takes off some of the enjoyment.

A year has slipped away since our winter journey through the Peace River Pass. Young Brick kept his promise of getting the *cache* right well, and a couple of months ago my jour-nals arrived in England, so that I have been able to put together this rough record of my Northern travels. On looking back one remem-bers only the good times, when meat was plenti-ful and a huge fire lit up the snow on the spruce trees; misery and starvation are forgotten as soon as they are over, and even now, in the midst of the luxury of civilization, at times I have a longing to pitch my lodge once more at the edge of the Barren Ground, to see the musk-ox standing on the snowdrift and the fat caribou falling to the crack of the rifle, to hear the ptarmigan crowing among the little pines as the sun goes down over a frozen lake and the glory of an Arctic night commences.

To the man who is not a lover of Nature in all her moods the Barren Ground must always be a howling, desolate wilderness; but for my part, I can understand the feeling that prompted Saltatha's answer to the worthy priest, who was explaining to him the beauties of Heaven. "My father, you have spoken well; you have told me that Heaven is very beautiful; tell me now one thing more. Is it more beautiful than the country of the musk-ox in summer, when sometimes the mist blows over the lakes, and sometimes the water is blue, and the loons cry very often? That is beautiful; and if Heaven is still more beautiful, my heart will be glad, and I shall be content to rest there till I am very old."

APPENDIX I

I AM much indebted to Professor Dawson, of the Dominion Geological Survey Department, for his kind permission to publish the following paper on the Unexplored Regions of Canada. It shows more plainly than any words of mine could tell how much yet remains to be done before this great portion of the British Empire is known as it ought to be.

ON SOME OF THE LARGER UNEXPLORED REGIONS OF CANADA.

(By G. M. DAWSON, D.S., Assoc. R.S.M., F.G.S., F.R.S.C.)

If on reading the title of the paper which I had promised to contribute to the Ottawa Field Naturalists' Club, any one should have supposed it to be my intention to endeavour to describe or forecast the character of the unexplored areas mentioned, I must, in the first place, disclaim any such intention. The very existence of large regions of which little or nothing is known, is of course stimulating to a fertile imagination, ready to picture to itself undiscovered "golden cities a thousand leagues deep in Cathay," but such unscientific use of the imagination is far removed from the position of sober seriousness, in which I ask your attention to the facts which I have to present.

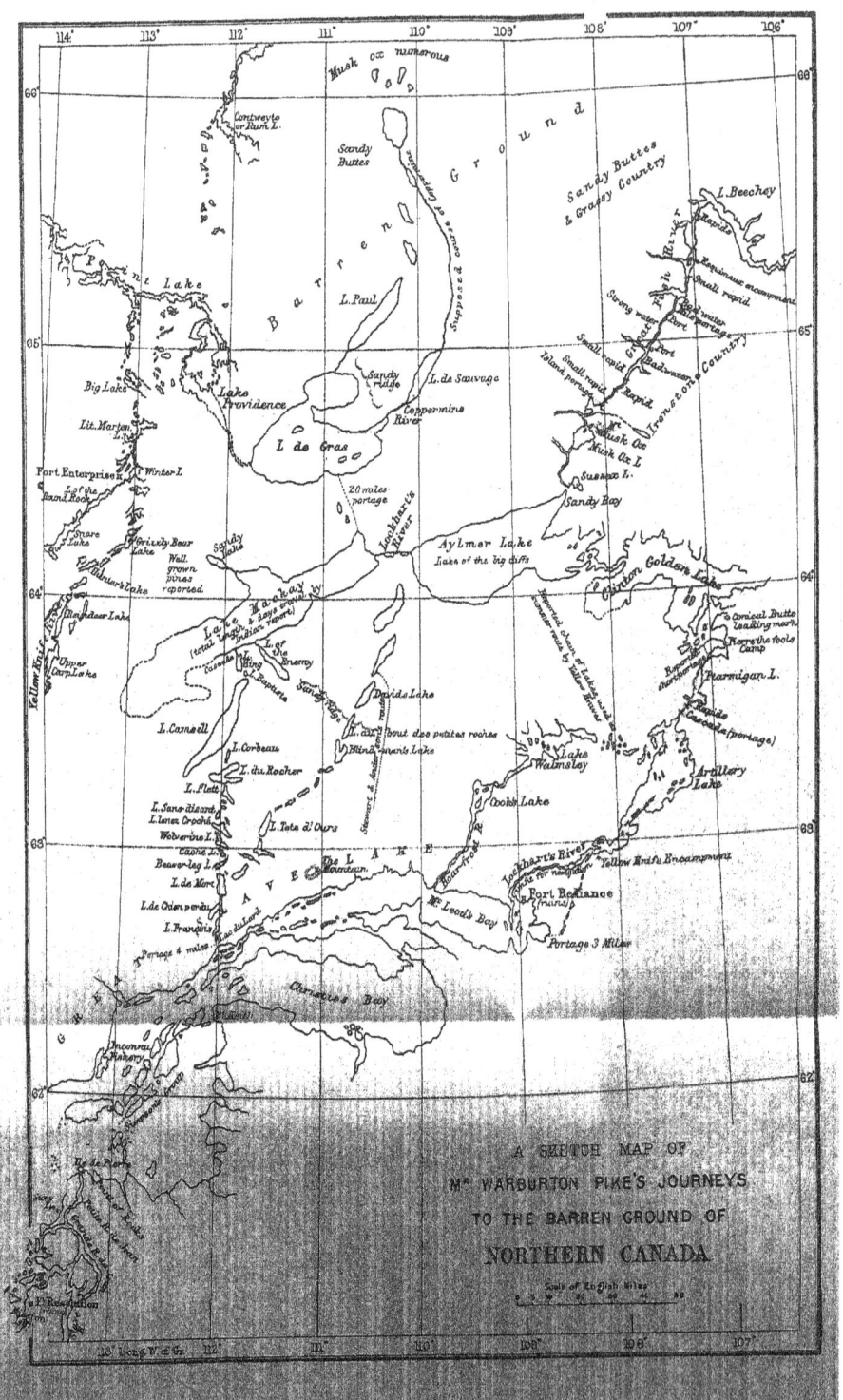

A SKETCH MAP OF
Mr WARBURTON PIKE'S JOURNEYS
TO THE BARREN GROUND OF
NORTHERN CANADA

Scale of English Miles

Fortunately, or unfortunately, as we may happen to regard it, the tendency of our time is all in the direction of laying bare to inspection and open to exploitation all parts, however remote, of this comparatively small world in which we live, and though the explorer himself may be impelled by a certain romanticism in overcoming difficulties or even dangers met with in the execution of his task, his steps are surely and closely followed by the trader, the lumberer, or the agriculturalist, and not long after these comes the builder of railways with his iron road. It is, therefore, rather from the point of view of practical utility than from any other, that an appeal must be made to the public or to the Government for the further extension of explorations, and my main purpose in addressing you to-night is to make such an appeal, and to show cause, if possible, for the exploration of such considerable portions of Canada as still remain almost or altogether unmapped.

What I have to say, in fact, on this subject resolves itself chiefly into remarks on the map exhibited here, upon which the unexplored areas to which I am about to refer are clearly depicted in such a manner, I believe, as almost to speak for themselves.

It is very commonly supposed, even in Canada, but to a greater extent elsewhere, that all parts of the Dominion are now so well known that exploration, in the true sense of the term, may be considered as a thing of the past. This depends largely upon the fact that the maps of the country generally examined are upon a very small scale, and that upon such maps no vast areas yet remain upon which rivers, lakes, mountains, or other features are not depicted. If, however, we take the trouble to enquire more closely into this, and consult perhaps one of the geographers whose maps we have examined, asking such awkward questions as may occur to us on the sources of information for this region or that, we may probably by him be referred to another and older map, and so on till we find in the end that the whole topographical fabric of large parts of all these maps rests upon information of the vaguest kind.

Of most of the large areas marked upon the map here shown, this is absolutely true, and the interests of knowledge with respect to these would be better subserved if such areas were left entirely blank, or, at least, if all the geographical features drawn upon them appeared in broken lines, in such a way as to show that none of them are certain. In other regions, the main geographical outlines, such as the courses of the larger rivers, are indicated approximately, with such accuracy as may be possible from accounts or itineraries derived from travellers or from officers of the Hudson's Bay Company; or from the descriptions or rough sketches of Indians or other persons by whom the region has been traversed, but who have been unprovided with instruments of any kind and whose knowledge of the country has been incidentally obtained.

There is, in the case of such partially explored regions, more excuse for the delineation of the main features on our maps, as these may be useful in imparting general information of a more or less inexact kind. We can scarcely, however, admit that such regions have been explored in any true sense of that term, while they are certainly unsurveyed, and very little confidence can be placed in maps of this kind as guides in travel. When, ten years ago, I struck across from Fort Macleod, on the west side of the Rocky Mountains, with the purpose of reaching Fort Dunvegan on the Peace, through a country densely forested and without trails or tracks of any kind, I had so much confidence in the existing maps of that region as to assume that Dunvegan was at least approximately correct in position on them. As often as possible I took observations for latitude, and each night worked out our position by latitude and departure, till at a certain point I was about to turn off to the north of the line previously followed with the confident anticipation of finding Dunvegan. Just here, very fortunately, we fell in with some Indians, and though our means of communicating with them were very imperfect, we gathered enough to lead us to accept the guidance of one of them, who promised to lead us to the fort, but took an entirely different direction from that I had proposed taking. He was right, but Dunvegan proved to be, as shown on the maps, nearly forty miles west of its real position. Fortunately no very great importance attached to our reaching Dunvegan on a given day, but none the less, this practical experience proved to me very conclusively the desirability of showing features in broken lines, or otherwise indicating their uncertainty when they have not been properly fixed.

It must be confessed, however, that most of the travellers ordinarily to be found in these unexplored regions, being Indians or hunters, traders and others travelling under the guidance of Indians, do not

depend on the latitudes and longitudes of places, or
on the respective bearings of one place from another. The Indians follow routes with which they
have been familiar since childhood, or, when beyond the boundaries of their own particular region
of country, go by land-marks, such as mountains,
lakes, and rivers, which have been described to them
by their neighbours. Their memory in this respect
is remarkable; but it must be remembered that
among their principal subjects of conversation when
sitting about the camp-fire are the distances in day's
journeys from place to place, the routes which they
have followed or have known others to follow, the
difficulties to be encountered on these, the points at
which food of different kinds may be obtained, and
the features which strike them as being remarkable
in the country traversed. Returning, however, from
this digression, which began with the statement that
accurate maps of such regions as are at present
merely traversed by traders and Indians, are not
imperative from the point of view of such travellers, it may with confidence be affirmed that such
maps and explorations upon which they are based
are absolutely essential to civilized society, to show
in the first place what the natural resources of these
regions are and how they may be utilized, in the
second by what highways such regions may be most
easily reached.

A glance at the map will show, that while many
of the larger unexplored areas may be affirmed to
lie to the north of the limit of profitable agriculture,
considerable regions situated to the south of this
limit still await examination. Large districts, again,
in which no farmer will ever voluntarily settle, may

afford timber which the world will be glad to get when the white pine of our nearer forests shall become more nearly exhausted, while, with respect to mineral resources, it is probable that in the grand aggregate the value of those which exist in the unexplored regions will be found, area for area, to be equal to those of the known regions, comparing each particular geological formation with its nearest representative. On the grounds alone, therefore, of geographical knowledge, and of the discovery and definition of the reserves of the country in timber and minerals, the exploration of all these unknown or little-known regions may be amply justified.

Taking a line drawn north and south in the longitude of the Red River Valley, which is, as nearly as may be, the centre of Canada from east to west, it may confidently be stated that by far the larger part of the country in which agricultural settlement is possible lies to the west, while the great bulk of the actual population lies to the east of this line. Looking to this grand fundamental fact, I believe it may safely be affirmed that some members of this audience will live to see the day when these conditions with respect to population will be boldly reversed, and in which the greater number of our representatives in Parliament gathering here will come from this great western region.

This disposition of the cultivable land depends partly upon the physical characteristics of the country, and in part on its climatic conditions. Beyond Winnipeg, and stretching therefrom to the west and north-west, is the great area of prairie, plain, and plateau, which, wider near the forty-ninth parallel than elsewhere on the continent, runs on in one form or other, though with diminishing width, to the Arctic Ocean. This is, generally speaking, an alluvial region, and one of fertile soils. Very fortunately, and as though by a beneficent provision of nature, the climatic features favour the utilization of this belt. The summer isothermals, which carry with them the possibility of ripening crops, trend far to the north.

Let us trace, for example, and as a rough and ready index of the northern limit of practicable agriculture of any kind, that isothermal line which represents a mean temperature of 60° Fahrenheit in the month of July. Passing through the southern part of Newfoundland and touching the island of Anticosti, this line runs to the north end of Mistassini Lake, and thence crosses Hudson's Bay, striking the west shore a short distance north of York Factory. Thence it runs westward, skirting the north end of Reindeer Lake, and then bending to the north-west, crosses Great Slave Lake, and touches the southern extremity of Great Bear Lake. From this point it resumes a westward course and crosses the Yukon River a considerable distance to the north of the confluence of the Pelly and the Lewes, turning south again almost on the east line of Alaska. We need not, however, further follow its course, as owing to peculiar climatic conditions on the West Coast, it ceases there to be any criterion as to the conditions of agriculture.

The character of much of the western interior country is such that its exploration and survey is comparatively easy, and it will be observed that here the larger unknown regions are to be found only far to the northward, leaving in the more rugged and inhospitable eastern region vast islands of unexplored country in much more southern latitudes.

It may be said, in fact, that comparatively little of the region capable, so far as climate goes, of producing wheat is now altogether unknown; but it may be added, that increasing as the world now is in population, its people cannot much longer expect to find wheat-growing lands unoccupied in large blocks. The time is within measurable distance when lands with a fertile soil though more or less rigorous climate, in which only barley, oats, hemp, flax, and other hardy crops can be matured, will be in demand, and we are far from having acquired even a good general knowledge of these lands in Canada.

For many of the unexplored regions marked upon this map, however, we can in reason appeal only to their possible or presumable mineral wealth as an incentive to their exploration, and if some of them should prove wholly or in great part barren when such exploration shall have been carried out, it will not be without utility to acquire even this negative information, and write upon them in characters as large as need be, "No thoroughfare."

I will now ask your further attention for a few moments while I run over and make some remarks in detail on the various unexplored areas as indicated on the map. It must first, however, be explained in what manner the unexplored areas referred to have been outlined. All lines, such as those of rivers, chains of lakes, or other travelled routes, along which reasonably satisfactory explorations have been made and of which fairly accurate route-maps are in existence, are given an approximate average width of about fifty miles, or twenty-five miles on each side of the explorer's or surveyor's track. The known lines are thus arbitrarily assumed to be wide belts of explored country, and that which is referred to as unexplored comprises merely the intervening tracts. By this mode of definition the unexplored regions are reduced to minimum dimensions. Neither are any comparatively small tracts of country lying between explored routes included in my enumeration, in which the least area mentioned is one of 7500 square miles; nor are the Arctic islands, lying to the north of the continent, referred to. Because of the empirical mode in which the unexplored areas have thus been delineated, it has not been attempted to estimate with more than approximate accuracy the number of square miles contained in each, my purpose being merely to render apparent the great dimensions of these areas.

In enumerating these areas, I shall not refer to the various explorations and lines of survey by which they are defined and separated one from another, as this would involve mention of nearly all the explorers who have traversed the northern part of the continent. I shall, however, note such excursions as have been made into or across the regions which are characterized as unexplored.

Beginning, then, in the extreme north-west of the Dominion, we find these areas to be as follows:—

1. Area between the eastern boundary of Alaska, the Porcupine River and the Arctic Coast, 9500

square miles, or somewhat smaller than Belgium. This area lies entirely within the Arctic Circle.

2. Area west of the Lewes and Yukon Rivers and extending to the boundary of Alaska, 32,000 square miles, or somewhat larger than Ireland. This country includes the head-waters of the White and probably of the Tanana Rivers, and, being comparatively low and sheltered from the sea by one of the highest mountain-ranges on the continent, the St. Elias Alps, doubtless possesses some remarkable peculiarities of climate.

3. Area between the Lewes, Pelly, and Stikine Rivers and to the east of the Coast Ranges, 27,000 square miles, or nearly as large as Scotland. This has been penetrated only by a few "prospectors," from whom, and from Indians, the courses of rivers shown on my maps published in connection with the Yukon Expedition Report are derived. It lies on the direct line of the metalliferous belt of the Cordillera, and its low lands are capable of producing hardy crops.

4. Area between the Pelly and Mackenzie Rivers, 100,000 square miles, or about twice the size of England. This belongs partly to the Yukon Basin and partly to that of the Mackenzie, and includes nearly 600 miles in length of the main Rocky Mountain Range. Many years ago, Mr. A. K. Isbister penetrated the northern part of this area for some distance on the line of the Peel River,[1] but owing to the manner in which he had to travel, but little

[1] *Some account of Peel River, North America*, by A. K. Isbister, Journ. Roy. Geog. Soc., vol. xv, 1845, p. 332.

accuracy can be attributed to his sketch of that river. Abbé Petitot also made a short journey into its northern part from the Mackenzie River side, but, with these exceptions, no published information exists respecting it.

5. Area between Great Bear Lake and the Arctic Coast, 50,000 square miles, or about equal to England in size. Nearly all to the north of the Arctic Circle.

6. Area between Great Bear Lake, the Mackenzie, and the western part of Great Slave Lake, 35,000 square miles, or larger than Portugal. With respect to this region and that last mentioned, it must be explained that I have felt some doubt whether they should be characterised as unexplored on the basis previously explained as that which is generally applied. Between 1857 and 1865, Mr. R. Macfarlane, of the Hudson's Bay Company, carried out an intelligent and valuable examination of part of the region north of Great Bear Lake, some results of which have lately been published,[1] and in both of these areas, between 1864 and 1871, the indefatigable missionary, Abbé Petitot, made numerous journeys, of which he subsequently published an account.[2] As Petitot's instruments consisted merely of a compass, and a watch which he rated by the meridian passage of the sun, it must be assumed that his mapping of the country does not possess any great accuracy. His work, however, considering the difficulties under which it was performed, is deserving of all praise, and his several descriptions of the

[1] *Canadian Record of Science*, Jan., 1890.
[2] *Bulletin de la Société de Géographie*, Tom. x, 1875.

character of the country traversed are most valuable. It does not appear from his account of these regions that they are likely to prove of great utility to civilized man, except as fur-preserves, or possibly from the minerals which they may contain. He writes: "Ce pays est composé de contrées silencieuses comme le tombeau, des plaines vastes comme des départements, des steppes glacés plus affreux que ceux de la Sibérie, de forêts chétives, rabougries comme on n'en voit que dans le voisinage des glaciers du Nord."

7. Area between Stikine and Liard Rivers to the north and Skeena and Peace Rivers to the south, 81,000 square miles, or more than twice as large as Newfoundland. This includes a portion of the western Cordillera, and, between the Liard and Peace Rivers, a large tract of the interior plateau region of the continent, parts of which, there is reason to believe, consist of good agricultural land. Its western extremity was crossed in 1866 and 1867 by the exploratory survey of the Western Union or Collins' Telegraph Company, then engaged in an attempt to connect the North American and European telegraph systems through Asia. No details of this part of their exploration have, however, been published, and if we may judge from other parts of their line, since checked, the survey made was of too rough a character to possess much geographical value.

8. Area between Peace, Athabasca, and Loon Rivers, 7500 square miles, or about half as large as Switzerland.

9. Area south-east of Athabasca Lake, 35,000 square miles. This may be compared in extent to Portugal.

10. Area east of the Coppermine River and west of Bathurst Inlet, 7500 square miles. This again may be compared to half the area of Switzerland.

11. Area between the Arctic Coast and Back's River, 31,000 square miles, or about equal to Ireland.

12. Area surrounded by Back's River, Great Slave Lake, Athabasca Lake, Hatchet and Reindeer Lakes, Churchill River, and the west coast of Hudson's Bay, 178,000 square miles. Much larger than Great Britain and Ireland, and somewhat larger than Sweden. The lakes and rivers shown in this great region depend entirely on the result of the three journeys made by Hearne in 1769-1772.[1] Hearne really wandered through parts of this region in company with Indians whom he was unable to control, his ultimate object (which he at length accomplished) being to reach the Coppermine River, in order to ascertain for the Hudson's Bay Company whether it was possible to utilize the native copper found there. Not even roughly approximate accuracy can be assigned to his geographical work. Referring to the position of the mouth of the Coppermine, he writes:—"The latitude may be depended upon to within 20 miles at the utmost." In reality it afterwards proved to be 200 miles too far north. This country includes the great "barren

[1] *A Journey from Prince of Wales Fort, in Hudson's Bay, to the Northern Ocean, 1796.*

grounds" of the continent, and is the principal winter resort of the musk-ox as well as of great herds of caribou. Hearne's general characterization of it is not very encouraging, but certainly we shall know more about it. He writes:—"The land throughout the whole tract of country is scarcely anything but one solid mass of rocks and stones, and in most parts very hilly, particularly to the westward, among the woods." The north-eastern extremity of this region was also crossed by Lieut. Schwatka in the course of his remarkable journey to King-William Land, but his geographical results possess little value.[1]

13. Area between Severn and Attawapishkat Rivers and the coast of Hudson's Bay, 22,000 square miles, or larger than Nova Scotia. Several lakes and rivers are shown upon the maps in this region in practically identical form since Arrowsmith's map of 1850, but I have been unable to ascertain the origin of the information.

14. Area between Trout Lake, Lac Seul, and the Albany River, 15,000 square miles, or about half the size of Scotland.

15. Area to the south and east of James Bay, 35,000 square miles, which also may be compared to the area of Portugal. This region is the nearest of those which still remain unexplored to large centres of population. It is probable that much of it consists of low land which may afford merchantable timber.

[1] *Schwatka's Search,* by H. W. Gilder.

16. Area comprising almost the entire interior of the Labrador peninsula or North-east Territory, 289,000 square miles. This is more than equal to twice the area of Great Britain and Ireland, with an added area equal to that of Newfoundland. Several lines of exploration and survey have been carried for a certain distance into the interior of this great peninsula, among which may be mentioned those of Professor Hind, Mr. A. P. Low, and Mr. R. F. Holme.[1] The limits of the unexplored area have been drawn so as to exclude all these. The area regarded as still unexplored has, however, it is true, been traversed in several directions at different times by officers of the Hudson's Bay Company, particularly on routes leading from the vicinity of Mingan on the Gulf of St. Lawrence to the head of Hamilton Inlet, and thence to Ungava Bay. These routes have also, according to Mr. Holme, been travelled by a missionary, Père Lacasse; but the only published information which I have been able to find is contained in a book written by J. McLean,[2] and in a brief account of a journey by Rev. E. J. Peck.[3] Mr. McLean made several journeys and established trading-posts between Ungava and Hamilton Inlet in the years 1838-1841, while Mr. Peck crossed from Little Whale River, on Hudson Bay, to Ungava in 1884. Something may be

[1] *Explorations in Labrador,* 1863; Annual Report Geol. Surv. Can., 1887-88, Part. J; Proc. Royal Geog. Soc., 1888; Ott. Nat., Vol. iv.

[2] *Notes of a Twenty-five Years' Service in the Hudson's Bay Territory.* London, 1849.

[3] *Church Missionary Intelligencer,* June, 1886; Proc. Roy. Geog. Soc., 1887, p. 192.

gathered as to the general nature of the country along certain lines from the accounts given by these gentlemen, but there is little of a really satisfactory character, while neither has made any attempt to fix positions or delineate the features of the region on the map. In all probability this entire region consists of a rocky plateau or hilly tract of rounded archæan rocks, highest on the north-east side and to the south, and sloping gradually down to low land towards Ungava Bay. It is known to be more or less wooded, and in some places with timber of fair growth; but if it should be possessed of any real value, this may probably lie in its metalliferous deposits. In this tract of country particularly there is reason to hope that ores like those of Tilt Cove, in Newfoundland, or those of Sudbury, in Ontario, may occur.

To sum up briefly, in conclusion, what has been said as to the larger unexplored areas of Canada, it may be stated that, while the entire area of the Dominion as computed at 3,470,257 square miles, about 954,000 square miles of the continent alone, exclusive of the inhospitable detached Arctic portions, is for all practical purposes entirely unknown. In this estimate the area of the unexplored country is reduced to a minimum by the mode of definition employed. Probably we should be much nearer the mark in assuming it as about one million square miles, or between one-third and one-fourth of the whole. Till this great aggregate of unknown territory shall have been subjected to examination, or at least till it has been broken up and traversed in many directions by exploratory and survey lines, we must all feel that it stands as a certain reproach to our want of enterprise and of a justifiable curiosity. In order, however, to properly ascertain and make known the natural resources of the great tracts lying beyond the borders of civilization, such explorations and surveys as are undertaken must be of a truly scientific character. The explorer or surveyor must possess some knowledge of geology and botany, as well as such scientific training as may enable him to make intelligent and accurate observations of any natural features or phenomena with which he may come in contact. He must not consider that his duty consists merely in the perfunctory measuring of lines and the delineation of rivers, lakes, and mountains. An explorer or surveyor properly equipped for his work need never return empty-handed. Should he be obliged to report that some particular district possesses no economic value whatever, besides that of serving as a receiver of rain and a reservoir to feed certain river-systems, his notes should contain scientific observations on geology, botany, climatology, and similar subjects, which may alone be sufficient to justify the expenditure incurred.

APPENDIX II

I HAVE to thank the authorities at Kew for the following list of a small collection of flowering plants that I found growing in the Barren Ground, chiefly in the neighbourhood of the head-waters of the Great Fish River.

Draba nivalis, Liljebl.?
Oxytropis campestris, L. (yellow and purple varieties).
Potentilla nivea, L.
Dryas integrifolia, L.
Saxifraga tricuspidata, Retz.
Epilobium latifolium, L.
Arnica angustifolia, Vahl.
Taraxacum palustre, DC.
Vaccinium uliginosum, L.
Cassiope tetragona, L.
Andromeda polifolia, L.
Phyllodoce taxifolia, Salisb. (*Menziesia cærulea,* Wahl.).
Ledum palustre, L.
Loiseleuria procumbens, Desv.
Rhododendron lapponicum, L.
Kalmia glauca, L.
Diapensia lapponica, L.
Pedicularis hirsuta, L.
Pedicularis lapponica, L.

INDEX

Tom Barrow's house, 290; he leaves Hudson's Hope for Edmonton, 295, which he reaches during an election, 298; he writes the last words in St. James's Street, giving advice to musk-ox hunters and longing for the Barren Ground, 299 seq.

Pierre, *see* Beaulieu, Pierre.

Pierre, Blind, *see* Fat, Pierre.

Pierre the Fool, 218, 219, 223, 224; his description of the country east of Clinton Golden Lake, 223.

Pierre, an Indian boy, the son of little François, 159.

Pierre, Ile de, 141, 142, 166, 229; a good spot for fishing, 27.

Pine River, 294.

Pine River Pass, 292.

Poplar Rapid, 262, 265, 287.

Portage, the Long, 12; the work of portaging described, 17, 18.

"Prairie, the bald-headed," a term of the cattle-men, 2.

Proverb of the North, a, 267.

Ptarmigan plentiful, 44.

Ptarmigan Lake, 219.

Quatre Fourches, 16, 237.

Quesnelle, 231, 246, 250, 258, 271, 292.

Rabbit and lynx, their periodic decease, 293.

Rae, Dr., vi.

Rae, Fort, 95, 148, 167, a good starting-point for the Barren Ground, 299.

Raven, a superstition concerning the, 66.

Red deer, the stream of, 2.

Reid, Mr., of Fort Province, told King Beaulieu that the earth went round the sun, 83.

Resolution, Fort, on the Great Slave Lake, the northern limit of the Athabasca district, 12, 22, 24, 50, 59, 97, 130, 150, 154, 163, 167, 185, 210, 225, 227, 228, 230, 232, 233; Mr. Pike returns to it, 143; its history and present life, 144, 145; it is not perhaps the best starting-point for the Barren Ground, 300.

Richardson, vi.

Riel, Louis, his rebellion, 83.

Rocher, Lac du, 38, 39, 63, 73, 91, 128; it is a haunt of the caribou, 39; trout are caught in it, 39; its products and geological structure, 41, 42; it is like the desert of Arnavatn in Iceland, 42.

Rocks, Point of, the end of the Muskeg country, 27.

Rocky Mountains, the, v, ix, 1, 143, 155, 209, 231, 237, 238, 241, 248, 250, 260, 265, 272, 281, 291, 294; the first glimpse of, 252, 253; Mr. Pike's attempt to cross them, 232-272.

Round, Mr., in charge of Dunvegan, 250.

Saint James's Street, 299.

Saint John, Fort, often called St. John's, 156, 249, 251, 252, 253, 294, 295.

Salt River, 19, 21.

INDEX TO APPENDIX I

The Codes Of Hammurabi And Moses
W. W. Davies

QTY

The discovery of the Hammurabi Code is one of the greatest achievements of archaeology, and is of paramount interest, not only to the student of the Bible, but also to all those interested in ancient history...

Religion   **ISBN: *1-59462-338-4***   **Pages:132**
MSRP $12.95

The Theory of Moral Sentiments
Adam Smith

QTY

This work from 1749. contains original theories of conscience amd moral judgment and it is the foundation for systemof morals.

Philosophy ISBN: *1-59462-777-0*   **Pages:536**
MSRP $19.95

Jessica's First Prayer
Hesba Stretton

QTY

In a screened and secluded corner of one of the many railway-bridges which span the streets of London there could be seen a few years ago, from five o'clock every morning until half past eight, a tidily set-out coffee-stall, consisting of a trestle and board, upon which stood two large tin cans, with a small fire of charcoal burning under each so as to keep the coffee boiling during the early hours of the morning when the work-people were thronging into the city on their way to their daily toil...

Pages:84

Childrens   ISBN: *1-59462-373-2*   *MSRP $9.95*

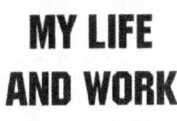

My Life and Work
Henry Ford

QTY

Henry Ford revolutionized the world with his implementation of mass production for the Model T automobile. Gain valuable business insight into his life and work with his own auto-biography... "We have only started on our development of our country we have not as yet, with all our talk of wonderful progress, done more than scratch the surface. The progress has been wonderful enough but..."

Pages:300

Biographies/   ISBN: *1-59462-198-5*   *MSRP $21.95*

The Art of Cross-Examination
Francis Wellman

QTY

I presume it is the experience of every author, after his first book is published upon an important subject, to be almost overwhelmed with a wealth of ideas and illustrations which could readily have been included in his book, and which to his own mind, at least, seem to make a second edition inevitable. Such certainly was the case with me; and when the first edition had reached its sixth impression in five months, I rejoiced to learn that it seemed to my publishers that the book had met with a sufficiently favorable reception to justify a second and considerably enlarged edition. ..

Reference   **ISBN: *1-59462-647-2***

Pages:412
MSRP $19.95

On the Duty of Civil Disobedience
Henry David Thoreau

QTY

Thoreau wrote his famous essay, On the Duty of Civil Disobedience, as a protest against an unjust but popular war and the immoral but popular institution of slave-owning. He did more than write—he declined to pay his taxes, and was hauled off to gaol in consequence. Who can say how much this refusal of his hastened the end of the war and of slavery ?

Law   **ISBN: *1-59462-747-9***

Pages:48
MSRP $7.45

Dream Psychology Psychoanalysis for Beginners
Sigmund Freud

QTY

Sigmund Freud, born Sigismund Schlomo Freud (May 6, 1856 - September 23, 1939), was a Jewish-Austrian neurologist and psychiatrist who co-founded the psychoanalytic school of psychology. Freud is best known for his theories of the unconscious mind, especially involving the mechanism of repression; his redefinition of sexual desire as mobile and directed towards a wide variety of objects; and his therapeutic techniques, especially his understanding of transference in the therapeutic relationship and the presumed value of dreams as sources of insight into unconscious desires.

Psychology   **ISBN: *1-59462-905-6***

Pages:196
MSRP $15.45

The Miracle of Right Thought
Orison Swett Marden

QTY

Believe with all of your heart that you will do what you were made to do. When the mind has once formed the habit of holding cheerful, happy, prosperous pictures, it will not be easy to form the opposite habit. It does not matter how improbable or how far away this realization may see, or how dark the prospects may be, if we visualize them as best we can, as vividly as possible, hold tenaciously to them and vigorously struggle to attain them, they will gradually become actualized, realized in the life. But a desire, a longing without endeavor, a yearning abandoned or held indifferently will vanish without realization.

Self Help   **ISBN: *1-59462-644-8***

Pages:360
MSRP $25.45

QTY

The Rosicrucian Cosmo-Conception Mystic Christianity by *Max Heindel*　ISBN: *1-59462-188-8*　**$38.95**
The Rosicrucian Cosmo-conception is not dogmatic, neither does it appeal to any other authority than the reason of the student. It is: not controversial, but is: sent forth in the, hope that it may help to clear...　New Age/Religion Pages 646

Abandonment To Divine Providence by *Jean-Pierre de Caussade*　ISBN: *1-59462-228-0*　**$25.95**
"The Rev. Jean Pierre de Caussade was one of the most remarkable spiritual writers of the Society of Jesus in France in the 18th Century. His death took place at Toulouse in 1751. His works have gone through many editions and have been republished...　Inspirational/Religion Pages 400

Mental Chemistry by *Charles Haanel*　ISBN: *1-59462-192-6*　**$23.95**
Mental Chemistry allows the change of material conditions by combining and appropriately utilizing the power of the mind. Much like applied chemistry creates something new and unique out of careful combinations of chemicals the mastery of mental chemistry...　New Age Pages 354

The Letters of Robert Browning and Elizabeth Barret Barrett 1845-1846 vol II　ISBN: *1-59462-193-4*　**$35.95**
by *Robert Browning* and *Elizabeth Barrett*　Biographies Pages 596

Gleanings In Genesis (volume I) by *Arthur W. Pink*　ISBN: *1-59462-130-6*　**$27.45**
Appropriately has Genesis been termed "the seed plot of the Bible" for in it we have, in germ form, almost all of the great doctrines which are afterwards fully developed in the books of Scripture which follow...　Religion/Inspirational Pages 420

The Master Key by *L. W. de Laurence*　ISBN: *1-59462-001-6*　**$30.95**
In no branch of human knowledge has there been a more lively increase of the spirit of research during the past few years than in the study of Psychology, Concentration and Mental Discipline. The requests for authentic lessons in Thought Control, Mental Discipline and...　New Age/Business Pages 422

The Lesser Key Of Solomon Goetia by *L. W. de Laurence*　ISBN: *1-59462-092-X*　**$9.95**
This translation of the first book of the "Lernegton" which is now for the first time made accessible to students of Talismanic Magic was done, after careful collation and edition, from numerous Ancient Manuscripts in Hebrew, Latin, and French...　New Age/Occult Pages 92

Rubaiyat Of Omar Khayyam by *Edward Fitzgerald*　ISBN:*1-59462-332-5*　**$13.95**
Edward Fitzgerald, whom the world has already learned, in spite of his own efforts to remain within the shadow of anonymity, to look upon as one of the rarest poets of the century, was born at Bredfield, in Suffolk, on the 31st of March, 1809. He was the third son of John Purcell...　Music Pages 172

Ancient Law by *Henry Maine*　ISBN: *1-59462-128-4*　**$29.95**
The chief object of the following pages is to indicate some of the earliest ideas of mankind, as they are reflected in Ancient Law, and to point out the relation of those ideas to modern thought.　Religion/History Pages 452

Far-Away Stories by *William J. Locke*　ISBN: *1-59462-129-2*　**$19.45**
"Good wine needs no bush, but a collection of mixed vintages does. And this book is just such a collection. Some of the stories I do not want to remain buried for ever in the museum files of dead magazine-numbers an author's not unpardonable vanity..."　Fiction Pages 272

Life of David Crockett by *David Crockett*　ISBN: *1-59462-250-7*　**$27.45**
"Colonel David Crockett was one of the most remarkable men of the times in which he lived. Born in humble life, but gifted with a strong will, an indomitable courage, and unremitting perseverance...　Biographies/New Age Pages 424

Lip-Reading by *Edward Nitchie*　ISBN: *1-59462-206-X*　**$25.95**
Edward B. Nitchie, founder of the New York School for the Hard of Hearing, now the Nitchie School of Lip-Reading, Inc, wrote "LIP-READING Principles and Practice". The development and perfecting of this meritorious work on lip-reading was an undertaking...　How-to Pages 400

A Handbook of Suggestive Therapeutics, Applied Hypnotism, Psychic Science　ISBN: *1-59462-214-0*　**$24.95**
by *Henry Munro*　Health/New Age/Health/Self-help Pages 376

A Doll's House: and Two Other Plays by *Henrik Ibsen*　ISBN: *1-59462-112-8*　**$19.95**
Henrik Ibsen created this classic when in revolutionary 1848 Rome. Introducing some striking concepts in playwriting for the realist genre, this play has been studied the world over.　Fiction/Classics/Plays 308

The Light of Asia by *sir Edwin Arnold*　ISBN: *1-59462-204-3*　**$13.95**
In this poetic masterpiece, Edwin Arnold describes the life and teachings of Buddha. The man who was to become known as Buddha to the world was born as Prince Gautama of India but he rejected the worldly riches and abandoned the reigns of power when...　Religion/History/Biographies Pages 170

The Complete Works of Guy de Maupassant by *Guy de Maupassant*　ISBN: *1-59462-157-8*　**$16.95**
"For days and days, nights and nights, I had dreamed of that first kiss which was to consecrate our engagement, and I knew not on what spot I should put my lips..."　Fiction/Classics Pages 240

The Art of Cross-Examination by *Francis L. Wellman*　ISBN: *1-59462-309-0*　**$26.95**
Written by a renowned trial lawyer, Wellman imparts his experience and uses case studies to explain how to use psychology to extract desired information through questioning.　How-to/Science/Reference Pages 408

Answered or Unanswered? by *Louisa Vaughan*　ISBN: *1-59462-248-5*　**$10.95**
Miracles of Faith in China　Religion Pages 112

The Edinburgh Lectures on Mental Science (1909) by *Thomas*　ISBN: *1-59462-008-3*　**$11.95**
This book contains the substance of a course of lectures recently given by the writer in the Queen Street Hall, Edinburgh. Its purpose is to indicate the Natural Principles governing the relation between Mental Action and Material Conditions...　New Age/Psychology Pages 148

Ayesha by *H. Rider Haggard*　ISBN: *1-59462-301-5*　**$24.95**
Verily and indeed it is the unexpected that happens! Probably if there was one person upon the earth from whom the Editor of this, and of a certain previous history, did not expect to hear again...　Classics Pages 380

Ayala's Angel by *Anthony Trollope*　ISBN: *1-59462-352-X*　**$29.95**
The two girls were both pretty, but Lucy who was twenty-one who supposed to be simple and comparatively unattractive, whereas Ayala was credited, as her Bombwhat romantic name might show, with poetic charm and a taste for romance. Ayala when her father died was nineteen...　Fiction Pages 484

The American Commonwealth by *James Bryce*　ISBN: *1-59462-286-8*　**$34.45**
An interpretation of American democratic political theory. It examines political mechanics and society from the perspective of Scotsman James Bryce　Politics Pages 572

Stories of the Pilgrims by *Margaret P. Pumphrey*　ISBN: *1-59462-116-0*　**$17.95**
This book explores pilgrims religious oppression in England as well as their escape to Holland and eventual crossing to America on the Mayflower, and their early days in New England...　History Pages 268

www.bookjungle.com *email: sales@bookjungle.com fax: 630-214-0564 mail: Book Jungle PO Box 2226 Champaign, IL 61825*

QTY

The Fasting Cure *by Sinclair Upton*　　　　　　　　　ISBN: *1-59462-222-1*　**$13.95**
In the Cosmopolitan Magazine for May, 1910, and in the Contemporary Review (London) for April, 1910, I published an article dealing with my experiences in fasting. I have written a great many magazine articles, but never one which attracted so much attention... New Age/Self Help/Health Pages 164

Hebrew Astrology *by Sepharial*　　　　　　　　　　ISBN: *1-59462-308-2*　**$13.45**
In these days of advanced thinking it is a matter of common observation that we have left many of the old landmarks behind and that we are now pressing forward to greater heights and to a wider horizon than that which represented the mind-content of our progenitors... Astrology Pages 144

Thought Vibration or The Law of Attraction in the Thought World　ISBN: *1-59462-127-6*　**$12.95**
by William Walker Atkinson　　　　　　　　　　　　　　　Psychology/Religion Pages 144

Optimism *by Helen Keller*　　　　　　　　　　　ISBN: *1-59462-108-X*　**$15.95**
Helen Keller was blind, deaf, and mute since 19 months old, yet famously learned how to overcome these handicaps, communicate with the world, and spread her lectures promoting optimism. An inspiring read for everyone... Biographies/Inspirational Pages 84

Sara Crewe *by Frances Burnett*　　　　　　　　　ISBN: *1-59462-360-0*　**$9.45**
In the first place, Miss Minchin lived in London. Her home was a large, dull, tall one, in a large, dull square, where all the houses were alike, and all the sparrows were alike, and where all the door-knockers made the same heavy sound... Childrens/Classic Pages 88

The Autobiography of Benjamin Franklin *by Benjamin Franklin*　ISBN: *1-59462-135-7*　**$24.95**
The Autobiography of Benjamin Franklin has probably been more extensively read than any other American historical work, and no other book of its kind has had such ups and downs of fortune. Franklin lived for many years in England, where he was agent... Biographies/History Pages 332

Name	
Email	
Telephone	
Address	
City, State ZIP	

☐ **Credit Card**　　　　　☐ **Check / Money Order**

Credit Card Number	
Expiration Date	
Signature	

Please Mail to:　Book Jungle
PO Box 2226
Champaign, IL 61825
or Fax to:　　　630-214-0564

ORDERING INFORMATION

web: *www.bookjungle.com*
email: *sales@bookjungle.com*
fax: *630-214-0564*
mail: *Book Jungle PO Box 2226 Champaign, IL 61825*
or PayPal *to sales@bookjungle.com*

Please contact us for bulk discounts

DIRECT-ORDER TERMS

**20% Discount if You Order
Two or More Books**
Free Domestic Shipping!
Accepted: Master Card, Visa,
Discover, American Express

www.ingramcontent.com/pod-product-compliance
Lightning Source LLC
Chambersburg PA
CBHW080951020726
47505CB00009B/2160